ACCLAIM FOR
CHELSEA FINE'S FINDING FATE SERIES

RIGHT *kind of* WRONG

"I love this book! There's something about a story of people fighting love that gets to me. I don't know why. All I know is that the sexual tension in this book is fabulous. I adore a man who isn't afraid to be in love, and I adore the way Jack fights for what he wants from Jenna. The great love story, quirky families, and scary action make this one a MUST READ!"   —SmutBookClub.com

"There's no better feeling than coming across a great road-trip story. I love those, and I loved RIGHT KIND OF WRONG for all the right reasons: great main characters, good storytelling, intense conflict, well-written plot…It was a journey I enjoyed from the beginning to the very end."   —LongandShortReviews.com

"Holy hot chemistry! *Fans self*…I read this book in one sitting because I could not put it down!"   —ABookishEscape.com

"I loved the way Chelsea Fine weaved Jenna and Jack's history into the story…In the end, this wasn't a story about Jack's (or Jenna's) family. It was about love. Believing in it. Giving it. Accepting it. Trusting it. And just letting it happen. And that made this book a highlight—and highlightable."   —GiveMeBooksBlog.blogspot.com

"Fine creates some amazing sexual tension between her characters, and this book is no exception. In fact, I think it may be the hottest of all three in the series!…I enjoyed the story line, felt the connection between the characters, and cannot wait for whatever Fine does next!"
                —LovinLosLibros.blogspot.com

PERFECT *kind of* TROUBLE

"I love that Fine has created a fun, sweet story that at the same time holds such emotional depth that I found my own heart breaking for these two characters." —LovinLosLibros.blogspot.com

"Chelsea Fine has a way of always managing to rip my heart out with some of her characters…*Perfect Kind of Trouble* is another beautiful, touch-your-heart story, and it will also have you rolling with laughter for Daren and Kayla's tough-love romance from the awesome author Chelsea Fine."

—IHeartYABooks.blogspot.com

"Wow, Chelsea Fine! She is quickly topping my list of favorite authors. She builds incredible stories and characters and she did it again with *Perfect Kind of Trouble*."

—LostinLit.com

"The narrative was pure bliss to read. The witty banter, the romance, the history, and the emotion lead a beautifully written play of heart and finding the unexpected in love. Fully, heartily a 5-STAR RATING and a highly recommended read for heart, love, fun, and just a beautiful read."

—BookLitLove.com

"Nothing short of absolutely total entertainment! Chelsea Fine takes the sadness out of death and fills the heart with romance— fun romance! Her sense of timing and her ability to encapsulate these two in their own little world is nothing short of true genius… Chelsea Fine is on a roll with this series!"

—TomeTender.blogspot.com

BEST *kind of* BROKEN

"By turns humorous and heartbreaking, *Best Kind of Broken* has become one of my favorites!"

—Cora Carmack, *New York Times*
bestselling author of *Losing It*

"You'll fall for Pixie and Levi, just like I did!"

—Jennifer L. Armentrout (J. Lynn), #1 *New York Times*
bestselling author of *Wait for You*

"Tangled with friendship, history, and heartbreak—not to mention a huge dose of humor—Chelsea Fine's New Adult novel is not to be missed! Beyond an incredibly HOT read, Pixie and Levi's longing for each other will have you rooting for them till the very end."

—Jay Crownover, *New York Times*
bestselling author of *Rule*

"This book destroyed me. Tore me into little tiny pieces. But somehow with lots of laughs and some very steamy times, Chelsea put me back together again! Chelsea Fine's style is witty, visceral, and fresh. All I wanted to do was crawl inside this book and live with the characters. And now all I want is MORE."

—Chelsea M. Cameron, *New York Times*
bestselling author of *My Favorite Mistake*

"Sandwiched between laugh-out-loud moments and some serious heat, *Best Kind of Broken* is an unforgettable story of loss and forgiveness that will leave your heart aching."

—Lisa Desrochers, *USA Today*
bestselling author of *A Little Too Far*

RIGHT *kind of* WRONG

A Finding Fate Novel

Book Three

CHELSEA FINE

FOREVER

NEW YORK BOSTON

Copyright © 2014 by Chelsea Lauterbach
Excerpt from *Best Kind of Broken* copyright © 2014 by Chelsea Lauterbach
Excerpt from *Perfect Kind of Trouble* copyright © 2014 by Chelsea Lauterbach
All rights reserved. In accordance with the U.S. Copyright Act of 1976, the scanning, uploading, and electronic sharing of any part of this book without the permission of the publisher constitute unlawful piracy and theft of the author's intellectual property. If you would like to use material from the book (other than for review purposes), prior written permission must be obtained by contacting the publisher at permissions@hbgusa.com. Thank you for your support of the author's rights.

Forever
Hachette Book Group
1290 Avenue of the Americas
New York, NY 10104

www.HachetteBookGroup.com

Printed in the United States of America

RRD-C

Originally published as an ebook

First trade paperback edition: March 2015
10 9 8 7 6 5 4 3 2

Forever is an imprint of Grand Central Publishing.
The Forever name and logo are trademarks of Hachette Book Group, Inc.

The Hachette Speakers Bureau provides a wide range of authors for speaking events. To find out more, go to www.hachettespeakersbureau.com or call (866) 376-6591.

The publisher is not responsible for websites (or their content) that are not owned by the publisher.

Library of Congress Cataloging-in-Publication Data

Fine, Chelsea, 1982–
    Right kind of wrong / Chelsea Fine. — First trade paperback edition.
        pages ; cm. — (Finding fate ; Book 3)
    "Originally published as an ebook."
    ISBN 978-1-4555-8319-5 (softcover) — ISBN 978-1-4555-8317-1 (ebook) —
ISBN 978-1-4789-8341-5 (audio download)   1. Young women—Fiction.
2. Man-woman relationships—Fiction.   I. Title.
    PS3606.I5335R54 2015
    813'.6—dc23
                                                            2014047098

To Kristen, who knows me so well and still hangs out with me.
You're the best "Jenna" a girl could hope for.

Acknowledgments

This series has been a whirlwind of fun and excitement to write and I couldn't have done it without my amazingly supportive readers. From the bottom of my heart, thank you! With every page you've read you've given me a gift I could never have imagined. I love your guts!

Thank you to Brett, my incredible husband, for being my soul, my spirit, and my sanity in this adventure we call life. You are better than I deserve and the best thing that's ever happened to me. Thank you for loving me. I'm yours forever.

Thank you to my sweet babies, who are no longer babies but almost tweens. You are the brightest lights in my life and I chase my dreams for you. Thank you for believing in me. Thank you for being proud of me. Thank you for all the things you give to me that are too big for words. I love your sweet souls with my whole heart.

Thank you to my wonderful mama. You have stood by me through all the many dreams I've chased and never doubted I would catch one. And look at me now! Dreams in my hands, spilling all over the place. Thank you for always believing that this day would come.

Thank you to Kristen, who is my "Jenna," for being a constant friend to me in all my seasons, and for making me laugh my head off. Seriously. I'm surprised my head is still connected to my body. Yours is the greatest friendship I've ever experienced, and I'm grateful beyond words for the joy you bring to my life.

Thank you to my good friend and fellow writer Shelly Crane, who is my partner in things to hope for. I love your guts—all of them.

Thank you to Suzie, my superstar agent. I couldn't have done any of this without your brilliance and patience! You're my superhero. For reals.

And thank you to my fantastic editor, Megha, for loving my characters just as much as I do! You felt what I wrote and made this book come to life. And you tolerate my crazy—which is no small task—and for that I'm forever grateful. Thank you for believing in this story, and all the ones before. You truly are incredible.

RIGHT *kind of* WRONG

I

JENNA

*L*ook at you. Being all in love like a grown-up. I'm so proud," I say, smiling at my best friend, Pixie, as we carry boxes into our joint dorm room. "And Levi," I add, turning to address Pixie's hot new piece of arm candy, "you're welcome."

He sets a box down. "Am I now?"

I nod. "If it weren't for me telling Pixie to suck up her fears and just let herself love you, you'd still be a miserable handyman."

"I am still a handyman."

"Ah, but you're no longer a *miserable* one." I grin. "Thanks to me."

He pulls Pixie into his arms and kisses her temple. "Then I guess I should thank you."

As they start kissing, my phone rings and I'm relieved for an excuse to leave them to all their lovebirding.

I slip out into the hall and close the door before answering my cell.

"Hello?"

"Hi, Jenna." The sound of my mom's voice makes me smile. "How's my baby?"

"I'm good," I say. "Pixie and I are almost all moved in. She came down here with her boyfriend tonight so we were able to get mostly unpacked. I just have a few more boxes left at the apartment, but I'm going to pick those up later. How are you?"

She pauses. "Well *I'm* okay."

It's the way she emphasizes the "I'm" that tells me exactly what this phone call is about.

"Grandma?" I sigh in exasperation. "Again?"

"I'm afraid so. She says she can feel the end coming close."

I sigh. "Mom. She's been saying she's dying for ten years and she's never even had a cough."

"I know, but she seems serious this time," Mom says.

Every few years or so, my grandmother announces to the family that she's going to kick the bucket at any given moment. The first two times it happened, I immediately flew back to New Orleans—where she lives with my mother and younger sisters in the house I grew up in—to be by her side, only to find Granny alive and well without so much as a sniffle. The last time it happened, I took a few days to get organized before flying back to New Orleans, where I found my "dying" grandmother singing karaoke at a local bar.

So as you can imagine, I'm not falling for her silly shenanigans this time.

"No way," I say. "I'm not spending my hard-earned money to fly out there again just so Grandma can get on my case about love and fate while belting out a verse of 'Black Velvet.' Tell her that I'll come visit when she has a doctor's note stating that she's at death's door."

"Oh, Jenna. Don't be so dramatic. I swear you're just as bad as your grandmother."

"I know," I say, in mock frustration. "And it's getting hard to compete for the title of Family Drama Queen with Granny declaring her impending death every two years. Could you tell her to just give it up already and let me be the shining star?"

I can hear the disapproval in my mother's voice. "That's not funny, Jenna."

"Sure it is." I smile. "And Grandma would agree."

"Please be serious about this," she says.

"I'll be serious about Grandma's death when she gets serious about dying," I quip.

A weary sigh feathers through the line. "Jenna, please."

"Why do we keep pandering to her, anyway? The only reason she keeps crying death is because she knows we'll all come running to her karaoke-singing side to hold her hand as she passes—which she never does. Why do we keep playing her game?"

"Because she's very superstitious and believes dying without the blessing of her family members is bad luck for the afterlife. You know that."

Now it's my turn to sigh.

I do know that. All too well. Since I was a child, the deep roots of Grandma's superstitions have wrapped their gnarled fingers around my family's every move. If her voodoo notions weren't so eerily accurate and, well, creepy, maybe we'd be able to ignore the old woman's ways.

But unfortunately, Grams has a tendency to correctly predict future events and know exactly what someone's intentions or motivations are just by shaking their hand. It's downright spooky. And I swear the old woman uses our fear of her psychic powers as a tool of manipulation.

Case in point? Her recurring death threats.

"Yeah, yeah," I murmur. "She deserves a pleasant send-off. I know."

I hear my mother inhale through her nose. "She does. But even if that weren't the case, your grandmother isn't feeling well and she'd like to see you. Again." When I don't say anything she adds, "And wouldn't you feel horrible if she was right this time and you missed your chance to say good-bye?"

The guilt card. A nasty tool all mothers use on their children.

"Fine," I say. "But I'm not shelling out the cash to fly there. I'll drive this time."

"All the way from Tempe to New Orleans?"

"Yes. And I will save big money doing it," I say. "I'll get my shifts covered at work and leave in the morning."

"Excellent. Your grandmother will be so happy."

I scoff. "Happy enough for karaoke, no doubt."

She clears her throat. "I'll see you here in a few days then. Love you."

"Love you too." I hang up the phone and head back into the dorm room to find Levi and Pixie making out against the wall.

"God. Seriously, you two?" I make a face. "I know you just got together in the middle of the road a few hours ago, but come on! There are other people here."

Levi doesn't seem to notice me as he continues kissing Pixie's face off, and Pixie takes her sweet time pulling back from her loverboy before acknowledging my presence.

She shoots me a hazy smile and nods at my phone. "Who was that?"

"My mom." I exhale. "Grandma claims she's dying."

"Again?" She bites her lip.

I nod. "So I'm going to drive out there this week and try to be home before school starts."

She pulls away from Levi, just slightly, but it's enough for him to stop smelling her hair—which I swear he was just doing. They're so in love it's almost gross.

"By yourself?" Pixie's green eyes widen.

Pixie and I met last year, at the start of our freshman year at Arizona State University when we were assigned the same dorm and became roommates. When school let out for the summer and Pixie and I could no longer live in the dorms, we split up. She moved to her aunt's inn up north—where she fell in love with Levi—while I moved into a local apartment with three of my cousins. It was a good setup, for the summer, but I'm happy to be moving back in with my bestie.

She and I are both art students—she's a painter and I'm a sculptor—so we have a ton in common and get along perfectly. She's the closest friend I've ever had, so I try my hardest to take the concern on her face seriously.

"Yep." I put my phone away. "By myself."

Levi reluctantly steps away from his girlfriend and busies himself by unpacking some of Pixie's things.

She frowns. "That doesn't sound like fun. Or very safe."

Levi glances at me. It's one of those big-brother protective glances and I have to bite back a smile. Aw…look at this guy. He barely knows me, but he's still worried about my safety. For the hundredth time, I silently rejoice that he and Pixie got together. She deserves a good guy who looks out for both her and her friends. A guy like that would drive me crazy. But he's perfect for Pixie.

"I'll be fine," I say to both Pixie's big eyes and Levi's concerned glance as I wave them off and grab my purse. "After I stop by work, I'm heading back to my cousins' apartment for the last of my boxes. I'll probably crash there for the night, so you two can get back to smooching against the wall or whatever." I wink at Pixie. "See ya."

"See ya," she says with a concerned smile as I exit the room.

Jumping in my car, I quickly head to the Thirsty Coyote, where I work as a bartender. It's a decent job for a college student. Good hours. Good money. And it suits me. Pouring drinks isn't my dream job or anything, but it gets me one step closer to finishing school and opening my own art gallery—which *is* my dream job.

I let myself inside and head to the back. It's just past dinner-time so the place is packed and I have to squeeze through the crowd just to reach the bar. When I get there, I lean in and call out to my coworker.

"Cody!"

He turns around and smiles at me. "What's happening, Jenna? Thought you had the night off."

"I do. But I need to get some shifts covered this week so I thought I'd come in and sweet-talk my favorite bartender…" I bat my lashes, knowing full well Cody isn't attracted to me at all. But he's still a sucker for making money, and more bar shifts means more money.

He grins. "I'm listening…"

I whip out my schedule and show him all the days I'd need him to cover. He agrees like the superhero that he is and heads to the back to make it official in the schedule log.

I wait at the counter, thinking about how long my drive to New Orleans will take if I leave tomorrow. Probably at least twenty hours. Ugh. Pixie was right. It really isn't going to be any fun.

My eyes drift over the crowd and fall on a tall figure in the corner. Gunmetal-gray eyes. Tousled black hair. Tattooed arms and broad shoulders. My body immediately goes on alert.

Jack Oliver.

It's not surprising he's here. He comes to the bar all the time, but usually he's with his friends and in a good mood. Right now, though, he's talking on the phone and seems very upset. His gray eyes are narrow slits and his jaw is clenched. But I'm not going to lie. Angry looks good on him.

At over six feet tall, with his broad shoulders and endless tattoos, Jack looks intimidating. But really he's a big softie. I hardly ever see him in a mood other than happy. So this angry version of Jack is a new experience for me. A very hot experience.

He catches me looking at him and tips his chin. His anger dissipates for a brief second as a lopsided smile hitches up the corner of his mouth, but then he turns his attention back to his phone and clenches his fist before ending the call.

In-ter-est-ing.

He shoves his phone into his back pocket and heads my way.

"What's up?" I say. "You seem upset."

He shrugs. "Nothing. Just family shit."

I snort. "God. Yes. I have plenty of that."

He nods and our eyes lock and hold.

One beat.

Two.

I hate this part of our friendship; the part that reminds me of what happened between us last year when we got drunk and carried away one very steamy night. The memory shouldn't still turn me on like it does. But Jack and those gray eyes of his—eyes rimmed with pale green and flecked with dark flints, looking almost silver at times—are hard not to respond to.

We never talk about it, which is better, but in moments like this, when his eyes are on mine with such command, I can almost feel his hands back on my body. Fingertips running the length of my skin. Palms brushing my curves—

"Here you go." Cody returns with the schedule book for me to sign and I silently bless the interruption.

No good comes from me reminiscing about Jack's hands. Or any of his other body parts.

"I switched our shifts and marked you down as *on vacation*," Cody says.

"Thanks," I say, taking the book and initialing by my traded shifts.

"Hey, Jack." Cody nods at him. "What can I get you to drink?"

"Just a beer," Jack says, sitting on the barstool next to me. He's so close I can smell his shampoo. It's a wooded scent, like sawdust and pine, and it plays at my memories in a way that makes my heart pound.

He looks at me. "So where are you going on vacation?" His warm breath skitters over my shoulder and sends a jolt of hot want through my veins.

Damn him.

On second thought, damn *me* for being such a swooner.

I'm not usually like this. I swear it. Guys are the last thing I give priority to in my life. It goes: chocolate, tattoos, a hundred other things…and then men. Because a woman doesn't need a man to have a full life. And I'm living proof of that.

I keep my eyes on the book. "New Orleans to visit my grandma."

He nods. "Is she dying again?"

Even my friends know how ridiculous my grandmother's yearly death threats are.

"Yep." I pop the *p*. "The drama queen just won't hand the spotlight over gracefully."

He smirks. "Like you'd wait to be handed anything."

Jack and I met two years ago, when I first started working at the Thirsty Coyote and Jack was my trainer, but we became friends almost immediately and now he knows me well enough to know that I'm not very patient, and if I want something I usually just take it.

Cody sets Jack's beer down and asks me, "Are you flying out tonight?"

"Nah." I finish signing the book and hand it back to him. "I'm driving there so I'll leave in the morning."

Jack swings his head to me and a slight wrinkle forms between his eyes. "You're driving all the way to Louisiana?"

Jack and I are both from Louisiana. I'm from New Orleans and he's from a small town just north of there, called Little Vail. The fact that we grew up so close to one another, yet met on the other side of the country at this bar in Arizona, was one of the first things we bonded over. That, and tequila.

"Yeah. Pfft. I'm not spending hundreds of dollars on a last-minute plane ticket. Grandma needs to give me at least a month's warning next time she decides to keel over."

Jack takes a swig of his beer, but continues looking straight at me, displeased.

"What?" I snap.

He shrugs. "That's just a long trip to make on your own."

"Yeah, well. Good thing I don't mind driving." I look at Cody. "Thanks for covering for me. I owe you. Later, Jack." I turn to leave just as a drunk guy stumbles into me, knocking me back into Jack's chest.

Jack's hands instantly go to my hips, and my hips instantly want to yank his hands down my pants. My hips can't be trusted.

"Watch it," I say to the drunk guy, giving him a little shove forward so I have room to pull away from Jack.

Jack's fingers slowly slide off my hips, trailing down just before ending contact with my body, and my eyelids lower in want.

Clearly, I need to have sex. Not with Jack—that would be a disaster. But with someone. Soon. So I can sex Jack out of my system. Again.

I've been trying to sex away Jack a lot lately.

I blink up and find Jack's eyes watching mine. He saw my moment of weakness; that split second of desire. Dammit.

"Be careful, Jenn," he says in a low voice, and his words trickle down my skin.

Jack's the only person I've ever let call me "Jenn." Why? I have no idea. I blame his voice, all sexy and deep and brushing along the sensitive places of my ears.

Damn him, damn him, damn him.

"Right." I step back and act casual. "So I'm going to go. I'll see you when I get back. Later."

I spin around and weave through the crowd with a huff, feeling Jack's eyes on me the whole time.

2

JACK

There are only two things I don't ever speak of. My crazy family and my history with Jenna. And both just fell in my lap.

I watch Jenna work her way to the front door and can't help the unease slipping through my veins. I don't like the idea of her going on such a long road trip by herself. She's independent and smart and I know she can take care of herself, but that doesn't lessen my concern any.

Her long dark hair is pulled back into a high ponytail revealing her golden eyes and high cheekbones. Her half-Creole heritage has kissed her skin with a permanent bronze, which only adds to her unique beauty as her shoulders, bare in the strapless shirt she's wearing, show off the numerous tattoos running the length of her arms. The intricate designs disappear beneath her clothes, where I know they continue to travel across other parts of her curvy body. She's beautiful and wild, and drives me absolutely crazy.

Her hips swing as she moves out the door and my gut tightens. If anything were to ever happen to her, if someone ever tried to hurt her, I . . . well I can't even think about it. Which is why I can't think about Jenna all alone in a car on a series of desolate freeways for three days.

I don't like it. I don't like it at all.

My friend Ethan plops down on the barstool next to me, reeking of cologne. "Hey, man."

"Hey," I say.

I've gone through a series of roommates this past year, but Ethan has been my favorite, so far, or at least the easiest to tolerate. He and I have been friends since I first moved to Arizona and, as very opposite as the two of us are, we get along pretty well.

"Was that Jenna I just saw leaving?" He nods at the door.

"Yep."

Ethan smirks. "What did you do to piss her off this time?"

I grin. I do have a way of getting under Jenna's skin. I can't help it. If she would just be a grown-up and address what happened between us last year then maybe I'd back down. But instead she acts like nothing ever went down and dammit, that's just insulting. Because she's not just some girl I hooked up with a while back. She's Jenna, for God's sake.

But she wants to pretend like we're nothing more than friends, so I go along with it. And occasionally I piss her off—because it's *something*. It's some sign that I matter more than she lets on.

"Surprisingly enough," I say, "I didn't do anything. This time."

Ethan shakes his head. "I don't know why you poke at her the way you do."

"Because it's funny." I shrug. "And it's not like she doesn't piss me off just as much, like when she goes off and sleeps with dickhead guys." I shift my beer mug around in a slow circle, one inch at a time. "When she knows she can do better."

"Yeeeah." Ethan purses his lips. "You care way too much about who Jenna sleeps with. That's not healthy, man."

I stifle a groan. "I know."

Ethan orders a drink from Cody while I stare into my beer. I really shouldn't care who Jenna sleeps with, especially since I'm no angel myself. But damn. I can't help it. I don't like her sharing her body with anyone else.

My phone rings again. I look at the caller ID and groan.

I've been fielding phone calls from my family members for a week now and it's grating on my nerves. Earlier, I was on the phone with my frantic mother, who was babbling about how concerned she is for my youngest brother, Drew. He's twenty and should be able to take care of himself by now, but apparently he's been acting shady lately and his behavior has my family on edge. Now Mom's flipping out and I'm running out of reassuring words.

I thought our last phone call would tide her over for a while, but now my other brother, Samson, is calling. Again.

Not a good sign.

I grudgingly take the call and snap, "What?"

"Easy, bro," says Samson. "I'm just the messenger."

"Yeah, well I'm getting sick of all your *messages*."

"What would you rather I do? Not call you? Let Drew go down on his own?"

I let out a frustrated sigh. "No."

"That's what I thought. Drew's in deep trouble this time, I can feel it. And Mom's losing her shit. I need you out here."

A year older than Drew and a year younger than me, Samson is the middle child, and the most laid-back. It takes a lot to stress him out, so the fact that he's been at my ear these past few days is a red flag in and of itself.

But as the oldest brother—and the only real male authority in my family—it's my job to keep everyone calm, cool, and collected. A task that's growing more difficult by the phone call.

"Not happening." I shake my head even though he can't see me. "I left for a reason, Samson. I'm not coming back."

His voice is strained like he's gritting his teeth. "And just what the hell am I supposed to do without you? You know I don't have the pull or the power that you do."

I run a hand through my hair. "Have Drew give me a call. I'll straighten him out."

"That's just the thing, man. Drew's missing."

My heart stops for a moment. "Mom didn't mention that."

"That's because she's in denial and refuses to accept that her baby boy is caught up in a mess. She thinks he's out roaming, but you and I know better."

Fuck.

I rub a hand over my mouth, trying not to panic. Or growl. This is exactly the shit I was trying to stay away from when I moved away from Little Vail, Louisiana, and toward Tempe, Arizona. And now here I am, getting dragged right back into it.

"Fine," I say, my decision made. "I'll come out there this week. Tell Mom to calm down, would you? Her freaking out will only make things worse."

"Got it. I'll see you later then."

"Yeah." I hang up and run a finger over my cold mug.

Drew is missing.

I knew something like this would happen, eventually. You can't play around with drug dealers and not get jacked down the road.

"You all right, dude?" Ethan asks as Cody sets his drink down.

"What? Yeah." I rub my mouth again. "I'm fine. Just family shit."

He takes a drink. "How come you never talk about your family?"

I stretch my neck. "Because there's nothing to say."

Actually there's a ton to say, but no one would want to hear it. And frankly, I like the life I've made for myself out here in Arizona. No baggage to weigh me down. No expectations lingering around me.

I pull up airfares on my phone and scroll through the prices with a grimace. Damn, it's expensive to fly. My eyes snap up as a thought hits me. Jenna's heading to New Orleans and I need to go to Little Vail, which is only two hours north and right on her way.

A slow smile spreads across my face.

I might just have to tag along on Jenna's road trip.

3

JENNA

A gaggle of girls meets me the moment I step foot inside my small apartment.

"Your mom called," Alyssa says, talking a mile a minute. "She said you're driving out to see Grams all by yourself because you think flying is too expensive but you really aren't, are you? Please tell me Aunt Sherry was just joking because you driving all alone across the states would be crazy."

"Crazy," Becca repeats, bobbing her head as they block me from walking any farther into the room. "There are like killers out there disguised as truckers and they will hunt you down on the road and like kidnap you and use your skin for like lampshades and stuff."

I crinkle up my face. "What—"

"It's true," Callie adds with a curt nod. "I always see these specials on TV about young girls who go on road trips by themselves and never make it back alive because some psycho roasted them like a turkey."

My cousins stare at me with their oversized eyes, waiting for me to ease their irrational fears and tell them that *of course* I'm not going to drive by myself across the country. Not without a suitor and a chaperone, and maybe a hoopskirt to match my corset. Because oh, the horror!

I roll my eyes and squeeze past them into the small living room. "You guys need to relax. No one is going to kill me. Or eat me."

"How can you be so sure?" Alyssa's eyes manage to grow even wider.

"Because unlike the three of you," I say, dropping my purse down on the coffee table and flicking a hand in their direction, "I wasn't raised by an overprotective daddy who put the fear of God in me about stepping foot outside without a *man* to protect me. I was raised by Sherry Lacombe and I can take care of myself."

I love my uncle Noah, but holy hell, he sure raised a skittish pack of scaredy-cats. I used to be jealous of my cousins, having a daddy around their whole lives who looked out for them and endlessly doted on them, but looking at their dreadfully concerned faces now I'm grateful I dodged that bullet.

There's nothing more dangerous than being afraid of everything.

"You should just fly, Jenna," Callie says. "With us. Then we'll get to Grams faster and at the same time."

Becca nods. "Yeah."

"Yeah," Alyssa echoes as the three of them close in on me again with their pouty lips and pleading eyes.

"And waste all my hard-earned money?" I snort. "Uh-uh. I'm driving—by myself—and that's final. So chill, all of you. And step back too." I push through them, again, and head for the kitchen. "God, you're like a bunch of needy hens. Peck, peck, peck. I pity the men you three end up with."

They follow me into the kitchen. Shocking.

It's times like these I wish ASU would let students live on campus over the summer. But noooo. I had to move my ass out of the cozy dorm I shared with Pixie and shack up with my three cousins, all of whom are in silent competition for the world's most girly girl ever.

Alyssa's dressed to the nines, as per usual, even though I'm almost certain she didn't leave the apartment today. Her hair is all done up, her makeup is far too dark and drastic for anything less than a Vegas outing, and her sparkly five-inch heels match the chandelier earrings flanking her high cheekbones. A typical Tuesday getup for my cuz.

Becca's no better, with her sleeked-back hair beneath a pink headband, and her button nose between her pink cheeks, and her very pink toenails. She's adorable in that sexy kind of way, which both perplexes and impresses me.

And Callie . . . well, Callie is hell on heels with boobs that would make a swimsuit model jealous and clothes so tight I'm surprised she doesn't need a scuba tank to breathe.

They're ridiculous, all of them, and it's hard to believe we're related. With my endless tattoos and piercings, and my tendency to dress like a punk rocker, I look like Amy Lee and Lara Croft had a half-Creole baby and gave her too much eyeliner for her birthday.

Needless to say, I look out of place among my cousins. But despite my best efforts, I inherited the Lacombe genes with our high cheekbones and small frames, and I have a tendency to wear a lot of jewelry—earrings dot my ears and I have at least one ring on each of my fingers—so I can't help but look somewhat girly.

"So what are you going to do, then?" Becca asks, hand on hip, jutted chin. "Just, like, pack a bag and drive, with just the GPS on your phone to guide you and your Charger through three states?"

My red Dodge Charger is my pride and joy. It's also half of my paycheck every month, but whatever. I love it.

"Yes," I say.

"That's insane!" She throws the hip hand up. "What if you get lost?"

"What if you get robbed?" Callie says.

"What if you get eaten?" Alyssa adds in a low voice laced with honest-to-God seriousness. She whispers, "I don't want anyone to eat you."

I stare at them. It's like living with Tweedledee, Tweedledum, and Tweedle-doom.

"Yeah." I turn to the freezer and pull out a carton of ice cream. "That would be a bummer. But look at the bright side. If I get eaten, you three can pillage my wardrobe and keep whatever you want." I grin.

Callie scoffs. "Like there's anything in there we would want. Ripped jeans and leather tube tops? No thank you."

I cock an eyebrow. "Your big ass wouldn't fit into my stuff anyway."

"You're just jealous of this delicious booty." She waves her hand at her plump rear.

"I have plenty of my own booty to go around." I take a bite of ice cream.

Alyssa, who's clearly still hung up on the possibility that someone on the highway wants to eat me, puckers her lips and says, "I still don't like the idea of you driving back home by yourself."

I smile. "Blame Grandma. Woman keeps 'dying' on us at the most inconvenient times."

Becca snorts. "That's the truth. You think she's really sick this time?"

Alyssa shrugs. "Who knows? But I have to admit, I'm kind of excited about flying home. I miss Dad."

"Me too," the other two say, nodding.

As they chat about their amazing father and how wonderful it is to have such a loving daddy, I put the ice cream away and head to my room to pack. It doesn't take me long, mostly because all I have to do is shove pretty much everything I own into the large purple suitcase my mom got me when I first moved out here and I'm good to go.

Sherry Lacombe wasn't thrilled about me leaving our home in Louisiana. She wanted me to stay nearby, and for good reason. I'm her beloved daughter and friend, of course, but I'm also her helper. I have three younger sisters at home: four-year-old Shyla, six-year-old Raine, and sixteen-year-old Penny.

When I was twelve, my mother decided to become a foster parent. It was supposed to be a temporary thing, but Mama couldn't help herself and just kept falling in love with the baby girls she took in and managed to adopt each one. By the time I was eighteen, she was a single mother of four.

My younger sisters are a lot of fun, but they can also be quite a handful. I know my mom really appreciated my help when it came to raising them and running the house, especially after Grandma started "dying" and moved in with us. We were a very happy—and very broke—female family of six, and my waitressing job in New Orleans provided just as much household income as my mom's job at the medical clinic. We were strapped for cash and I was going nowhere, looking at a future of waiting tables and living paycheck to paycheck just like my mom.

I'd been out of high school for almost two years and was starting to lose hope in myself, and my dream of someday opening a gallery to display my sculptures, so when Arizona State University offered me an art scholarship—and the prospect of a better future—I couldn't pass up the opportunity for free schooling.

Mom was not pleased when I announced that I wanted to go to school out of state. But once she accepted the fact that I needed to move away, not just for school, but so I could make something of myself and secure some kind of future for my family, she was completely on board. Hence, the awesome purple suitcase.

And it ended up being better than I could have imagined because I met Pixie. Even though I'm a year and a half older than she is, we'll both be starting our sophomore year of art school this fall and I couldn't be happier. Arizona was definitely a good move for me.

I pack until it's overflowing and I have to sit on the luggage to get it zipped up. Then I change into my jammies, say good night to the gaggle of hens in the living room, and crawl into bed.

4

JACK

*W*hy do you insist on looking like a douche bag every time you leave the apartment?" I say, frowning at Ethan's attire.

After we left the bar, we came back to our shitty apartment where Ethan immediately changed into what he calls his "Peacock Smock"—yes, it's as horrible as it sounds—and started making faces at himself in the mirror of the single bathroom we share. And because I keep walking past the bathroom on my way up and down the hallway as I start packing for the road trip Jenna doesn't know I'm joining her on, I can't *not* look at him.

"This," Ethan says, gesturing to his skintight purple jeans and the black dress shirt he's left deeply unbuttoned to reveal the three gold chains hanging down his chest, "is an attention grabber. First I capture the ladies' eyes with my outfit. Then I reel in their hearts with my charm."

I shake my head as I yank my duffle bag from the hall closet. "I don't know where you read that bullshit, but you look ridiculous. Which in turn makes me look ridiculous. Please stop making me look ridiculous."

"Sorry." He places a fedora on his head at a very precise angle and shucks his shoulders at his reflection. "No can do. I'm going clubbing tonight and I don't want to jeopardize my game."

I roll my eyes and, turning away, head down the hall for my room, calling back, "Clubbing? What are you, a teenage pop star?" I snort. "Jenna was right, dude. You have no game."

I hear him scoff. "At least I have my own balls."

I drop the duffle bag on my bed and glare at him through the doorway. "What's that supposed to mean?"

He flicks up his open collar. "It means Jenna has your balls in her hand and you let her squeeze them as tightly as she wants."

"Fuck you."

He raises his hands. "Hey man, I'm not saying it's a bad thing. I'm just saying that Jenna could claim bird shit was delicious and you'd probably think she was 'right' about that too."

I scowl and turn away. "This has nothing to do with Jenna. You have no game, Ethan. Own it."

He mocks, "*Own it*," as I start shoving clothes in my bag.

My pocket vibrates and I pull out my phone only to frown at the screen before answering, "What?"

Samson clucks his tongue. "We really need to work on your telephone greetings, man."

"What do you want?"

"It's not me this time. Mom wanted me to call and remind you to bring an umbrella, in case it rains."

I scoff. "Did she want you to call me about an umbrella or did she want you to check up on me and make sure I was really heading out there?"

"Both, probably."

I sigh. "Right. Well, tell her to relax. I'm leaving tomorrow." A pause. "How's she doing?"

Samson hesitates a moment. "Not good."

Of course she's not doing good. Her son is missing. Missing.

Where we come from, there are only two reasons a guy goes missing: He's either on the run or in the ground. Neither of which sound like Drew.

Drew's not a fighter or a dealer. If anything, he's the opposite. A mama's boy, who follows the rules and stays out of trouble.

I stop packing. "I don't like this, Sam. Something feels wrong."

"I know," he says. "I'm trying my best to figure all this shit out, Jack. I swear. But you know how it is out here. No one will talk to me—because I'm not you. I don't have your connections. Your associations."

"Damn straight, you don't," I snap harshly, red-hot protectiveness and fear burning beneath my skin.

"Right," Samson says slowly. "My point is that I can only do so much without you, but I'm working my ass off to find any leads on Drew. I really am."

"I know you are, Sam." I quiet my tone. It's not his fault, all this shit. It never was. "Drew's lucky to have you there." A wave of guilt crashes into me and I ride it out until it hurts just enough for me to surface for air.

I shouldn't have left Little Vail. I shouldn't have left my family.

But I needed to leave. I *had* to.

It was my only chance to get out.

I shouldn't have left—

"No. Drew's lucky to have *you*, bro." Samson's words cut open a fresh wound and smooth it over at the same time. Guilt's a fickle bitch. "We all are."

With a thick swallow, I go back to shoving clothes in my duffle bag. "How's Mom doing on money? Does she need more? I can send more—"

"She's fine. We're all fine," he says. "We don't need anything but your overprotective ass out here to help with this Drew situation. How are you coming out? You flying?"

"Nah. I'm hitching a ride with a friend."

"Why don't you take your motorcycle?"

I go back to stuffing items into the duffle. "Because it's a long trip to make by myself. Can't risk getting delayed by bike troubles and shit. Besides, what if it *rains*?" I mock.

"What, are you scared of getting wet?"

"No. I'm just not a reckless moron like you."

He scoffs. "So then fly."

I zip up my bag and toss it by my bedroom door. "I thought about it. But I've got a friend driving out to NOLA anyway so I figured I'd make the best of it. You're good until later this week, right?" I say. "Mom doesn't need me sooner?"

"No, she'll be cool until you get here," he says. "Besides, she's got me to keep her company now, remember? I'm living with her again. You know, because of the whole thing with Trixie kicking me out."

"God, you're horrible with women."

He scoffs. "You're one to talk. You haven't had a woman like... ever."

I scowl. "*Had a woman?*"

"You know what I mean. You never date anyone. Not seriously."

"Right," I say. "And no one's ever kicked me out. Funny how that works."

"Asshole," he mutters. "On that note... I'm signing off. I'll be seeing you later this week, I guess. I'd tell you to ride safe but since you're too much of a baby to ride in the rain..."

"Fuck off."

"That's the spirit. See you later, bro." The line goes dead and

I shove the phone back into my pocket before getting a pack of cigarettes out of my other pocket. Then I haul my bag out to the living room.

"Damn." Ethan eyes my bag as he slips a flashy watch over his wrist. "How are you going to fit that thing on your Harley?"

"I'm not," I say, finding a lighter in the key tray we keep in the kitchen. "I'm going with Jenna. Her grandma isn't doing so well so she's driving out to Louisiana to visit and I'm thinking about hitching a ride."

Slipping out the back door, I step onto the small apartment balcony and light up. Ethan stands in the doorway, watching me inhale.

"Seriously?"

I nod.

"Have you asked Jenna?"

I shake my head.

"Why not?"

I swear, it's like living with a girl, all the questions.

"Because." I let out a long cloud of smoke. "If I *ask* her, she'll say no. If I just show up... well, she'll still say no, but it'll be a hell of a lot easier to talk her into saying yes when she's caught off guard and looking at me."

He shakes his head. "You need to stop fucking with her, Jack. That's not cool."

I stare at him. "Me? If anything, she's fucking with me." I inhale through my nose and look away.

"I like Jenna, dude," Ethan says. "And if her grandma's not doing well then you shouldn't be adding to her stress. She's not as tough as she looks—"

"Don't you—" I snap, then relax my shoulders and calm my

tone. "Don't talk to me like I don't know shit about Jenna. I need a ride and she's thinking about driving across the whole fucking country by herself." I take another drag and try to push out all my fear over Jenna traveling alone with a long exhale. "It's a win-win situation."

Ethan slowly nods, remains silent for a moment, then retreats back into the apartment, leaving the balcony door open. "Good luck, dude," he calls out as he leaves through the front door, then adds, "You're going to need it."

I stay on the balcony and stare down at the noisy Tempe traffic around ASU's campus.

In a way, I guess he's right. Jenna's going to be pissed. And when she's upset she's hell on heels and fierceness on fire. But frankly, I don't give a damn. She can claw at my face if it means I'll get to accompany her on this reckless little cross-country jaunt of hers.

Damn Jenna. She's too brave for her own good. Don't get me wrong, I like her backbone. I like the fight in her veins and the sharpness of her talons. But that doesn't mean she's invincible. None of us are.

Taking a seat on the lone plastic chair on the balcony, I lean back and puff again on my cigarette. Tomorrow's going to be a challenge, talking her into letting me tag along on her trip, but as long as I show up with my nice-guy face on—and keep my hands to myself—I know she'll cave. And if she doesn't, well...then I'll have no choice but to use my hands. And Jenna's never been able to say no to my hands.

5

JENNA

One positive aspect of living with three girly girls is that no one gives you crap when you load half of your possessions into your car for a quick road trip.

Three suitcases might seem like overkill for a visit back home but I really had no choice. The first suitcase is for my clothes. The second for my hair and makeup supplies, because beauty takes time—and lots of tools. And the third, of course, is for my shoes. Shoes get their own piece of luggage since they are practically works of art. Or at least mine are.

Cramming everything into my trunk, I slam it closed before heading back upstairs to the apartment to grab the last thing I need: my purse. Stepping inside, I am once again bombarded by the hens.

"Call every three hours," Becca says, biting her thumbnail.

"And don't pull over unless it's a total emergency," Callie adds, pointing a long manicured finger at me.

"And whatever you do, don't talk to strangers." Alyssa's eyes are even more wide this morning than they were last night.

I let out a long exhale as I pick up my purse then turn to my well-meaning but completely obnoxious cousins.

I look at Becca. "I'm not calling every three hours. That's

ridiculous. I might call once a day. Maybe." Pointing back at Callie, I say, "I will pull over whenever I damn well please. But I promise I'll try not to pull over on desolate strips of freeway littered with signs that say Watch Out! Killer Nearby! Sound good?" She glares at me as I turn to Alyssa. "I won't talk to strangers—unless they're hot and offer me candy, in which case…" I smile. Her eyes bulge even more. "Girl, you need to stop doing that with your eyes or they're going to pop right out of that pretty little head of yours and accidentally get stomped on by my boots." I gesture to the high-heeled boots I'm wearing.

Are they practical for driving? Certainly not. But they're red and made of awesome so I shall sport them cross-country.

"Just please be careful," Callie warns in the big-sister voice she typically reserves for her younger sisters.

She and I are pretty much the same age so she rarely takes that tone with me, but I'm well aware of the seriousness built up behind it so I place my hand on her shoulder and get real for a minute.

"Callie. I promise I will be safe. You don't need to worry." I meet her eyes with a silent look of sincerity and she nods. Opening the door, I smile at the three of them. "I will see you guys when I get to Grams, okay? Love ya." We exchange hugs that are extra squishy, then I make my way back down the apartment stairs to my red car.

The Tweedles stare down at me from their perch on the mid-point landing and I wave a final good-bye before unlocking the doors and sliding into the front seat. Pulling the door closed behind me, I turn to put the key in the ignition and—

"Ahh!" I jump back, startled and pissed, then thwack my open palm against the gigantic body of pure muscle seated in the passenger seat. "God damn you, Jack! You scared the shit out of me!"

Okay, so maybe hitting him wasn't very mature but I couldn't help myself. My nerves are a little on edge and, honestly, Jack's just so...big, anyone in their right mind would be terrified to be caught off guard by his presence.

"What the hell?" I snap, throwing him some serious stink eye.

He grins. "Good morning."

"What are you doing in my car?" I glance up through the windshield at where my cousins still stand on the landing, captivated by Jack's sudden appearance.

Great.

"I'm going with you," he says.

I whip my eyes back to him. "What?"

"To Louisiana." He points to a large duffle bag in the backseat.

I blink. "Uh, no you're not."

"Uh, yes I am."

"Like hell."

He crinkles his brow. "I've never understood that phrase. But okay. I'll go with you 'like hell,' whatever that means."

"Get out of my car." I point to his door.

"Oh, Jenna." He clucks his tongue and his eyes flash. "This will be good for both of us."

For a moment, I stare at him, not sure how to interpret his words. He watches me carefully, clearly enjoying the fact that my mind went anywhere other than his sentence.

I cock an eyebrow and cross my arms. "What are you talking about?"

He casually leans against the passenger window like he belongs in my car, like he's perfectly comfortable horning in on my space, and pierces me with his gray eyes. "It's like this. For reasons beyond my control, I need to go back home. And for reasons beyond your control, so do you. So since our 'homes' are right next door to one another, I figured we'd carpool to Louisiana and you can just drop me off at Little Vail on your way to New Orleans."

He gives me that little-boy smile of his and it's all I can do not to lean forward and soak it in. I hate me.

"I don't see how that's good for me," I say. "At all."

He shrugs. "You get some company on the road."

I nod with a clenched jaw. "And you get a free ride."

His eyes meet mine and I instantly realize that was the wrong thing to say.

His smile grows. "Precisely."

I shake my head. "I don't need any company."

I don't like spending excessive time with Jack. Not just because we fight, but because of what *happened* last year. It was one crazy night when we were both drunk, and we never spoke of it after the fact, but our "friendship" has been tense ever since.

Nevertheless, I haven't been able to shake my attraction to Jack since that night, and sitting two feet away from him for an entire road trip certainly won't help anything. I need him to get the hell out of my car. Immediately.

"Sure you do," he says easily. "Everyone needs company."

"Not me. So get out."

He grins. "No."

God I hate him. But not really. God I hate that I don't hate him.

I jut my chin, stare him over, then suck air in through my teeth. "Fine. If you won't remove yourself…" Exiting the driver's-side door, I stomp around the hood of the car over to his door, yank it open, and wrap my hands around his bicep. Then I start pulling.

He doesn't budge. Like, he literally doesn't move an inch as I tug at his oversized arm and grunt like I'm trying to move a massive piece of hardwood furniture and not a human being.

His eyes dance as he watches my struggle. "What's your plan here, Jenna? Haul me out of the car and leave me in the street?"

"Yep." I catch sight of my cousins watching with rapt attention from the stairs, Becca still biting her thumbnail.

"Well, now. That doesn't sound friendly at all," he says, flicking the lever to recline the seat a bit so he looks even more relaxed than before.

I try pulling him out again, to no avail. He's giant and solid, and honestly, just touching him is turning me on. I drop my hands and take a steadying breath as I think about the scene my cousins are watching. A grown woman trying to yank a six-foot-four-inch tattooed male from a car? This must look ridiculous.

Taking a step back, I swipe a lock of my sleek dark hair away from my face and glower at the gray eyes smiling at me. "I'm not trying to be friendly."

"Clearly."

Callie's voice chastises me from the top of the stairs. "Just let him go with you, Jenna. It'll make everyone feel better."

He grins up at Callie then at me. "See? I have supporters."

I sneer. "Just because my cousins think you're some kind of motorcycle god doesn't mean I'm putty in your hands. You can't just *tell* me that you're coming along on *my* road trip."

"Would you feel better if I asked?"

"Not especially."

"Jenna." He leans forward and sinks his eyes into mine in a way he's only done a handful of times since I've known him. It's an intimate look, a meaningful gaze, and I can feel his eyes boring right through me and down into the deepest parts of my being. "Will you please let me join you on your trip to Louisiana?"

For a moment, I'm lost in his eyes. Speechless. Vulnerable. Then I pull back, straighten my shoulders, and slap on a scowl as I stare at him, pissed.

I don't trust myself around Jack. And he drives me crazy. Crazy in a way I've never been able to control.

But I *did* spend half the night tossing in my sleep with nightmares about being eaten by some crazy highway psycho—thank you, cousins—and all morning I've had doubts about traveling alone. Having Jack tag along might not be so bad. He's obnoxious, sure, but he'd never let anything bad happen to me. Surely I can manage to keep my panties on around him for a few days...right?

I relent, as per usual when it comes to Jack, but refuse to make eye contact with him as I stomp back to my side of the car. "Fine. But no talking."

Seeing my concession, my cousins clap their hands in glee and I roll my eyes. The sooner I'm out of Arizona, the better.

"No talking?" he says as I get back in the car and start the engine. "That doesn't sound reasonable. Or polite."

I wave good-bye to my onlooking cousins as we pull away. "Shut up."

"Now that *definitely* wasn't polite."

"Are you still talking?"

"Are you still being rude—"

"Shh!"

He chuckles and lifts the lever on his seat so he's seated upright again. "Oh, this is going to be fun, Jenna. You'll see."

"Shut up."

"Ask nicely."

"*Please* shut up."

He considers for a moment. "No."

And that's how the first ten minutes of our "fun" road trip go down; with me snapping at him to *shut it*, and him defying me with a happy smile.

Ten minutes down, twenty-one hours to go. Louisiana has never felt so far away in my life.

But once we're on the freeway and headed out of town, the reality of my situation sets in—as does my jaw—and I want to slap myself for letting Jack talk me into this nonsense. I do not need a chaperone, or any other kind of accompaniment, on this trip. I'm a big girl and I can take care of myself.

I bite back a curse and grip the steering wheel tighter than necessary. Damn Jack. How does he manage to get his way with me time and time again? And why do I always cave? Damn me.

From the corner of my eye, I see him glance at me for the fourth time since we left Tempe, and a warm current rushes through my veins. Damn, damn, damn.

We pass a sign that reads COPPER SPRINGS 100 MILES, and I switch lanes to pass a slowpoke car in front of me.

My agreement to this couple's road trip was a momentary lapse in judgment and, frankly, I blame Jack and his all-knowing eyes. He knows what he does to me. He knows I can't resist the way he looks at me when he's being real. Yes. This is *his* fault, and I'm not about to spend the next few days cooped up in a small space with him just because he has manipulative eyes. We're turning around.

I glimpse at the endless freeway in front of me and frown.

Okay, at the next stop, we're turning around. End of story. And co-ed road trip.

I fidget with one of the rings on my left hand, spinning it around my finger as I think up a smooth way to inform Jack that our joyride has come to an end. He's going to pitch a fit, I already know it.

Clearing my throat in the pleasant silence we've shared for the past, oh, twenty minutes, I use my sternest voice and say, "Listen, Jack—"

"No."

"No?" I glance at him. "You don't even know what I was going to say."

"Yes, I do." He fixes his gaze out the windshield. "You were going to say this was a mistake and that you're turning this car around, or something to that effect, so I'm saying no. It's too late to change your mind." He looks out the side window. "And besides, I need to get to Louisiana. I don't have time for your fickle behavior, Jenna. Not today."

With his face turned away, I can't read his expression, but his tone tells me all I need to know. That was a jab, meant to pierce the thickest shields of denial I've built around my heart, and it shot straight through each one.

It shouldn't hurt the way it does, the past, the truth. But I can't seem to guard myself against Jack's thoughts on how I've handled— or rather, refused to handle—the topic of *us*.

"Please, tell me how you really feel," I say bitterly. "Don't be subtle on my account."

A beat passes where he doesn't look at me. "I'm never subtle."

I snort. And isn't that the truth.

I could fall for his bait—that's what it is, bait to start a long-overdue conversation—but that would mean bringing up feelings and fears and, even worse, what happened last year, and I don't have the heart or the stomach for any of that. So instead I settle for blaring angry-girl music on the radio.

Jack sits still for exactly fifteen seconds before changing the station to something akin to angry-*boy* music. Like that's happening. I change it back. So does he.

"Quit it, or I will voodoo you so you don't wake up in the morning," I snap.

"Already threatening to kill me?" He sighs dramatically. "I thought for *sure* we'd make it until sundown before you played the voodoo card."

I ignore him and tune the radio to '90s rock. "My car. My music."

Alanis Morissette comes on singing "You Oughta Know," and Jack groans. For a split second, I feel for him. I know how much he despises Alanis Morissette.

"Can we please listen to something else?" he says. "I swear I'm not trying to be a dick this time."

I lift a brow. "Oh, so you admit you were trying to be a dick a second ago?"

"Of course." He shrugs. "Angry-girl music? Come on. Could you be any more obvious?"

I try not to overthink that as I flick a hand at him. "You'll listen to polka if I so desire. That's the cost of inviting yourself into my vehicle."

He looks at me. "Fine, diva. I'd rather listen to polka than to a scorned woman screaming about how all men are no good."

With a sugar-sweet tone, I say, "Too close to home?"

He smiles sharply. "You tell me."

Yeaaah. There's no way I'm spending another hour with this

man, let alone another week. We have more unresolved issues than the characters on *Gossip Girl*.

"That's it," I say, veering right for the nearest exit ramp.

"What are you going to do, pull the car over and give me a firm talking-to?" he mocks.

"Ha. We're way beyond talking."

He looks out the window again. "Oh, I know."

I glare at him. "See? That's what I'm talking about. You keep alluding to shit, trying to provoke me, and I'm done."

"What?" He crinkles his brow in confusion. "No one in their right mind would try to provoke you, Jenna. You're like a caged cat in heat. All claws and teeth. You're already provoked—and you have been since the moment I met you. So why don't you just calm down and get back on the freeway." He looks around. "Where are we, anyway?"

"Oh, I'll tell you where we are." I point a finger in the air and lift my chin, utterly pissed that he just referred to me as a cat in heat. I whip into the parking lot of Willow Inn and skid to a stop. "We're at your final destination."

Thank God Willow Inn is out here in the middle of nowhere and, therefore, an ideal drop-off station for unwanted passengers. I couldn't have handled one more second with Jack and his laid-back attitude.

I throw the car in park and look at him, waiting.

A small smile peeks at the corners of his mouth, but otherwise he doesn't move. "You think you're dropping me off at this..."— he peers up at the quaint-looking building—"large replica of Snow White's cottage in the middle of nowhere?"

I nod once. "This is where Pixie works—or worked—this

summer and I'm sure her aunt can make arrangements for you to catch a cab back to Tempe. Or to Little Vail, if you so desire. But Jenna's Chauffeur Service is officially closed for business. Now get out."

He scans my face and inhales slowly, then lowers his voice. "I know it's not easy, this thing with you and me, and I'm sorry if I've been more of a dick than usual, but Jenna..." He shakes his head. "I'm not leaving you."

His tone, his words, everything about his presence in this moment completely contradicts everything about him so far today. And this is where the Jack Conundrum comes into play. It's easier when he's acting like an ass. More simple when he tries to annoy the hell out of me. But when he's *this* person...this deep, genuine, intense soul with gunmetal eyes and a determined jaw...that's when things get complicated.

And I don't want complicated.

"I wasn't asking," I say. Then, exiting the car, I grab his duffle bag from the backseat and march for the inn's front doors. Good God his bag is heavy. What did he pack in here, barbells?

Behind me, I hear the passenger door open and close. "It'll be a lonely trip without me, you know." Jack's voice rumbles up my back and over my shoulders. "There's only so much companionship your angry-girl music can give you."

I make a face at the inn's front porch steps as I climb them. Companionship, my ass.

"I'll pay for all the gas," he sings, like that's worth tolerating his presence for days on end. "And I'll drive when it gets dark."

I slow my steps. I hadn't thought about how exhausted I might be driving at nighttime. Having another driver to help ease that burden would be nice...What? No! No. I scoff, more at myself than at Jack's words, but he perceives it differently and responds in typical Jack fashion.

"Oh, come on," he says. "You hate wearing glasses when you drive and we both know you're pretty much blind as a bat at night without your glasses on."

"I am not *blind as a bat*."

I hear the smile in his voice. "Okay. Blind as a cat, then."

I growl in frustration. "I can't believe I even considered driving back home with you. I would've ripped your head off long before we crossed the Texas border." Heaving open the inn's front door, I charge through and shoot my eyes to him over my shoulder. "Frankly, I'm impressed we made it this far without me killing you."

He grins. "What's with all the death threats? Is that how you handle all of life's problems? By committing murder?"

Dropping the duffle bag, I spin around and sneer at his tall body. "Just the really big ones." Briefly—like so brief it's not even a second—I glance him over in an appreciative way. Because he really is gorgeous, with his broad shoulders and square jaw and dark tattoos covering his big arms—but then I pull it together and lift my chin in anger. But it's too late.

He caught my wandering eyes and now *his* eyes know. They always know, dammit.

His smile goes crooked. "First of all, there's no need to take your frustration out on my luggage." He points to the bag on the floor, then leans down so our faces are close together. Too close. Close enough to smell the woodsy scent of his shampoo and feel his warm exhaling on my cheeks. "Second," he says with playful eyes. "Is that your way of telling me I'm big?"

We lock gazes and my heart beats against my chest. Ugh. If only I could hate this infuriating man. Life would be *so* much easier.

6

JACK

*B*ehind the check-in counter, an attractive woman with long, dark hair clears her throat, clearly not entertained by our little spat, and smiles at Jenna.

"Jenna," she says. "Welcome to the inn. I didn't know you were stopping by. Pixie's not here, though."

Jenna whips her eyes away from me and focuses on the woman. "Oh, I'm not here for Pixie. I'm here to drop off this bozo"—she points to me in a dramatic way—"so I can be on my way to New Orleans."

Bozo. Wow. She's so flustered she can't even come up with good insults.

Biting back a smile, I turn to the woman behind the counter and nod at the feisty cat who is now seething in my general direction. If only she knew how hot that was.

"Jenna's not big on road trip buddies," I explain. "And she has a hard time being enclosed in small spaces with me. I'm Jack, by the way." I hold out my hand.

"Ellen," the woman says, slowly shaking my hand as her hazel eyes dart to Jenna with silent questions.

I wink at Jenna.

She throws her arms up and growls, "You infuriating man."

I just smile at her. "You're adorable. I'll just take my bag *back* to the car and wait for you until you're done throwing your temper tantrum." I nod again at Ellen. "It was so nice meeting you."

Picking up the duffle bag, I exit the inn with Jenna's glaring eyes trained on me until the front door closes between us.

She's frustrated, and I take that as a good sign. I know Jenna better than she'd ever admit so I know she's not really upset with me. If she were, she wouldn't bother talking to me at all. I'd be suffering her silent treatment right now, and probably her eternal scorn, if I'd truly pissed her off.

Instead, she's frustrated with herself, for caring when she doesn't want to care, and a part of me feels bad about that.

Who am I kidding? I don't feel bad at all. She can drown in her own confusion for all I care—just as long as she surfaces with a clear head and some inner honesty.

After putting the bag away, I check my phone. Another four missed calls from back home.

Shit.

Walking back up the inn's front steps, I stand in the shade and light a cigarette. Just as I take my first drag, a guy rounds the porch from the side of the inn and slows his walk when he sees me.

"Hey," he says.

I tip my chin. "Hey."

He looks like a frat boy, with short brown hair, dark eyes, and eyebrows that are too perfect to belong to a dude.

He furrows those girly brows in confusion as he looks around. "Are you a guest here?"

I shake my head. "Nah. Just making a quick stop on my way out of town. I'm Jack."

"Daren," he says.

I nod at the front door of the inn. "My friend Jenna knows the owner."

His eyebrows rise. "Jenna's here?"

My pulse instantly hammers and I feel the hot sting of jealousy prick just beneath my skin. How the hell does this pretty boy know Jenna? And more importantly, how *well* does he know her?

I nod once. "You guys know each other?"

"Yeah, we met briefly a few weeks ago at the lake, through her friend, Pixie."

I nod, satisfied that his knowledge of Jenna extends only to meeting her once. In public.

"I know Pixie," I say. And then, because I know Pixie's from a small town, I ask, "You guys grow up together, or what?"

"Something like that," he says. "How do you know Jenna?"

"We used to work together." It's the simple answer.

He scoffs. "I bet that was interesting. That girl's got some claws on her."

I smirk, oddly proud of the fact that Jenna scares this pretty boy. "Tell me about it. You on her shit list, or what?"

He lets out a breath and slowly nods. "I'm afraid so. I'm pretty sure she'd cut my balls off if she had the chance."

"Yeah." I scratch my cheek. "She's not the kind of girl you should piss off."

He snorts. "Is there any kind of girl you should piss off?"

I grin. "Spoken like a guy with experience." I take a drag of my smoke. "You fuck something up with a girl?"

He looks through the inn's front window at where Jenna is talking to a pretty blonde girl and inhales. "Yep."

I turn away and exhale a thin cloud of smoke. "That sucks."

He shrugs and looks hesitantly at the inn's front door, as if he's scared to go inside, but not sure if he wants to stay outside either. "I wasn't good enough for her anyway."

I take another drag and cock my head. "Girls don't want guys that are good enough for them." I exhale slowly. "They want guys that know what they want."

Daren looks off to the side. "Then I'm screwed."

I stare at my burning cigarette. "You're only screwed if you give up."

He narrows his eyes with a sneer. "Yeah, that's not cheesy. What, is that your motto or something?"

"No." I scoff. "But it should be."

He nods knowingly. "Jenna got you running circles, or what?"

I flick the ashes from the cigarette and nod. "Jenna's hard to walk away from."

"Aren't they all?"

I look at him, then through the window at the blonde. "You tell me."

He looks through the window as well and I swear I see true pain in his eyes. "Maybe we're both screwed."

I take a final drag. "Maybe."

Shaking himself from whatever memory it is that has him so haunted, Daren straightens his shoulders with a smirk. "Well good luck to you, then."

"Same to you," I say.

He moves across the porch, bypassing the front door, probably to avoid the blonde girl inside, and disappears around the corner.

I put out my finished cigarette and pop a piece of gum in my mouth. Jenna is going to bitch when she smells smoke on me. I already know it. But the gum might buy me a little time.

Then, cracking open the large inn door, I poke my head inside. Spying Jenna across the lobby, I watch her for a moment. She's speaking in hushed tones with the pretty blonde Daren's so hung up on, and leaning in with a mischievous smile.

All I can think about as I watch Jenna's eyes light up is how much I want that smile pointed at me.

The way I felt about Jenna used to piss me off. I've never been one to need or even want a girl messing up my life. Just the opposite, in fact. The Lone Wolf role suited me well and I was perfectly content with my world of solitude. But Jenna came along and twisted everything up. She turned me inside out and made me feel complete in a way that made no sense. I fought the sentiment, of course. There's no room for anyone in my fucked-up life—especially not a wild, stubborn, reckless girl like Jenna.

But fighting proved futile, and somewhat self-destructive, so I did what all good leaders do when they realize losing a battle could mean winning the war: I surrendered. Not to Jenna, exactly, but to the way she made me feel. It's not a pretty or romantic thing. It's a truth with scars and holes—and it commands me completely.

Does that make me weak? I used to think so. But then I see Jenna, still in the throes of a battle I've long since succumbed to, and I wonder which of us is stronger. Which of us sleeps well at night and which of us tosses in the moonlight.

Strength isn't about what you can and cannot achieve. It's about what you will and will not do *in order* to achieve. And on that, I know exactly where I stand.

Watching Jenna across the lobby, I take a deep breath and prepare for round two of what is sure to be a memorable—if not fatal—trip back home.

I call out, "I'm ready when you are, diva!"

Complete agitation covers her face as she whips around with narrowed eyes and yells, "Don't. Call. Me. DIVA!"

I grin. "It never gets old."

"God!" she exclaims, thrusting her arms up again.

The look on her face is priceless. I could do this all day. I might, actually.

Wagging my eyebrows in a totally inappropriate and suggestive manner, I slip back outside and let the door fall shut.

A moment later, the inn door flies open and Jenna stomps down the porch steps to meet me by the car. I quickly shove my phone in my pocket, wanting to put as much distance as possible between my present circumstances and the mess waiting for me in Little Vail, and climb into the car at the same time she does.

She's huffing and puffing and cursing under her breath like a spoiled teenager, but when her eyes finally flick to mine there's no hostility there, just impatience.

"You're paying for all the gas," she says, sliding a pair of dark sunglasses over her golden eyes. "And I mean every single drop."

I lean back in the passenger seat, repressing the joyous satisfaction I feel at the haughtiness on her face. "Yes, ma'am."

If buying Jenna's gas keeps her safe by my side then I'll purchase every last drop in the country. And then some.

7

JENNA

I'm well aware that I caved. Again. Which just proves that I really am putty when it comes to Jack. Not a good sign, especially considering the extensive amount of quality one-on-one time we'll be spending together now that I've misplaced my backbone and bent to Jack's every whim.

A shiver runs through me, and not the unwelcome kind. Damn Jack.

Jack makes things interesting. And I like having him around. These things are both true, despite my best efforts. But Jack can't know that. Not just because it would ruin my grand life plan—which by the way, largely depends on me not getting involved with a guy, like ever—but because it would screw with his head. And I don't screw with guys' heads.

Do I flirt? Sure. Do I sleep with guys I'm attracted to? Absolutely. But I never lead guys on. It's something I'm quite proud of, actually, and if I slip up around Jack that's exactly what will happen. He'll think one thing and I'll be sure to do another. That's the risk I'm taking, here on this journey across the states. And honestly, I'm not sure if it's worth it. If I were to hurt Jack more than I already have... well, I might never recover.

Which is precisely why sitting so close to him in my little red car is a bad idea. But whatever. The chips have been laid, the bet called, and now we're in a spinning roulette. Here's hoping we don't both come away from this empty-hearted.

My phone rings. It's Pixie.

"Hey, Pix," I answer.

"Hey! How's the road trip going?" She sounds ridiculously happy, which is a symptom of her being ridiculously in love, no doubt.

I wonder, for like a nanosecond, if I'll ever be so in love that I sound that happy. But I quickly banish that thought. Not because I'm anti-love or anything, but because I have other priorities.

"It's going…okay," I say, sneaking a peek at Jack. "How's our dorm room looking?"

"Great. Levi has us pretty much all unpacked and moved in."

I smile. "Bless that boy."

"So…" she says. "Ellen just called me."

I groan. "She told you about Jack?"

He glances at me across the car, but I ignore him.

"Yep," Pixie says. "So what's the deal? I thought you were driving solo to New Orleans."

"I was. But Jack needed a ride back home too and one thing led to another and now he's sitting beside me."

"Hey, Pixie!" Jack shouts at the phone with a smile.

"Hey, Jack!" she calls back then sighs cheerfully. "I love how everyone is calling me Pixie now, instead of Sarah."

"It suits you better," I say. "So what did Auntie tell you about us?"

"Just that you tried to dump Jack at Willow Inn," she says. "Come on, Jenna. It can't be that bad. Personally, I think it's a good thing you have someone with you. And the fact that it's Jack is even better."

I narrow my eyes. "Why?"

She laughs. "Uh, because he's your friend? And even though you guys have weird sexual tension—"

"We do *not* have weird sexual tension—"

"Yes, you *do*. Don't deny it."

Jack watches me with amusement and I purposely look away.

"All I'm saying," Pixie continues, "is that even though you guys have weird sexual tension, you still get along well."

"What are you talking about? We fight all the time." Now I *do* look at Jack.

Pixie scoffs playfully. "My point exactly."

"Whatever."

"Fine. Be in denial. It won't change anything." I hear the smile in her voice. "But drive safely, okay? And come back soon! I already miss you and you probably haven't even crossed the border yet."

I laugh softly. "I miss you too. Later, Pix."

We hang up and Jack cocks his head at me.

I scowl. "What?"

He grins. "Weird sexual tension, huh?"

I roll my eyes and turn up the radio. "Whatever."

He looks away from me, but his grin stays in place.

We don't speak for the rest of our journey through Arizona and I'm grateful for the reprieve. Don't get me wrong. I like talking to Jack. Truly. He's fascinating in his own way. Part trouble, part mystery. Playful and pensive. He's one of the few males on this planet I enjoy conversing with—when he's not being a dickhead, of course. But at this particular moment, I appreciate his silence. Mostly because it means I'm spared from the sound of his voice.

It's a manly voice, husky and rough, yet somehow beautiful as it drifts my way and caresses my ears. It's always been kryptonite for me, much like his omniscient eyes, and in many ways it's more powerful than even his hands, which is saying something.

But eyes I can turn away from, and hands I can pull back from, but a voice...

A voice is an inescapable lover, unbidden and undeniable. You cannot unhear an enticing phrase or a whispered word, just as you cannot unfeel the heated breath that accompanies such things. And Jack's voice, especially when saying my name, is my total undoing.

So the silence is welcome as we travel beyond the Arizona border, and even more so when the sun falls behind the mountains in the rearview mirror and dusk sweeps across the desolate New Mexico desert. But as darkness crawls out from the extended shadows of the sunset and slowly ushers in the coming night, the silence starts to grow thick and my mind starts to wander to naughty memories.

Nightfall does this to people, reminds them of darkness and all the things done therein. Activities that evoke pleasure and passion.

Suddenly feeling hot, I crack my window and let a thin wave of warm summer air stream in from the pink-and-purple-streaked sky. I slowly inhale. Even though the air does nothing to cool me down, I still welcome the breeze moving over my skin. Like soft fingertips, gliding inside my elbow...trailing up over my arm... sliding up my neck and along my jaw...

Another shiver moves through me and I curse the sun for setting so soon. Then I curse myself for not living in a place where the sun stays out all day and night during the summer. Like northern Russia. Or Alaska. Yeah, that's how upset I am with the damn sun. I'm wishing I lived in frigid Alaska.

"You seem antsy," Jack says.

From the way he reclined his seat when we crossed the Arizona/ New Mexico border, I was hoping he'd fall asleep by sunset. No such luck.

I force my shoulders to relax as I roll my neck. "I'm not antsy. Just tired." That's not true at all, but explaining to Jack that his mere presence makes me think of sex would just make the descending darkness hotter.

"Perfect timing, then." He moves his seat back up and stretches his neck. "Since it's my turn to drive."

I glance at him. "Seriously? I thought you were joking about that."

"I never joke about blind people driving."

The comfort I drew from his silence these past few hours instantly dissipates. "I am *not* blind."

"Oh, really," he says, pointing out the windshield. "Then why don't you read that neon-green sign way up there?"

I squint at the freeway lights, all of which seem to be glowing. "I don't see any green sign."

"My point exactly," he says. "Pull over."

I continue searching and frown. "Knowing you, there probably isn't a green sign at all. Don't mess with me, Jack. I'm totally fine to drive."

"There absolutely *is* a green sign and you are not fine to drive." When I don't respond he adds, "Please don't be stubborn about this. I know your vision gets soft at night, like every light has a halo around it, and I know that makes it difficult to drive."

Now that I think about it, it does look like there are halos surrounding every light on the freeway. But damn him, I'm still totally fine to drive!

All the blurry halos start to bleed into one another.

Ah, crap.

He sighs. "I know you're used to doing things on your own, but this is one of those circumstances where having someone with you is actually beneficial. You don't have to drive at night. It's safer if you don't, actually. But if you let me drive, we can cover more ground each day. Why don't you take the next off-ramp and we'll stop for some dinner. Then I'll drive us for a few hours before we stop for the night."

He's right. I know it. And honestly, the bleeding halos are starting to freak me out.

"Okay." I nod then veer right onto the off-ramp, cruising past a neon-green sign as I do.

Dammit.

I take the single exit road to a small strip mall of eating establishments, gas stations, and retail stores then park in front of a burger place. Getting out, we stretch our legs from the long drive.

Jack nods at the trunk. "Where are your glasses?"

I wrinkle my nose. "If you're driving then I don't need them."

"Yeah, well I don't feel like watching you squint at dinner just so you can see a menu, or your hand in front of your face." He grins, fully aware that my vision isn't that bad.

I smile sweetly. "Yeah. It would be a real shame if I mistook you for a salad and accidentally stabbed you with my fork."

"A crying shame. Now get your glasses."

"Oh, I'll get my glasses," I bite out, popping the trunk. "Not because you told me to but because I don't feel like trying to decipher a glowing menu."

"Right. Of course."

Digging through one of my bags, I search for my glasses,

expecting Jack to make some comment about the amount of luggage I have jammed in the trunk. He says nothing, however, and
soon I find my glasses and slam the trunk closed, and we enter the
restaurant.

It's smells like onions and ranch dressing as we walk inside,
which should gross me out but instead has me salivating. Apparently, lunch is a meal I should take seriously while on the road. We
slide into the nearest booth and my skinny jeans squeak against
the sticky red vinyl as I situate myself.

The waitress comes, takes our drink orders, then hurries away
as I slip on my glasses. They're horn-rimmed, hot pink, and stud-
ded with rhinestones at the corners—clearly the coolest glasses ever
worn—but I still squirm as I move them over my face.

Jack watches me in amusement and I eye him sharply. "What?"

He cocks his head. "What's your deal with wearing glasses? If
you hate them so much why don't you just get contacts?"

I push the pink frames up my nose with all the sass one can
muster when wearing bedazzled glasses. "Oh, I have contacts. Purple ones, neon-green ones, copper ones that make me look like a
hungry vampire...But those are for recreational purposes only."

He lifts a brow. "Oh, I know."

And...all my naughty desires from earlier suddenly crowd into
the booth with me.

Damn him.

As if my natural eye color wasn't odd enough, I sometimes like
to play dress-up with my irises. One of those times was last year.
With Jack. Yada, yada, yada.

"But because I only need my glasses at night or for reading," I
continue, sidestepping more bait, "and popping in a pair of gooey
contacts before every meal is inconvenient, I carry these babies

around." I tap a finger to one of the rhinestone corners. "At least until I can afford laser surgery."

He props an arm over the back of the booth. "And surgery will correct your vision so you no longer need glasses?" The mural of inked images twisting around his forearm and bicep demand my attention for a moment, inviting me to run my fingertips over their designs and, you know, *other* places on Jack's body. But I quickly recover, like the non-horny, class act I am.

I nod. "Twenty-twenty, baby. Then these librarian spectacles are gone for good."

He considers that for a moment and a shadow of disappointment passes his eyes. "And it'll just be your golden cat eyes against the world."

I don't know why people always compare me to a cat. Maybe it's the way I slink about when I walk, or my dark features, or the exotic angle of my yellow-hued eyes. Whatever the reason, people seem to think of me as catlike. And while I typically hate that, there are two people I don't mind thinking of me as a feline. Pixie is one. The dark-haired, gray-eyed tattoo show sitting across from me is the other.

"Isn't it always?" I smile smugly.

He stares at me, his gaze penetrating my pink glasses and diving straight through me. "No."

I let myself stay caged in his silver arrows. It's warm here. Safe. It's all the things that I refuse to need, which is precisely why I hate the silky haze it brings.

I snap my attention to the waitress headed back to our table with our drinks, grateful for the distraction.

She sets the ice-cold beverages down. I don't look at Jack and he doesn't look at me. Informing us that she'll be back momentarily to take our orders, the waitress leaves and I have no choice but to look up, where Jack's eyes wait for mine.

The silky haze returns. Sighing heavily, I banish it from our table with a scowl that could sear a pigeon mid-flight and dart my eyes away.

Flicking our menus up like thin plastic barriers, Jack and I study the restaurant's dinner selection like we're prepping for the SATs. The tension slowly dissipates, like it always does, and eventually I relax.

The waitress returns and we give our orders to her waiting pen, hovering over a skinny notepad, poised to scribble down our every wish. It does just that and she reaches for our menus with a cheerful smile.

I reluctantly release my plastic shield and calmly fold my hands on top of the table as she walks away. "So I was thinking we'd drive through Burksbend to get to Little Vail."

He shakes his head. "Rayfort is faster."

"Are you sure? I think Burksbend is faster—and it's a straight shot."

"It's not a straight shot. It's a two-lane highway through mountains. Rayfort is the way to go."

I think for a moment then shrug. "We're going through Burksbend anyway."

He juts his jaw. "Are you always this controlling? God." He scoffs. "It's like you can't relinquish control for even a second. You always have to be in charge. You always have to call the shots. I bet you're always on top during sex too."

He says it jokingly, but the truth in his statement catches me off guard and it must show in my face because his eyebrows go sky-high.

"Are you kidding me?" he says in a quiet voice. "You're always on top when you have sex?"

I shrug. "I like being on top."

"Yeah, but...you've been in other positions before too, right?" When I don't answer he repeats, "Right?"

I look at the table. "No."

His mouth falls open then closes as his face crinkles in disbelief. "Even your first time?"

I snap my eyes to him. "I don't know why this baffles people so much. Girls being on top their first time makes total sense. It gives them the power to control when and where, and how, uh... *comfortable* things are." I flick a hand. "Total sense. So yeah. Even my first time."

He just stares at me.

"Look," I say, leaning in. "I like to be the power player during sex. The hurricane. The idea of being at some guy's mercy is just...not sexy. I want to be the queen and absolute authority. So I'm always on top." I shrug and lean back. "Get over it."

He shakes his head. "Oh, I'll never get over it. I can promise you that."

I don't know why he's making a big deal about this. It's not like I'm a total weirdo because I like to be in control during sex. But still, my cheeks heat with embarrassment and we eat the rest of our meal in silence.

8

JACK

Dinner with Jenna was awkward but checking into the dinky motel just outside of Las Cruces is worse. The motel itself doesn't seem bad. Clean rooms. Fresh paint. A friendly old man at the front desk. It's the room situation that tops the uncomfortable tension we shared at dinner.

The kind motel clerk looks more than happy to have guests staying at his humble establishment. "Good evening, folks, and welcome." He greets us with a smile that could triumph over any hard time, and probably has. "I'm Leroy. Two of you checking in tonight?"

We nod, both too exhausted to form words after our long day on the road.

Leroy grins down at a computer screen. "Would you like a queen bed or double bed?"

"Oh. We'll actually need two separate rooms," Jenna says.

Leroy looks at us, puzzled. "What for?" His eyes bounce from Jenna to me then back to her. I can understand his confusion. We match, Jenna and I. Or at least people think we do.

She's covered in tattoos. I'm covered in tattoos.

She looks feisty. I look fierce.

She has bronze skin and golden eyes. And I have...well, my

skin is two shades paler than hers and my eyes nearly colorless. But we both have dark hair and attitudes, so people tend to assume we're together, which doesn't bother me one bit. Jenna, on the other hand...

"For...privacy?" she says, glancing at me like I'm some kind of Peeping Tom she's desperate to get away from.

I scowl at her. "Really?"

"Okay, two rooms." Leroy types something into his computer then looks up. "How many beds?"

Jenna blinks in confusion. "Uh, two."

Nodding, he mutters to himself while clacking away at his keyboard, "One room with two queen beds..."

"No." Jenna shakes her head. "We don't want two queen beds in one room."

Leroy frowns at her. "Oh you'll want queen beds, honey." He gestures at my height. "Your fellow isn't going to fit well on a double bed."

I watch Jenna's jaw clench and bite back a smile. Now I know why the old man is confused, and it's not because of our appearance. I'm just waiting for Jenna to figure it out.

"This is not my fellow," she says. "This is my friend. Just my friend. So we'd like two separate rooms, each with one bed. Please."

Leroy scratches his head. "You two aren't engaged?"

"Engaged? What?" Jenna turns to me with an incredulous look, her mouth falling open as a wrinkle forms between her pretty little eyebrows. But then she glances down and her expression freezes in place.

Ah, there it is.

"Oh." Turning back to Leroy, she holds up her left hand and points to the diamond band on her ring finger. "Yeah, this isn't an engagement ring." She shakes her head and pinches her lips. "This is a family heirloom, of sorts. I just wear it on this finger because it doesn't fit on any others."

Every finger on both of her hands is adorned with a ring of some sort. Jenna is a bit of a jewelry lush, which is only a problem in situations such as these.

Leroy looks at me and I shrug, used to this happening from time to time when I'm with Jenna. The first time it happened it freaked me out. I had just moved to Arizona and the last thing I wanted was some clingy girl parading me around with a ring on her finger. But now it doesn't bother me at all. And if I'm being totally honest, I kind of like it. Guys see that ring and don't approach Jenna like they would if she didn't have it on. I call that a win.

"So do you have two *separate* rooms we can check out for the night?" Jenna asks, leaning against the front desk's counter.

The old man glances at the screen. "Sort of."

She blinks. "Sort of? How can you sort of have two rooms?"

He smiles and hands a key to each of us. "You'll see."

Ten minutes later, we're all checked in and headed to our "separate" rooms. Jenna walks a few feet in front of me, clearly not over the engagement thing. As per usual.

I let out a tired exhale. "If you don't like people thinking you're engaged then just stop wearing the damn ring."

She shakes her head and her sleek black hair tosses from side to side. "It was my grandma's ring and she gave it to me with specific instructions to wear it until I feel settled in life, which I don't—yet. And I'm not going to stop wearing it just because people in our culture think the two of us are dumb enough to be engaged."

I glare at her swinging hair. "I realize you're not my biggest fan, but you don't have to be a bitch about everything."

She stops walking and turns around, big eyes filling with regret. "Sorry." She shakes her head with a sigh. "I wasn't trying to be a bitch to that guy in the lobby. I was just trying to get us our own rooms."

It's this side of Jenna—the part that wants to be softer—that reminds me why I try so hard to stay in her life.

"You weren't a bitch to the front desk guy," I say. "But saying that being with me would be a dumb move is kind of bitchy."

Her eyes flash with a spark of something...sadness? Desire? I'm not sure, but it's gone in an instant.

"It *would* be dumb." She shrugs. "For us, or for anyone else our age to be engaged."

"Says the girl who willingly wears a diamond on her ring finger."

She points at her hand. "This isn't a real diamond. It's just mirrored glass. See?" She slides the top of the "diamond" to the side and it swings out like the lid on a very small container. But the diamond shell isn't empty.

"What's that?" I point to a small piece of brown material wedged inside the fake diamond.

She snaps the mirrored lid back into place and smirks. "The world's smallest gris-gris bag."

Without further explanation, she starts walking again, her long black hair swishing from side to side as she moves.

I follow after her. "And...what's a gris-gris bag?"

She sighs. "A Voodoo love potion thingy."

I bite back the smile that so desperately wants to burst through my face. "You have a Voodoo love potion on your ring finger?"

She spins back around, eyes flashing as she points at my chest. "It was my grandma's idea, okay? Not mine. She's just...like...

really superstitious and when I moved away she got all weird about me finding love so she asked me to wear this ring and I couldn't say no, because she's super intense and thinks I'll be cursed if I don't."

The whole time she's talking, I nod. "Uh-huh. So tell me"—I cross my arms—"has this magical Voodoo ring brought you love since you put it on?"

She looks me up and down—a brief glance—but I catch it anyway and a bolt of triumph rushes through my veins.

"No," she snaps. "Of course not."

"And, uh…" I run a hand over my almost-smiling mouth. "When did you first start wearing this love potion ring?"

"When I moved to Arizona."

"That exact day?"

"No. I first put it on…" Her eyes widen, just barely, and she purses her lips. "I don't remember."

I finally let my smile loose and break into laughter, knowing she must have first worn the ring sometime around meeting me.

Oh, this is rich.

"Liar," I tease.

"Whatever." She lifts her nose in the air like she's so far above this conversation and all her very inconvenient truths.

But I let it go. Pushing the subject will only force her to lie to me. And besides, it's enough to know that her love potion is in some way related to her introduction to me. It's enough.

For now.

"This is me," she says, stopping in front of a room with a white number eight drilled into the door. Sliding her key into the handle lock, it clicks and she pushes the door open.

I walk past her and stop at the next door over. When she frowns at my stopping I explain, "This is me," and point to door number nine.

"Oh." She pulls her suitcases inside her room. "Right. Well, see you in the morning."

I nod and let myself inside my room. Our doors close behind us at the same time with a loud *clunk*. Looking around, the small room isn't bad. It's old and has a faint smell of smoke, but everything else about the place is new and fresh.

I toss my bag on the bed and move toward the small bathroom in the back of the room. After today's long car ride, a hot shower would be nice. I catch a reflection of myself to the left and pause. Turning, I realize it's not a reflection at all but Jenna walking across a small hallway from me, headed to the back of her own room.

She turns as well and we stare at each other through an open doorway that attaches the two rooms.

"Oh, you've got to be kidding me," she says, crossing her arms.

"I guess this is what he meant by 'sort of.'" I smile at the adjoining doorframe. "This probably used to be one big suite."

Jenna steps forward and nudges the stopper away from the base of the door, then lets it fall closed between us. The door squeaks as it falls back, but instead of stopping at the doorjamb it swings into my room then back into Jenna's.

I catch it on its return to me and hold it at the doorframe. I try to lock it, but there's no latch of any kind to keep the door in place so it just hangs between us, slightly squeaking as it struggles to stay still.

"Perfect," I hear Jenna say through the door. "A room with no real privacy."

I flex my jaw in agitation. "Would you relax, already? It's not like I'm going to barge into your room uninvited. And I don't know why you keep bitching about privacy. I've seen you naked, Jenna. I think our privacy boundaries were compromised a long time ago."

"That's exactly my point," she mutters then huffs as her footsteps retreat. "Whatever. Good night."

"Night," I say to the door, then head for the shower.

The hot water refreshes me, and for the first time all day I'm able to think clearly. Being around Jenna muddles my mind, and sitting beside her for hours on end makes it nearly impossible for me to think about anything other than her. Things like what the hell is happening back home.

I don't know how bad a shit storm I'm walking into. It could be a minor misunderstanding where Drew is just being a dumbass and hiding out of precaution. Or it could be a repeat of what happened with my father before I left Louisiana. As water falls over my head, I rub a hand down my face and flick it away from my eyes. I certainly hope it's the former.

After I towel off and pull on some pants, I hear the air conditioner kick on with a soft hum. The hanging door between Jenna's room and mine begins to sway back and forth as I turn off every light except for the lamp by the bed. The door squeaks with each swing. *Screech, screech.*

Well that's going to be annoying as hell to sleep through.

Sitting on the edge of the soft mattress, I scroll through the missed calls on my phone.

Samson.

Samson.

Mom.

Samson.

Mom.

Mom.

Samson.

Dear God, they're needy. I'm not a phone person but I understand why they choose to call instead of texting me their complaints. When your family participates in shady activities, you learn not to leave evidence in your wake. And text messages would be a blaring testimony to just how fucked up my situation back home is.

Bracing myself for what's to come, I dial my mom's number and rest an elbow on my knee as I hold the phone to my ear. She answers on the first ring.

"Jack," she says breathlessly. "Where have you been all day? I've been calling and calling."

No shit.

"Sorry, Mom. I've been on the road with shitty service." It's not a complete lie but a zing of guilt courses through me.

Lilly Oliver loves her children and only wants us to be safe. I need to loosen up and be a better son. Or at least a more comforting one.

Screech, screech.

The swinging door continues to squeak and I hear Jenna curse as my mom spills her concerns into my ear. "On the road? So Samson was telling the truth?" she says, with a tremor of panic. "You left Tempe? You're really coming out here?"

"Yeah. Should be there in two days." I frown. "Isn't that what you wanted?"

"What? Yeah, baby. Of course. I just...I didn't think you'd actually do it. I was hoping there wasn't anything to worry about—that Samson and I were just overreacting—but now...I knew it," she says with a quiet curse. "I knew bad was brewing. Drew wouldn't just take off and not call for five days."

He's been gone five days? Fuck.

"He's an adult, Mom," I say with more assurance than I feel. "He's probably just out getting wasted with some new girl of his." I glance at the noisy door.

Screech, screech.

"Don't patronize me, Jack," she scolds. "I know he's in trouble. If he weren't, you wouldn't be hauling your ass back here, especially after your promise to never return to this *hellhole.*"

I knew it was coming. It needed to. But if anyone has the right to call me out on bailing, it's my mother, so she gets a free pass on throwing my decisions in my face.

"I had to leave, Mom," I say, my lungs pulling tight with something dangerously close to remorse. "You know I did."

Screech, screech.

A frustrated Jenna yanks the door inward and presses it against the wall then tries to kick the stopper back in place. She's wearing a thin shirt with skinny straps that hangs to just above her belly button with a pair of tiny black shorts. The outfit shows off the many tattoos on her legs, stomach, and arms, but I know there are more hidden beneath the small scraps of material she has on.

Her eyes meet mine and neither of us moves for a second. Her hair is wet from the shower she must have taken and the dark strands cling in wild tangles to her bare shoulders and flushed cheeks. The primal part of me that wants to own her, to tame her, comes alive and claws at my rib cage. She must sense it because she instantly breaks contact, dropping her eyes to the stopper and kicking at it again. But her kicks aren't strong enough to wedge it in place.

Through the phone, I hear my mom's weary sigh. "I know you did, baby. I just wish you and your brother would quit pretending like this is no big deal. I already lost your father. I can't lose Drew too."

I walk over to where Jenna is still cursing at the door and, with one solid kick, wedge the stopper under the base so the door stays locked against the wall, wide open between our rooms.

"I know, Mom," I say. "You won't lose him. I promise."

At my words, Jenna looks up at me in concern. I wave it off, giving her a reassuring nod. The last thing I need is Jenna flipping out. At least with my mom and brother I can ignore their calls. If Jenna were to jump on board the freak-out train, I'd have no way to turn her off.

Jenna gestures to the doorstop and mouths, *Thanks*.

I mouth back, *No problem*, then listen as my mom sighs again through the phone.

"I hope you're right," she says wistfully. "I'm glad you're coming back home, baby." She pauses. "Really glad."

I look at the floor, struggling to find the right words to say, but I come up with nothing. Mom must realize this because she carries on without hesitation.

"Drive safe, baby," she says. "I'll see you soon. Good night."

"Good night, Mom," I say and the line goes dead. I lower the phone.

Jenna's eyes catch on my bare chest for a moment before she nods at the phone. "Your mom, huh?"

I drop the phone in my pocket. "Yeah."

She furrows her brow. "Who's she afraid of losing?"

I smile sadly, half of me wishing Jenna knew everything about me, the other half wishing she knew nothing at all.

"Everyone," I say. Jenna doesn't seem satisfied by my vague answer so I add, "But at this particular moment, she's worried about my brother."

"Samson?"

I shake my head. "Drew."

The corner of her mouth lifts in a small smile. "Baby brother got himself into some trouble, then?"

"I'm afraid so." I glance at the doorstop. "I guess you got fed up with all the screeching?"

"It was driving me insane."

"Yeah, patience and tolerance have never been your strong suits."

"Please." She rolls her eyes. "Like you weren't just as annoyed by that damn squeaking as I was."

I grin. "Oh, I was annoyed. Just not enough to come over here and kick the shit out of this poor plastic wedge"—I tap my foot against the stopper—"to prop it open."

I pull my eyes up, tracing the ink patterns on her thighs, then over to where the cherry blossom branches from her back wind to her stomach and dot her lower belly. I've touched those branches and kissed those blossoms. It's burns me a little that I may never have the pleasure of doing that again.

Jenna clears her throat and tips her chin. "Then good thing I was. Now we'll actually get some sleep tonight. And I don't care how long it makes our trip each day, I'm sleeping in tomorrow— and every other day we're on the road. This is as close as I've gotten to a vacation since I started working at the Thirsty Coyote and I'm not about to set an alarm clock."

I smile to myself. Jenna isn't a morning person, not in the slightest. She's definitely a night owl, which suits her personality perfectly. The intense darkness. The changing moon. The glinting stars. They're far more "Jenna" than the happy morning sun and clear blue sky.

"So our departure time is dependent on you waking up out

of your own free will?" I whistle. "Okay, then. I guess I'll see you around noon."

She narrows her eyes. "I'm not *that* bad at waking up."

"You sleep like a hibernating bear."

"I do not," she says sternly, but there's a sliver of teasing in her eyes that fills me with pride. I know her well, and I like it.

"You do, but it's okay." I shrug. "We'll leave when we leave."

I look down into her golden eyes, just inches from mine, and wonder if there will ever be a time when I can stand this close to her and not feel so undone, so unguarded. Then I wonder if that's even something I would want.

"Thanks," she says quietly then draws in a slow breath before shifting her eyes away. She takes a step back. "Night."

I retreat from the door as well. "Night." And we go to our own beds.

As I get in mine, my thoughts turn to Drew and the mess that waits for me in Little Vail. He'd better not be mixed up too deep with the wrong kind of business. I'll be pissed if he is. I love Drew—hell, I practically raised the kid—but I worked too hard to give him a better life for him to throw it away.

I thought I'd gotten my family free and clear before I left Louisiana, paying for their release with my service, my blood. But maybe I was wrong. Drew's disappearance is probably him paying for my sins, in one way or another, and it's all my fault. Samson's stress. My mother's worry. Drew's absence. All my fault.

Running a hand through my damp hair, I inhale deeply through my nose and stare at the bed. There's no way I'll be able to sleep tonight, not with my mind racing like it is, or my chest pounding the way it has since I took Samson's call yesterday. Restful sleep won't come until I know my family is safe. And free.

I almost snort. If that's the case, I may never sleep again.

I hear Jenna pad around her motel room and watch as, one by one, each of her lights go out. Then I shut off the last lamp beside me and the only light left behind is the glow of the yellow bulbs outside our motel doors, shining in through the thin fabric of the window curtains. It's faint, but in the darkness it's enough to see through to Jenna's room.

Our beds mirror one another across the propped-open door so I can see her lying on her side facing me and she can see me on my back with my head turned in her direction. Our eyes are glinting bits of dark marble, trained on one another in the soft yellow light, as if we're sleeping side by side in a single bed instead of thirty feet apart in separate ones.

The last time we looked at one another across bedsheets was last December, but it feels like years have passed since then. I turn away and stare at the ceiling, remembering the first time I saw Jenna.

She was a new hire at the Thirsty Coyote, and I'd heard only intriguing things about her from coworkers. She was from New Orleans, born and raised, with both Creole and French in her blood, which accounted for her "exotic" look, as everyone called it. She was rumored to practice Voodoo, and had more attitude in her soul than she had tattoos on her body. All of these things, along with the fact that she was one of the best bartenders my boss had ever seen, had me curious to meet the mysterious new hire. And when I finally did, I wasn't disappointed.

She was just as feisty and headstrong as I'd been told, but far more attractive than anyone had described. When I first saw Jenna, with her mile-long eyelashes, long graceful neck, and diamond stud in her nose, "beautiful" wasn't the right word. "Striking" was more like it. Looking at her was like being hit by something powerful. A force. A bolt of fire.

She had her back to me at first, as she reached for a tequila bottle high above her head, but then she turned around and struck me with her golden eyes, and I was scorched on the spot.

And I've been burning ever since.

9

JENNA

I absently turn the fake diamond band on my ring finger and frown into the dark. The day I met Jack also happened to be the first day I'd ever worn my grandmother's gris-gris ring. When Jack asked about the ring earlier, I realized, for the first time, that the day I started wearing the gris-gris ring was the same day we met—and a thick combination of fear and hope knotted my stomach at the realization.

But there was no way in hell I was going to let Jack know that. He'd probably just use it as a sign that we're supposed to be together. And it's not a sign. It's not.

The ring had nothing to do with Jack's attraction to me—or mine to him.

If anything, it was Jack's voice that first drew me in. Long before his silver eyes took me captive, long before his art-stained skin named him my comrade, the sound of Jack's voice poured into my ears and dripped down my spine, melting me one syllable at a time, until the sound of him was permanently embedded in my being.

The first time I heard him speak was my second day at the Thirsty Coyote, back when Jack used to work there. I was straining for a bottle of high-end tequila on a shelf just out of my reach when his voice brushed over me from behind.

"We have stepladders for this very reason," he said in that husky tone that is uniquely Jack.

I spun around to face a tall, dark, and handsome heartthrob and tried not to react to how attractive he was.

"Yeah, well. What fun is a ladder when I can earn the satisfaction of grabbing it on my own?" I hopped up, nearly grasping the bottle before landing, then jumped again.

He glanced at the bar top crammed with patrons. "I'm sure our customers think watching you jump up and down is more fun too." I stopped jumping as he easily lifted the bottle from its shelf.

"See, this way," he said, handing it to me, "I don't have to worry about you knocking the bottle down and breaking it. There's no risk."

I shrugged. "And no satisfaction."

A slow grin stretched out his face. "I'm Jack, by the way. Your new trainer."

I didn't flinch but inside all I could think was how fan-fucking-tastic it was that I'd just sassed off to the guy I was going to be stuck training with for the next two weeks.

But then Jack started talking about bar menus and scheduling policies and all I could think about was how I was ever going to learn anything from this beautiful man when he kept talking to me with that voice of his. That raspy, deep, alluring voice. But I did, eventually, learn a thing or two from Jack.

And some of it was even work-related.

A few months later, Jack got a job as a bartender at a nicer bar, which meant better pay, and he quit the Thirsty Coyote. He's finishing his master's in psychology because he wants to be a counselor for at-risk kids—I know; he's too good to be true—but putting himself through school has been a constant battle for him, so the opportunity to make more money while still keeping his same bartender hours was a no-brainer for him. Even still, I was disappointed that we weren't going to work together anymore.

But we were good friends and continued hanging out together, along with Pixie, Ethan, and a few of our other friends from school. But Jack and I . . . we had a connection, from the very beginning. It was like we were soul mates, but not in a stupid, obsessive way. There was no silly flirting, no jealousy, no awkward tension between us. It was always easy.

Jack and Jenna: friends.

Jack and Jenna: work buddies.

Jack and Jenna: partners in crime and late-night tattoo decisions.

But then one night, everything changed and we became something entirely different.

Jack and Jenna: drunk and naked in Jack's bedroom.

The night started out harmless enough. We were at Jack's apartment—where he lived alone at the time, since this was before Ethan moved in—and drinking with our friends. I was wearing my colored contacts that night—a blue color that made my eyes look *really* green—and I was the happy kind of buzzed, not too drunk but tipsy enough to find everything amusing. And I guess Jack was too, because we were the happiest people in our posse.

Our friends slowly called it a night, one by one crawling back to their homes, until it was just Jack and me laughing in his kitchen as we fed each other carrot sticks.

Don't ask me why. That's just part of being drunk. You do weird shit like feed people carrot sticks like they're a donkey you're trying to win favor with.

The point is we were having a good time. I always had a good time with Jack. He was easy and I was free, and we made each other laugh.

But then, in my buzzed kitchen silliness, I tripped over his foot and fell into him. My chest sank against his as I lost my balance and stared up into gunmetal-gray eyes alight with laughter. My smile grew, matching his, and then I kissed him. Just for fun. Just because I could. But then I fell into him in a whole different way.

I pressed my lips to his and our smiles melted into mouths of want, of passion, of things I couldn't control—things I didn't want to control. Letting the kiss be my master, I surrendered to the desire inside me and wrapped my arms around his broad shoulders. He took me against him easily, tucking my body into his as he kissed me back with those lovely lips of his. So full and red. So hard when he scowled yet so soft against mine in that moment.

Jack. This was Jack.

The reality didn't slow my passion. If anything, it enticed me more as I lifted up on my tiptoes and rolled my hips into his hot body. It was crazy. It was reckless. It was *Jack*, for Christ's sake. But I couldn't stop, didn't want to stop.

So I thought, what the hell? A night playing naked with Jack might not be bad. It could be fun.

So I pulled away with a teasing smile and walked backward as he tried to reach my mouth again and again. Before I knew it, we were in his bedroom and his lips were on mine again.

With swift and sure movements, he took my ass and hoisted me into his arms, shoving my back against the nearest wall as he pressed himself between my legs and sucked at my mouth. I was instantly wet and aching, desperate for more touch, more want, just...more.

I exhaled loudly, letting my hot breath flit over his ear as I tilted my head back for air and exposed my throat. Guys love the throat, so vulnerable, at the mercy of their mouth.

But instead of kissing along my windpipe, Jack cupped my throat with his hand and held my head to the wall as he continued to kiss me. He pulled at my lips and pushed his tongue into my mouth. My nipples hardened in excitement but my mind whirled, not sure what to make of my neck in his grasp. He squeezed lightly, then ran his thumb down my windpipe. Slowly. Softly. The juxtaposition had me panting and arching my back, wanting more.

Moving his mouth to my ear, Jack's husky voice fluttered over me. "Jenna."

It wasn't a question. It wasn't a statement. It was just my name, on his tongue, and I felt a sharp burning behind my eyes. The sound of his voice in my ear, along with the feel of his hands running over my back and thighs and his mouth kissing at my jaw, tugged at something inside me. Something undeniable, with teeth that sank deep into my emotions and confused me.

I shook my head away from my name on his lips. I couldn't have Jack—or anyone—saying my name in the middle of this. I couldn't be me, fully free, if I was reminded of who I am. Of my flaws and weaknesses. That wasn't how it worked.

I ran my hands over his shoulders to his chest, then slid them down to his pants, grabbing at the button of his jeans until it was undone and I could pull open the waistband.

"Bed," I commanded, breathless. I blinked away from the haze he'd put me in and stared directly into his eyes. "Now."

I was over the up-against-a-wall shit. I had far too little control like that. His hand stayed against my throat and moved upward, forcing my chin to tip backward even farther so I was completely at his mercy. It didn't scare me or make me uncomfortable, but it certainly made me eager to be on the bed where I could climb on top of him.

Jack's eyes traced the lines of my face, warm steel seeing me, wanting me, knowing me. He released my throat and whipped us around, and then my back was on the soft mattress. He reached into the nightstand and quickly pulled out a condom. I took that opportunity to quickly slip out from under his large, eager body and pushed him down under me.

He smiled up at me. "So it's gonna be like that?"

"Shut up." I straddled him, momentarily jerking as his hardness rubbed against just the right spot, then refocused my attention to his shirt. I yanked it off. Then my shirt. I pulled it away from my body with one quick movement. Same with my bra, then I pressed my naked chest against his as I kissed him again.

He gripped my hips, hugging my backside against him as we bit at one another's lips and licked our way around each other's mouths. It was a feeding frenzy of kisses, our hungers both desperate and unfulfilled. Both too powerful to concede.

Pulling away, I pulled his pants off his body—he had no underwear on, much to my happy surprise—only to have him grab my waist and pull me up against him, my back to his chest, pinning me with the bar of his forearm. He shoved my pants down until my legs were free then slid his hand down between my breasts, over my belly, and into my panties where he firmly cupped my wetness.

I bucked against the touch, loving it but wanting more control.

His deep voice fluttered over my ear again. "Jenna."

I whimpered at the emotional tug that hearing my name incited. Hating it. Loving it. Wanting to undo it. I tried to twist around to face him, but he locked me in place, working his fingers over my slippery folds so I was all but immobile. I placed my hand over his with the intention of pulling his delicious touch away from my sensitive areas, but found myself holding him to me more firmly. Wanting his touch to linger.

Sliding my wetness all around, he found my clit and gently plucked at it. I tipped my head back where it rested on his shoulder and my eyes rolled into the back of my head as he touched me. One of my hands stilled against his, pushing him into me even more while my other hand bent around and grabbed the back of his head. Slipping my hand into his hair, I grasped a chunk at the back of his neck and pulled as he worked me closer.

I don't know where my control went, but it was long gone now as his clever fingers slipped inside my core, filling the aching need between my legs. One finger then two, sliding in and out of me as I stayed pinned against him. But it wasn't enough. I wiggled and moaned, wanting the hard erection I felt at my back to be buried deep inside me. Not his fingers.

He went back to my clit, rolling over it with the soft, wet pads of his fingers until I was gasping into the dark room. I slid my hand up from his and sank my fingernails into his forearm as he worked me to the brink.

Then a white-hot orgasm ripped through me, blinding me to everything but his touch as he moved his hand against me and I arched my back, bucked my hips, moaned and whimpered, until I was a complete puddle in his arms. For a moment, I was limp and weak, drained and satisfied, with my thighs trembling and my belly in spasms against his hold.

It was the best I'd ever felt, but also the weakest I'd ever been.

Drawing a shaky breath, I whipped around and shoved him back on the bed. Willing myself to recover from the shattering orgasm, I pulled off my soaked panties and straddled him with my jaw locked. Jack would not own me with his hands, his touch, his soft gray eyes looking up at me like he knew I felt something deep...like he knew...

No. He would not control me.

Slapping the condom off the nightstand, I quickly tore it open and rolled it over his hard, thick erection. Then I lifted myself over him, placed him at my entrance, and slowly slid down onto him. As I descended, I made the mistake of looking at him and found his eyes watching me with something I wasn't ready to see. Sure, there was lust in his eyes, there was desire and hunger, but there was also something that couldn't be—something frighteningly close to love—and I was locked in the hot gaze of it as I connected our bodies and filled myself with his hardness. The moment his erection tapped the back of me, stretching me out and rubbing against every desperate nerve inside my core, I let out a gasp and my eyes fluttered.

He felt so good. Closing my eyes, I moved over him, up and down, bringing more pleasure to both our bodies and working up a sweat as I sat atop his large penis and rode. He was just a body, I told myself. A hot body. This was just pleasure. Nothing more. No emotions needed to be involved.

My heart pounded as I tipped my head back, giving in to the lust and animal instinct inside with small moans and light whimpers. Soon, I was just a creature, drawing pleasure from another creature. All was how it was supposed to be.

But then I heard it. "Jenna." And the black hole of lust I'd leaped into spit me back out and my eyes flew open. Jack set his hands to my hips and held me in place on top of him, roughly sliding his hand up my spine while at the same time pushing me down to him. When my face was right in front of his, with our bodies still hot and feverish and joined together, his jaw set and his eyes steeled over.

"Look at me," he said. His hand wound around my shoulder and took my chin. Gripping it sternly he said, "I want your eyes."

My core flexed in desire, squeezing his long erection inside me, and a whimper escaped my mouth. I didn't want to look at him. I didn't want to see him. To see *Jack*.

Because then Jack would see me, and surely see the emotion I was trying to keep at bay inside me.

"Please, Jenna," he said, his raspy voice raking over my mouth as he trapped me in a kiss and pulled at my lips until I was nodding in agreement. Then he released my chin and lips and relaxed his head as I lifted up again.

Now straddling him with my eyes directly on his, I slowly pulled my core up his thickness then slid back down. And again. He watched me without expression, just his eyes on mine, watching my naked body pull pleasure from his and give that pleasure right back. It was personal. It was intimate. And it was so unfamiliar that I could hardly contain the emotion blossoming inside my soul.

Trying my best to concentrate on the pleasure, not the sentiment, I gained momentum and rode him more fervently until my hair was a mass of black strands whipping about my face and sweat dripped down my spine. My swollen breasts swung with my movements and I sank my nails into the large pecs of his chest. I was powerful above him, completely in control. A hurricane. A fierce storm. I was the owner of his body and pleasure. I was the queen. I was his master.

But my eyes stayed on him as promised, and with every stroke of pleasure came another tug at my soul, at that deep dusty place inside me. Until looking at him burned my eyes and choked my throat. As if his hand was against my windpipe again, I couldn't watch his eyes without suffocating.

I blinked away the stinging. I rode him like an animal. I moaned. I blinked again.

"Jenna," he said, but this time it was a soft word, as he watched my emotions seep through. It was a word of permission and under-standing, and it completely unraveled me.

A single tear fell down my face as I moved above him, followed by another. The emotional thing inside me was now awake and unrelenting, fighting with the beast of pleasure, and losing. I kept my eyes on Jack and he kept his eyes on me, a million silent words between us as tears streamed down my face.

Somewhere along the way, I'd lost all my control when it came to Jack. But maybe I never had any to begin with.

Blinking back to the present, I stare at the motel ceiling. So much can happen in so little time. So much can change.

Turning my head to face the open door between our rooms, I stare across the darkness at Jack. I can't tell if he's awake or not, but a small part of me wants to crawl into the sheets beside him. Not to recreate the hot—albeit emotionally confusing—sex we had a few months ago, but because…because…he's my friend. And sleeping a door-frame away from him feels wrong, which is weird because I sleep sev-eral blocks away from him every night back home in our apartments.

God, Jenna. You're so weird. Get it together.

Rolling onto my side, I turn my back on the doorway between us and let out a long, slow breath. Eventually, I fall asleep to visions of hot tears, slick body parts, and a pair of deep gray eyes sinking into my soul.

———

By the time I'm dressed and ready to go the next morning, Jack's already waiting for me at the car with a smug look and a to-go cup of coffee in his hand as he leans against the hood.

"Told you so," he says, handing me the hot drink.

"You were wrong about me not waking up until noon," I defend. "I actually woke up at 11:35 a.m. So there."

"No, I said I'd see you at noon and…" He looks at his phone. "It's 12:01 p.m. right now." He looks up. "So yeah. I told you so." There are shadows under his eyes like he's exhausted, but his grin is anything but.

"Whatever," I mumble, taking a sip of coffee and thanking all the coffee gods for creating this amazing beverage that instantly gives me happiness. I nod at Jack's empty hands. "Where's your coffee?"

Pulling away from the hood, he straightens to his full height. "Unlike you, I woke up at the crack of dawn so I've already had three cups and checked us both out of our rooms. You got the keys?" He holds out his hand. "I'll drive first today."

Pulling them from my purse, I place the keys in his big hand and frown. "You couldn't sleep?"

Jack might not sleep in the way I do, but he certainly doesn't wake up with the roosters.

We get in the car, me in the passenger seat and Jack in the driver's, and he starts the engine. "I slept fine."

He doesn't look at me as we back out of the motel parking lot and I know something's wrong.

"Did the stuff with your brother keep you up?" I ask.

Pulling onto the freeway, we head east. "I told you. I slept fine."

I watch him for a moment. "You never talk about your family so I never pry, but you're obviously stressed-out." Tucking my coffee into one of the console cup holders, I turn to face him. "What's going on?"

"Nothing." He shakes his head. "Just family drama. That's all."

Irritation courses through my veins at his refusal to confide in me. "Family drama. Okay. Sure. Be vague. That's cool."

He smiles humorlessly. "What, you want to bond now? That's ironic."

My blood pressure rises at what he's insinuating. "If you have something you want to say, Jack, just say it already. I'm sick of dodging these softballs you keep throwing my way."

He glances in the side mirror and switches lanes. "That's just it, Jenna. It doesn't matter what I say, you'll just find a way to step around my words. Because that's what you do. *Dodge*."

If he wasn't so totally right, I'd pop him in the jaw.

Of *course* I dodge him. If I didn't dodge him, I'd end up throwing myself at him. And if I thought that would help matters, trust me, I'd do it. But after what happened the last time I let my guard down around Jack and his hot body, I don't trust myself.

Why I let him get so close to me, to my heart, I'll never know. But I've been trying for months to undo the emotional connection I inadvertently created that night, and here Jack is, drudging up the past like it's common conversation for us.

I can't risk getting any more attached to him than I already am—or worse, falling in love with him. And the only way I can be sure to avoid such things is by staying away from anything and everything that might suck me in—including conversations about what happened between us.

But here I am, scrambling to find some sort of comeback that will beat him down and save me from responding at the same time, and I've got nothing.

"You don't want me to dodge? Fine." I shrug in frustration. "So we slept together. Once. And it was…" *Hot. Erotic. Amazing. Intense.* "Different," I finally say. "It was different."

A muscle flexes in his jaw. "It was different."

I shrug angrily. "For me, at least. It was probably same ol' sexy time for you."

His eyes dart to mine. "What's that supposed to mean?"

My temper rises. "It means I'm not going to sit here and debate the right adjectives for what happened between us because I don't feel like pinning myself to your board of sexual conquests."

"You think I consider you a conquest?"

"It's fine. Really. You have conquests, I have conquests. It's all the same thing. That's just how it goes. I'm not pissed about it. I just don't feel like chatting about it."

He nods darkly. "So you sleeping with me is the same as you sleeping with that lousy bartender—what was his name? Greg? Gary? Some shit like that."

"Gee, I don't know," I snap. "Am I the same as Angela, or Olivia, or that Heather girl with the purple hair?"

He scowls. "What, are you keeping tabs on everyone I go to bed with?"

"Well it's not hard to do when you're parading them through the Thirsty Coyote."

His eyes flash. "At least I never slept with any of your roommates."

I point at him. "I had *no idea* Tyler was your roommate. That was a complete coincidence."

"And what about Davis? Was that a coincidence too?"

I smile sharply. "Davis was just as much a coincidence as you going home with Bella was."

A beat passes. We pretty much just listed off all of our sex partners since the two of us hooked up, and that can't be normal. Clearly, we have jealousy issues. And the fact that we're not a couple yet we still have jealously problems is a sure sign we're completely dysfunctional.

"This is why us sleeping together was a mistake," I say, leaning back in my seat. "It changed everything."

"It didn't change anything," he says. "It just brought the truth to the surface. You're just too chickenshit to admit it."

"Admit *what?*" I shout, throwing up my hands. "What is this mysterious thing I'm supposed to be admitting, Jack?"

"The way you feel about me. About *us*," he shouts back.

I roll my eyes. "Not again. I'm not hashing this out again."

"*You* never hashed anything out in the first place. *I* did," he says. "You know exactly where I stand, but I have yet to hear a single real thing come out of your mouth as far as you and I are concerned."

My heart begins to pound and my eyes burn. "Because you and I aren't part of my plan!"

His knuckles turn white as he grips the steering wheel. "Your plan." He nods angrily. "Because God forbid anything happen outside of your precious plan. God, Jenna." His jaw clenches. "You're so obsessed with controlling everything in your life that you can't even consider that maybe 'your plan' isn't the best thing for you."

"My plan is perfect for me—"

"No. I know your plan." He shakes his head. "And it's a fucking dead end for you." I open my mouth to protest, but he carries on with flared nostrils. "It will drive you to boredom and suck the life out of you until you either die, safe and old and absolutely miserable, or break your own damn rules and live, wild and free, and without any goddamn plan."

I fall back in my seat, stunned, and face forward, watching the lines on the road race by in yellow and white blurs. "What do you want me to say, Jack?"

He visibly swallows. "It's not about what I want you to say. It's about the truth, Jenna. That's what I want." Glaring at the road, he mutters, "That's all I've ever wanted."

Shaking my head, I slowly inhale and try to keep my emotions locked down. Damn Jack and his truth. Damn this whole thing.

"I don't know what the truth is," I say after a few long seconds, "so I guess you're out of luck."

His lips form a thin line as he stares out the window as dozens more yellow and white blurs skate by. When he finally responds, his voice is low and bitter. "I guess so."

We don't speak for the next hundred miles, and a screaming silence hangs between us. And with the silence comes more memories of that night, last year.

After Jack and I had had sex, I rolled off his body and stretched out beside him in bed. We stared at each other for a moment, both of us breathing heavy, and I tried to get my ridiculously happy heart under control. An impossible task, considering it was hammering away with a contentment I'd never experienced before.

I traced a finger down his thick bicep, where a fierce-looking hawk clutching a snake in its talons was tattooed against his muscles. Then I glanced at his back where, among a dozen other designs, a mighty eagle soared at me with determination in its eyes.

"I like your tattoos," I said softly, trailing a fingertip over the eagle's spread wings.

"Mmm," he murmured as he lightly brushed the shooting-star tattoo on the inside of my thigh. "And I like yours."

"Which one was your first?" I smiled. "Your first tattoo."

He turned onto his back to show me his chest. "This one," he said, pointing to a silhouette of a small bird flying against the moon.

It wasn't the most detailed ink on his body, but it was captivating in its own simplicity, and a little faded.

"Why that?" I asked. "Why a midnight bird over your heart?"

He looked at the bedsheets and smiled sadly. "A midnight bird. I like that." He pulled his eyes back up. "When I was sixteen and decided to get a tattoo, I wanted something that represented hope, and a bird seemed like the right symbol."

"Sixteen?" I scoffed. "What kind of tattoo shop lets a minor get inked?"

"The kind in my hometown," he said seriously.

"Huh." I stroked my thumb over the midnight bird of hope, memorizing every line and curve of the design. "So you were hoping for something."

He nodded.

I met his eyes. "And did you get it?"

He smiled. "Yep."

I smiled back. "Then I guess it's a lucky tattoo."

"I guess so." His grin grew and our gazes locked for a long moment before he suddenly said, "Pancakes."

I laughed. "What?"

"We should make pancakes."

My heart danced as I grinned from ear to ear. "We totally should."

So we made pancakes, in the middle of the night.

I wore one of his T-shirts—nothing else—and sat cross-legged on his kitchen counter as he fed me bites of freshly made pancakes. All his forks were dirty, otherwise we might have used utensils instead of our fingers, but it was more fun with our hands anyway. Our hands were sticky with syrup, our bodies were sated from our time in bed together, and I was the most content I've probably ever been.

And then Jack said the worst possible thing.

"I like you, Jenna." His eyes were serious and cutting into me like hot blades. "A lot."

My first instinct was to say, *I like you too.* But my next instinct was to shout, *No, I love you!*

And then shit got real.

Because my heart wanted to scream, *I want you forever!* And that wasn't a truth I was ready for. I stared down at his oversized shirt and went into complete panic mode. Shaking my head. Denying that I felt anything for him.

He called me on my bullshit and tried his damnedest to yank the truth from my mouth, but I was stubborn. I had every shield up, ready for battle, because I had big goals for myself.

What if Jack's goals didn't cooperate with mine? What then? Which one of us would get to fulfill our dreams? How many compromises would we have to make? Love doesn't accommodate dreams; it crashes into them. And even though I wasn't ready to admit it out loud, I knew pursuing something—anything—with Jack would lead to *love*, if it wasn't swimming in it already.

And here he was, asking me to be okay with that. It just wasn't fair. Jack couldn't just come in and undo all my best-laid plans. I was protective of those plans for a reason and I couldn't afford to let my guard down.

I would not be my mother. Single. Poor. Heartbroken with dusty dreams that will never be achieved. And I wouldn't be my grandmother either. I saw what loving a man had done to them, and I refused to follow in those footsteps.

My grandpa left my grandma when she was eight months pregnant for a waitress half her age, and Grams raised my mama in such poverty that she didn't even know what a ten-dollar bill looked like until she was fourteen years old.

Mama worked her booty off, saving money so she could go to medical school and become a doctor. She had a dream—a plan. Then she fell in love with a handsome man and got pregnant with me four months later. My father promised her he'd be there. Promised her that she could finish school and accomplish her goals. He said he'd stand by her side and help her.

And then he woke up one day and told her he'd changed his mind. That being a father was too hard and that his dreams were more important than hers. He left her—he left *us*—and Mama was completely broken. We never had a secure income so we moved constantly, always getting evicted. Always behind on bills. The electricity would get shut off. The water. I moved from school to school, always having to make new friends and hope they didn't notice that my clothes were too small for me because we couldn't buy new ones that fit. That my shoes were worn with holes and muck. That my hair was dirty because sometimes we lived in Mama's car without a bathroom to shower in.

I had no control, no certainty. As a child, I vowed to find a way to provide for myself. To make a life for myself where I could fall asleep easily each night without worrying about when I might get to eat again.

Things got better, eventually. When I was sixteen, Mama got a good job as a medical assistant at the local clinic. It didn't pay a lot, but it was a steady paycheck with guaranteed health insurance. And as a bonus, it was in the medical field, so Mama was happy about that. I was able to get a job waitressing at a neighborhood café, and with our combined paychecks we were able to make a somewhat stable life for ourselves. Together.

Soon after, Mama began fostering children and ended up adopting the three most amazing little girls in the whole world.

Life turned out okay for my mother. But I didn't want to go through all she did just to get to be "okay."

So the moment I felt myself falling into Jack's eyes, tripping into his heart, I knew I had to shut it down. Too much was at stake.

He told me he was crazy about me. He told me we were good together. He told me I was everything he ever wanted. He said all the things any girl would appreciate.

But all I heard were the broken promises of my dad and the betrayal of my grandfather. So I said no. I stopped eating pancakes and left Jack's apartment with his scent still on my skin and fresh tears running down my cheeks.

Across the car, I glance at his profile as we cross the Texas border and my heart clenches. I wasn't lying when I said I didn't know what the truth was, but I wasn't exactly being honest either.

What I feel completely contradicts what I want. I feel more attracted to Jack than I do to anyone else, but I don't want him to be my boyfriend. I feel possessive of Jack when he hooks up with other girls, but I don't want to be one of the girls he hooks up with. I feel empty when we go a few days without seeing one another, but I don't want him to be the source of my contentment.

I have a plan for my life, my future. A good plan. A solid plan.

I'm going to graduate college. I'm going to sell my sculptures and promote my artwork until I raise enough money to open an art gallery. Then I'm going to showcase artwork until I have enough money to buy myself a home. And a car. And health insurance. And maybe then I'll get a small pet. Like a black cat or a little pig.

But Jack doesn't fit into those plans.

So when he asks me for the truth, and I'm caught between my need to explain why I don't want him and my desire to rip his clothes off, it messes with my head.

If I were a stronger person, I'd stay away from Jack completely. But I can't. I don't want to. Cutting him out of my life, at least right now, isn't an option. He's too important to me—even if he's being kind of weird about his family situation.

My phone rings and I glance at the screen. Speaking of family...

"Hey, Mom," I answer, lifting the phone to my ear.

Jack glances at me for the first time in at least an hour then looks back at the road, where endless miles of dry, empty desert surround us on all sides. There is literally nothing out here in nowhere, Texas. No trees. No signs. Nothing.

"Hey, sugar." The sound of my mother's cheery voice makes me suddenly eager to get home. "How you doing?"

"Doing good," I say. "How's Grams?"

"Oh, she's hanging in there. But she's sure looking forward to seeing you. How's the trip going?"

Staring out the window, I blow out my cheeks. "Long? Boring? Dry? Pick one."

"That good, huh?"

"That good," I repeat blandly.

"Well at least you're not alone," she says. "Your cousins flew in today and informed me that you left with a passenger. They weren't sure how long he'd last, but since you answered your actual phone instead of putting me on your car's speakerphone I'm assuming you still have your travel companion."

My mom prides herself on her powers of deduction. When I was a teenager, I used to call her Sherrylock Holmes because I could never pull one over on her. The woman was just too damn intuitive, and she always knew when I was lying. It made sneaking out at night and other getting-up-to-no-good shenanigans rather difficult, but I managed.

"Yes, Mama, I do have a *travel companion*," I mock. "What are you, seventy? Why are you talking like Andy Griffith? Ner-dy."

She huffs. "Mm-hmm. Who's more of a nerd, the forty-five-year-old woman who says 'travel companion' or the twenty-one-year-old girl who knows who Andy Griffith is?"

A small smile pulls up my mouth. "Touché."

"So are you bringing Jack home with you or what?"

I frown. "What makes you think my travel companion is Jack?"

Jack looks at me again, his gray eyes curious as they scan my face. Feeling my skin grow hot, I turn away from his gaze.

"Because he's the only guy I ever hear you mention by name so I figured he'd be the only guy you'd tolerate on a road trip," she says.

A beat passes where my heart completely flips out, shifting into full-on panic mode as I try to come to terms with my mother's words.

Do I talk about Jack that much? Am I one of those silly girls that calls home and blabs about the boy she likes? AM I?

"Your cousins also might have mentioned that it was Jack they saw in your car," she adds, instantly relieving me of the code red protocol my body was preparing for. "So should I be expecting both of you later this week?"

I let out a small breath. "Uh, no. Jack's family lives in Little Vail so I'm just dropping him off on my way home."

"Mm-hmm," she says, clearly not believing me. "Well I'm just glad you're not alone. I hope your day on the road goes smoothly. Call me tomorrow?"

I nod, even though she can't see me. "I will. Love you, Mama."

"Love you too, baby."

Our call ends and I put my phone away, wondering if an hour of tense silence qualifies as "going smoothly." It's certainly better than an hour of fighting or having sex...okay, it's not better than an hour of sex. But really, what *is* better than an hour of sex? Nothing, that's what. Except maybe *two* hours of sex. And wow, I need to start thinking about something else.

"How's your grandma?" Jack asks.

"She's doing good," I say, pulling my hair back and stacking it on my head. After my shower last night, I let it air-dry so now it's a mess of thick black waves that insist on sticking to my skin. "She's glad that I'm coming home."

He nods. "It's been a while since you've been back."

"Yeah. Almost a year and a half." The breeze from the air conditioner pleasantly cools the back of my neck. "But you've been gone even longer than me. You were in Arizona way before I was so you haven't been home for at least..." I do the math in my head. "Two years?"

"Three," he says.

I lift my brow. "Wow. This thing with Drew must be serious."

He shrugs. "Maybe. Maybe not."

His shoulders tense with his casual words, giving him away, and worry trickles through my veins. If he's worried, I'm worried. That's just how it always is with me when it comes to Jack.

I watch his big fingers, loosely wrapped around the steering wheel, and follow the curves of his scarred knuckles. Jack has lots of scars. Not so many that it's alarming, but enough to elicit questions from anyone who might study his skin for longer than a few seconds. I've studied his skin before. All of it. Questions sat on my tongue, but I never asked them.

My eyes trail over the lines of dark ink that lick out from his sleeves of tattoos, barely reaching the backside of his hands. The licks tangle up into more intricate patterns of design on his thick forearms, shifting with his muscles when he grips the steering wheel or makes a turn. But his large forearms are nothing compared to his even larger biceps, which are nothing compared to his great shoulders. The designs twist into even more detailed images as they climb up his arm and disappear under the sleeve of his black shirt, but I know underneath are dozens more tattoos that probably tell stories about Jack that no one has ever heard.

That's what tattoos are: storytellers. Not always, but most of the time. Some stories we tell with our tongues, in words and kisses and sometimes even the food we make for others. Other stories are just for ourselves and are told in tattoos and scars and the shields we erect around our hearts.

Jack has many stories. Maybe even more than me.

We stop for lunch somewhere in the middle of Texas and eat in silence at a run-down café. After lunch, we switch places and I take over the steering wheel while Jack sleeps in the passenger seat. At least, I think he's sleeping. He pulled a hat from his bag and set it over his face so I can't see his eyes, which is just as well.

My stomach is in knots and my heart unsettled. I feel like I'm at war with myself and losing on both sides. The heavier my soul gets the more I want to be home.

Somewhere around four p.m., Jack pulls his hat off and sits up. We manage to have a civil conversation about where to stay for the night and how best to get there. I stop for gas and Jack pays. We look at each other twice when we're back on the road, but otherwise we keep our eyes out the windows.

The knots in my stomach loosen a bit and soon my soul feels less heavy. I'm not sure why. Maybe just because we're not snapping at each other. But then sexual tension dawns with the setting sun and suddenly the car feels small and cramped.

Nothing happened or changed to bring my dark desires to life. It's just the idea that the bright light of day will soon be gone again and the soft light of night will wrap around us that has me thinking and wanting naughty things.

Jack has me pull over so he can drive, and after we switch places, I try to do what he did—pretend to sleep. I can hear him breathing. I can hear the sound of his rough hands sliding over the steering wheel. I can hear all the pieces of Jack, alive and awake next to me, and I know sleep will be impossible.

———

Looking up at the San Antonio motel I directed us to, Jack frowns. "This place is a dump."

He's right. It's not gross and horrible, but it's certainly no more than a two-star place to sleep. Paint is peeling off the building, the lit-up vacancy sign is missing two letters, and the roof is sagging in the center.

Grabbing my luggage, I straighten my shoulders and inhale. "Yeah, well. The only way my driving to New Orleans instead of flying makes any sense is if I stay at cheap—very, very cheap— motels along the way. You're welcome to go check yourself in at the nearest Ritz Carlton if this isn't up to par for your highbrow taste."

He shrugs his shoulders and heads for the lobby. "If you're staying here, I'm staying here."

I roll one of my suitcases behind me as I follow, leaving the other two in the car since I only need the one for tonight. Jack pulls the lobby door open and a loud chime sounds as he holds it open for me. I step inside and approach the front desk where I'm greeted by a bubbly middle-aged woman with curly brown hair and thick eyeglasses.

"Good evening!" She waves at us even though we're standing right in front of her. "Welcome to San Antonio. Looking for a place to stay for the night?"

I nod. "Two rooms, please."

Her cheery smile falters. "I'm sorry. We only have one room available at the moment. Will that be okay?"

Not even a little.

I sigh. "No. We'll just keep looking. Thanks, though."

As I turn to leave, the woman says, "I'm afraid you might have trouble finding a room in this area tonight." I look back at her and she bites her lip apologetically. "It's the big art festival this week, you see. So most of the nearby hotels are completely booked."

Fantastic.

I rub a hand down my face, too exhausted and annoyed to reply in a civil manner.

"Should I book the one room then?" the woman asks.

"Yes, please," Jack says.

I shoot my eyes to him. "What?"

"You said you needed to save money to make this trip worthwhile," he says, lifting a shoulder. "What better way to save money than to share the cost of a room with me? And besides, I'm exhausted and don't feel like driving around searching for a better option."

The smug grin on his face aggravates me, but the fact that he has a good point aggravates me even more.

I turn back to the woman at the desk. "I guess we'll take the one room, then."

The happy woman gets us a room key and we shuffle back out the chiming door and down the cracked sidewalk to our motel room. Jack inserts the key and opens the door to reveal a small bathroom and, much to my relief—or maybe my disappointment, I'm not sure—two double beds.

"See?" he says, shutting the door behind us and locking it. "Two beds. You were stressing out for no reason. And this is really just the same scenario we had last night in New Mexico, but at half the price."

I sigh. "You're right. It's fine." I toss my suitcase on the bed farthest from the door. "You want to take a shower first or what?"

He checks his phone with a frown then looks up. "You go ahead. I've got to make some calls." Tapping the screen a few times, he slips outside and holds the phone to his ear. Before the door latches shut, I hear him say, "Hey, Samson. How bad is it now?... Fuck...No, I haven't had contact with anyone..."

The door cuts off the rest of his sentence and I stare at the empty motel room as a wave of unease washes over me. He's really stressed-out.

Grabbing my stuff from my suitcase, I head into the bathroom and turn the shower on. Even though driving all day with the air conditioner on isn't filthy or sweltering, I still feel like I'm coated in grime and sweat as I peel off my clothes and step under the spray.

The water washes away the day's drive but doesn't rinse the worry from my gut. Next to Pixie, Jack's the closest thing I have to a true friend. And I'd bet I'm pretty damn close to being one of his good friends too. So you'd think I'd know exactly what was going on with him and his family. But our real shit, the deep stuff that makes up who we are and where we come from, isn't something Jack and I talk about.

Though now I'm starting to wish it were. Everything inside me wants to assure Jack, or support him in some way. But I can't do that when I'm in the dark about whatever he's dealing with.

Finished with my shower, I turn off the water. The room is still empty when I exit the bathroom so I peek outside. But Jack's nowhere to be found. Huh.

I take my time straightening my hair and getting dressed. I make my obligatory call to my cousins so they know I'm not chopped up in a trunk somewhere. I call Jack and listen to his husky voice as it goes straight to voice mail. I pace the room a few times. I paint my toenails neon purple.

When Jack's still not back after all this, my worry begins to spread like the mutant roots of a giant tree, stretching into my limbs and wrapping around my chest. Just when I'm about to slip on my shoes and go hunt for him, Jack pushes into the room with his arms full of bags.

"Hey," he says casually. Like he hasn't been gone for an hour and a half. Like he hasn't had me panicking over his whereabouts and whether or not *he's* chopped up in pieces in somebody's trunk.

"'Hey'?" I put a hand on my hip. "Where the hell have you been?"

He sets the bags on a small table by the door and cocks his head with an almost smile. "Why, did you miss me?"

"I'm not kidding, Jack." I thrust an angry hand in his direction. "You just took off without telling me and I had no idea where you went or when you would be back. And then I tried calling you but it went straight to voice mail—"

"Hey." He gently wraps his hands around the tops of my arms. "My phone died and I didn't have a way to charge it, and honestly I didn't think I was going to be gone as long as I was. I'm sorry. I didn't mean to freak you out—"

"You didn't freak me out," I snap, pulling out of his grasp. "I just didn't know where you were."

He eyes me carefully then steps over to the bags. "I was out getting us dinner since this town is crawling with tourists for that art thing and I didn't feel like fighting traffic and waiting lists for a meal." He pulls out a few takeout boxes and sets them on the table with some utensils. He doesn't look at me. "Thai food. I got you that curry shit you like and some spring rolls."

The fury and fear that lit my veins just moments ago instantly dissolves as the smell of chicken curry meets my nose.

"You hate curry," I say, walking up beside him.

He nods. "Yeah, but I love pulled pork. At first I went to this barbeque place to get us dinner"—he pulls a container stuffed with a pulled pork sandwich and French fries out of another bag—"but then I saw the Thai place next door and thought you might appreciate that a little more so I went there after, which is why it took longer than I expected to get back here." He sets a box of spring rolls in front of me.

Of course he went out of his way to get food that I like. Must he always be so good to me? Even when he's being a dickhead, he's always so damn good to me.

I look up at his gray eyes apologetically. "I'm sorry I snapped. Thanks for getting us food."

He grins. "Thanks for freaking out about me."

I roll my eyes and sit down. "I was not freaking out."

He sits down across from me. "Sure you weren't."

We eat in comfortable silence, both of us clearly starving, until all our food has pretty much vanished and we're both in better moods.

"What time are you planning on waking up tomorrow?" he asks as he cleans up the empty boxes and bags. "Or do you plan to wake with the afternoon sun?"

"Ha. Ha." I stab the last bite of chicken on my plate. "I was actually thinking about setting an alarm, believe it or not."

He scoffs. "I'll believe that when I see it."

"I'm being serious." I swallow the last bite and clean up my mess as well. "I want to get an early start so we'll be in Louisiana by sunset."

I feel his eyes on me as I haul the rest of the bags and napkins to the small trash bin. "I guess you're pretty excited to be going home, then."

I shrug. "It'll be nice to see my mom. And my grandma, of course." Seeing a rare opportunity of having Jack in both a good mood and in a willing conversation about "home," I go fishing a little.

"What about you?" I ask innocently. "Are you excited about being home tomorrow?"

He leans back in one of the small dining chairs and his big

body dwarfs the seat like he's a giant and we're in a miniature land. "Not really."

I tuck my feet underneath me and cross my legs on my own chair, which looks just my size. "Because of things with Drew?"

He nods. "Yep."

I drift my eyes to the to-go cup of iced tea he brought for me and pick at the lid as I carefully ask, "So what's going on with him?"

Silence.

"He's just in some trouble."

"What kind of trouble?"

"Jenna."

I look up and find his eyes zeroed in on me like a hawk facing off a predator. "What?"

"Why are you prying?" he asks.

I lift a brow. "Why are you being so secretive?"

"Because my family shit doesn't concern you." He doesn't say it in a mean way, but his words still sting.

"But it concerns *you*," I say, then quietly add, "And you concern me."

He scans my face. "Do I?"

A thick warmth has suddenly entered the room and I shift in my chair to accommodate it as it licks around my body.

"Yes," I say with a single nod. "I care about you. A lot."

Too much.

His eyes are still studying me so I look away with a short exhale.

"Whatever's going on with your brother is obviously weighing on you and stressing you out." I shrug. "Maybe if you told me what it was you wouldn't feel so...heavy."

He shakes his head. "Trust me, you don't want any part of what I'm dealing with."

I harden my features. "And if I *did* want some kind of part in . . . whatever it is you're dealing with?"

His eyes darken. "I would do everything in my power to keep you out of it."

We stare at one another for several seconds, confusion and frustration pouring from my side of the table. What in the hell has him so angry and fierce?

"I need a smoke," he says, abruptly standing from the table.

He slips out the door without looking back and I stare at my to-go cup of iced tea, the knots in my stomach returning with more fervor than before.

Jack only smokes when he feels out of control. He only smokes when he's unsure, or doesn't trust himself.

He only smokes when he feels like he's failing.

And here I am, feeling like I've disappointed him so greatly that I've now forfeited my rights to care about him, and I can't help but feel like a failure as well.

10

JACK

*T*hree cigarettes later, I return to our room and quietly step inside. Every light is off except the small lamp on the table and Jenna's shadow seems to be sleeping in the next bed over.

"How was your smoke?" Jenna says into the darkness, clearly not asleep.

I sigh, emptying my pockets on the lit table. "Don't start."

Jenna's never been a fan of smoking, or smokers, and has made that clear to me on several occasions. And while I've pretty much quit, with a few rare exceptions, she still sneers when I light up.

I hear her sheets rustle and chance a glance in her direction. The glow from the lamp is enough to cast the lines of her pretty face in a soft yellow light.

"I don't give a damn if you smoke," she says, running her cat eyes over my face.

I unzip my bag and pull out a clean shirt before meeting her eyes. "Then why are you looking at me like that?"

She tilts her head. "Because I'm worried."

I scoff and head for the bathroom. "I would have guessed worrying about others went against your *plan*."

I don't know why I'm poking at her. Jenna's not the one I'm mad at right now. I'm angry with myself. With the situation back home that I can't control. With all the wrong decisions I've made in my life. Not the pretty girl in the motel bed who refuses to love me out loud.

Turning on the sink, I pull off my smoky shirt and toss it on the counter before bending down to rinse my face. The cold water feels good against my skin. Clean. Fresh. When I straighten back up, Jenna's standing right beside me with a hand on her hip and a mean scowl on her face.

"You don't have to be an asshole," she says.

"About your plan?" I blink. "Yes, I do." My pulse rises like I'm preparing for a fight.

"Why?" She huffs.

"Because that fucking plan of yours is the reason you won't admit that what happened between us wasn't just sex."

She steps back and lifts her hands. "I can't do this with you right now."

"Fine by me," I say, going back to the sink. "You never can, anyway."

God, I really am an asshole. But even so, the fact that she can't engage in an honest conversation about us offends me.

I hear her scoff before she climbs back into her bed and pretends to fall asleep.

Jenna's ridiculous, yet predictable reaction to being asked about us plays on repeat in my mind and I inwardly sigh. I thought if I played it cool for a few months and didn't push the subject, Jenna would come back around, and we could eventually have a grown-up conversation about things. I knew it wouldn't be fast or easy—nothing with Jenna is—but I didn't foresee how painful it would be to sit idly by in the meantime, watching her hook up with other guys and stick to her "plan."

She's doesn't do relationships. I get that. She doesn't ever want to be tied down to a guy. I get that too. But treating me like I'm an interchangeable piece in her chess game of a life and her big master plan isn't fair. Because I know that she cares about me in a way that scares the shit out of her. And that means something.

She's crazy about me, and I'm crazy about her, which makes this whole thing that much more infuriating. If Jenna would just accept that we have a good thing together I'd back off. I truly would. But the girl is stubborn and obsessed with control. And while I admire her boldness and hardheadedness, it also really pisses me off sometimes. Like right now.

————

"Ooh! Ooh!" Jenna jerks the car to the right and pulls over.

"What now?" I say groggily.

I didn't sleep well last night—surprise, surprise—so the moment we left the motel I shut my eyes and hoped for a nap. No such luck.

I look around. "We've only driven two miles from the motel. Do you have to go to the bathroom already? My God. You have the world's smallest bladder."

"No, Jack. Look!" She points out the window at the sidewalk, crowded with people and paintings. "It's the art festival that woman was talking about last night."

I open my mouth to object, because going to a morning art festival is pretty much the last thing I want to do at the crack of dawn, but when I see the joy in Jenna's eyes my lips press together in silence.

God, she's beautiful when she's happy. Why can't she be beautiful *and* easy to deal with? Is that so much to ask?

"Can we check it out?" She looks at me like a three-year-old asking for candy and I already know I'm at her mercy. "Please?"

I sigh. "Sure."

"Really?" Her eyes sparkle and it does something to my chest. Something irritatingly wonderful and I want to make her eyes sparkle like that all the time.

God, I'm so lost to her, it's pathetic.

"Really." I nod.

We get out of the car, Jenna leaping out like she's heading to a carnival, and me stiffly unfolding myself from the passenger seat, and she leads me by the hand down the sidewalk.

I look down at our adjoined hands and smirk. She's so giddy, she doesn't realize she's holding my hand. This little art festival detour might not be so bad after all.

We go from tent to tent to vendor to tent to vendor, looking at paintings and sculptures and jewelry and metalwork. Blown glass and quilts and every other form of art seems to be on display at the festival, dotting the scenery with bright colors and shapes.

Jenna looks like she's in heaven, smiling at every tent and cooing over every sculpture. She touches a silver necklace and a ring with a red stone, and stares at melancholy paintings and dancers in the street. Then she cheerfully moves along, chatting with every artist she sees and smiling for no reason.

I don't think I ever realized how happy art made her. I know that it's her passion, of course. But passion and happiness are different things—sometimes even rivals—so I never thought to connect the two.

But seeing her now, here, surrounded by all these colors and works of creation, I want nothing more than to bring her to an art festival every day.

"Ooh! My sisters would love these." She picks up a few hand-held fans, each painted with a different colored peacock, and opens them up. She smiles as she fans herself with one. "My mom calls us girls her little peacocks, because we're loud, colorful, and filled with attitude."

I snort. "That's you, spot-on." I think about my friend Ethan and bite back another snort because it's also him, spot-on. "How many sisters do you have again?" I ask.

"Three." She nods. "I'm my mom's only biological child, but she fostered Penny, Raine, and Shyla when they were all younger and ended up adopting each one, which was great because I was attached to them the moment I first saw them."

I nod. "Was that after your dad left?"

"Yeah," she says. "He took off when I was little and Mom could barely afford to feed me."

"Whoa," I say quietly to this new information. "That sucks."

I had no idea Jenna's childhood faced any struggles like that.

She shrugs. "We were better off without him, you know? Eventually Mom got a decent job, though. Then we were able to move into a little house. That's when Mom started fostering."

I smile. "It sounds like your mom is pretty amazing."

"Oh, she is." She smiles back. "She definitely is."

She buys a few of the painted fans then we head back toward her car. We pass the jewelry tent again and she stops to admire the red-stoned ring once more. Her fingers turn it over and her lips part as she takes it in.

"Do you like it?" the woman behind the makeshift counter asks.

"Oh, yes," Jenna says. She looks at the price tag and tries to hide her grimace.

I glance at the price. It's an exorbitant amount of money, but I can understand why it's priced so high. It's really unique.

"It's the only one I've ever made," the woman says. "There is no other ring exactly like that one anywhere in the world."

"It's beautiful," Jenna says in a hushed tone. "It's red like fire, but has a streak of blue down the center, like water. A perfect blend of two opposite elements."

The woman nods in proud agreement. "It's quite rare."

I cock my head at Jenna's examining eyes. I rarely see her so fascinated with things. She's typically so guarded and sharp. But watching her look into the ring is like seeing a glimpse of her as a child. Lost in wonderment. Believing in unicorns. Chasing rainbows.

"I'll take it," I say, looking at the woman.

Jenna's big golden eyes turn to me. "What?"

I shrug. "You like it. I can afford it. Let's get it."

She keeps staring at me, her mouth slightly open. "But that's not—I can't—"

I look right at her. "Do you want the ring?"

She blinks. "Yes."

I look back at the woman and hand her my debit card. "We'll take it."

The woman charges an insane amount of money to my card before carefully untying the price tag from the ring. Then holds it out to Jenna, who stares at it with such reverence that I'm afraid she's going to freak out.

Jenna looks back to me. "You just bought me a ring."

Oh shit. She really is going to freak out.

"Don't overthink it, Jenn," I say. "Just take the damn ring and let's go."

Carefully, Jenna takes the ring from the woman and slides it onto her left hand. We don't speak about it again, but as we get into the car, Jenna examines the ring on her hand and her eyes sparkle.

Worth every penny.

———

Because of our unexpected stop at the art festival, we don't reach Little Vail until nearly ten p.m., and I'm exhausted. My phone rings and I glance at the screen before answering.

"Hey, Mom. I'm almost home. I'll be there in twenty—"

"I need you to go get Samson," she says, irritated. "He took my car to Vipers and got completely wasted, and now Jonesy won't let him drive home and I have no way to pick him up."

I inwardly groan. "I don't get it. He knew I was almost home and we have serious shit to handle. Why the hell would he go get wasted?"

"I don't know, Jack. He was fine this afternoon, but then he got a call tonight and started freaking out and then took off with my car."

"Why didn't he take his Harley?"

She pauses. "Because he sold it. Didn't you know?"

"No." I shift lanes and make a U-turn, heading toward Vipers, a bar at the edge of town. "He failed to mention that."

Drew's missing. Mom's out of her mind. Samson's selling his goddamn bike? What the fuck is going on with my family members lately?

"Can you please go pick him up so Jonesy doesn't throw him out?" My mother's pleading voice isn't something I'm good at saying no to, so I answer the way I normally do.

"Of course. I'll see you soon." I hang up the phone and look at Jenna with a sigh. "I have a huge favor to ask."

She nods. "You need to pick your brother up from some bar called Vipers?" I frown and she explains, "Your mom was talking kind of loud. I heard her through the phone."

"Right." I turn my eyes back to the road. "I know it'll mean you won't get to New Orleans until later, so if you say no that's totally fine. I've got friends you can drop me off at who will give me a lift to Vipers."

"No, it's fine. It's just a few extra minutes. It won't make that much of a difference anyway."

"Are you sure?"

"I'm sure."

I nod and let out a slow breath. "Thanks, Jenn." From the corner of my eye, I see her glance at me, but she doesn't say anything else as we drive through the small-town lights of Little Vail to the shadiest bar in four counties.

Vipers is known for being a hub of criminal activity, complete with police raids and the occasional murder, and it's where I practically grew up. Not one of my proudest personal facts.

Pulling into the gravel lot, I park us in the back, more out of habit than convenience, and kill the engine. Then, as I watch the comings and goings of the who's who of big crimes in small towns, I ponder which is safer—the dark parking lot adjacent to a run-down industrial park, or the crowd comprised of questionable individuals inside the bar.

"You wait here," I say to Jenna as I get out of the car. "I'll be right back."

"Uh-uh." She opens her door and climbs out as well. "I need to pee."

I look at her, trying to conceal my panic. "Can't you hold it until we get Samson back to my place?"

She arches a sassy brow. "Hold it? No, *Dad*. I've been holding it for three hundred miles."

"You don't want to use the bathroom in this place. Trust me."

She scrunches her face in confusion and annoyance. "What's your deal right now? Let a girl pee, okay?" She starts marching for the front doors.

In three quick strides I'm beside her and talking in a hushed tone so my words come across less scolding than I mean them to be. "If you go in here with me, I need you to stay by my side. Do you understand?"

She snorts. "In the bathroom? Yeah, I don't think so."

"I'm being serious." I pull her arm and she spins to face me. But her look of irritation quickly dissolves into bafflement when she sees my expression. "This isn't a bar like the Thirsty Coyote. Hell, this isn't really a public bar at all. And you..." I glance her over and hot possessiveness courses through my veins. "You are going to draw attention."

She's wearing a tight black tank top, which molds to her chest in an all-too-delicious way, with a pair of tiny red shorts that show off her long, flawless legs. Rings cover her fingers and climb up her ears, while a diamond stud marks the side of her nose and the arch of her eyebrow. Her long lashes are thick and dark, sweeping over amber eyes filled with spirit. And tattoos wind over her shoulders, down her arms, and peek beneath the hem of her shorts, curving around her left thigh with the bottom half of a mermaid's tail.

My eyes trail up and over every inch of her and I swallow. "I need you to stay right by me when we go inside." I lower my voice. "Please."

She shifts her jaw back and forth, like she's not sure what to think, but finally shakes her head. "Fine. Whatever. But so help me Jesus, if you try to follow me into the bathroom stall I will yank off your balls and flush them. Understood?"

I narrow my eyes and move forward for the door. "Murder. Castration. You're a violent little thing, you know that?" My tone is relaxed but I'm anything but as we near the door.

Not just because I know what waits for us inside, or because I hate who I'm about to turn back into, but because there is a very good chance that I might have to follow Jenna into the bathroom stall to keep her safe. And I really don't feel like guarding my balls.

11

JENNA

So...Jack's being weird.

I get it. This isn't a girly bar and he doesn't want guys to mess with me and blah blah blah, but come on. *Stay by my side?* I'm an adult with an overstuffed bladder, not a toddler wandering around Disneyland.

He opens the door to the bar, but unlike usual, he doesn't hold it open for me. Instead, he steps inside and pulls me in behind him, keeping me hidden behind his massive shoulders as the door closes at my back.

Okay, not cool.

I start to move around him, curse words ready to leap from my tongue, but stop in my tracks when I realize the loud chatter inside the bar has significantly quieted. Peeking out from behind the big shoulder in front of me, I watch people, one by one, turn their heads to the door and park their eyes on Jack.

An odd tension fills the air, almost dangerous and definitely careful, but curious as well as more of the crowd turns our way.

These are Jack's people, apparently, and they all look...hard. Like, motorcycle-gang hard. Even the women look like they could slice my head off with a single swipe of their excessively long, acrylic fingernails. I look at Jack and frown.

His playful smile is gone, replaced by a hard scowl, and his chest is puffed out more than usual. I'm suddenly not as desperate to pee anymore. I can hold it for another few minutes. Hell, I can hold it for another few hours, if need be.

And need might very well *be*.

A hefty man, who I assume is the bartender, stands behind the bar with his dark eyes trained on Jack in a confrontational way. He looks to be in his fifties, with leathery skin and fat knuckles, and his shoulder-length gray hair is pulled back into a neat knot, matching the gray handlebar mustache curving out beneath his nose.

One second passes. Then two. Three.

"So the prodigal son has returned," the hefty bartender says, and the quieting chatter fades even more as ears perk up in every corner.

"I hate to disappoint," Jack says in a rough voice I've never heard him use before, "but I'm only here for Samson."

This is clearly some kind of standoff. I'm not sure if I should be worried, scared, or on my way to getting the hell out of Dodge. But one thing's for certain: Everyone in this bar knows Jack. And not in a friendly way.

"I wasn't sure if we'd ever see you again," the bartender continues. "Especially after…" He shrugs. "You know. But I was hoping we would."

A tight smile pulls out Jack's lips. "I was hoping you wouldn't."

The legs of a chair screech as a tall man with a long red scar down his cheek scoots out from a nearby table and stands. He slowly steps up to Jack, gets right in his face, and meets his gaze with violence in his eyes. Jack's gray eyes stare back with matching danger.

"You want me to take care of this, Jonesy?" the scarred man

says, his words tumbling over the bulge of chew wedged in his bottom lip as his eyes stay on Jack. He deftly slides a set of brass knuckles over his thick fingers before making a fist and cupping it into his other hand—and all the while, his eyes never leave Jack.

Yeah, Jack's definitely not friends with these people.

A thread of nervousness weaves through the crowd as people here and there shift in their seats, waiting for the bartender—Jonesy, apparently—to answer.

But Jack speaks first. "You sure that's a good idea, Murray?" he says to the scarred man. His voice is so low I can barely hear him as he nods at the thick red gash marking his opponent's face. "Things didn't work out *well* for you the last time you tried to 'take care' of me."

The Murray guy snarls. "You son of a bitch—"

He lunges at Jack, plowing into his chest with the full force of his body weight, but Jack doesn't budge. He simply grabs the guy by the throat, with one hand, and squeezes, his dark gray eyes glinting in the dim bar lights. Then he calmly says, "I suggest you back down." Murray gurgles and sputters as Jack puts more pressure on his windpipe. "What do you think, Jonesy?" Jack's gaze stays on Murray's beet-red face.

My eyes widen in shock. *What the . . . ?*

Is Jack really choking some biker guy right now? Is this really happening?

"I think you've made your point," Jonesy says, slightly amused.

Jack releases Murray and the scarred man coughs and wheezes as he stumbles backward. "Fuck you, Oliver."

I stare at Jack. Who the hell *is* this guy?

"I appreciate your eagerness, Murray," Jonesy says to his lackey, "but you can stand down. I'm sure Jack isn't here to cause any trouble. Are you, Jack?" The bartender's dark eyes drift to me, still half-hidden behind Jack's broad back, and flash with intrigue.

"That depends," Jack says, shifting closer to me as he addresses the bartender. "Are you looking for trouble?"

An uneasy trickle makes its way down my back as I scan Jack's face. Everything about him is suddenly unfamiliar, different. His body language. His tone. His entire demeanor. As if he's just stepped into someone else's personality.

Jonesy the bartender pulls his gaze away from me and curls a smile in Jack's direction. "Not particularly."

Jack lifts his chin. "Where's Samson?"

Jonesy nods to a red door at the end of a dark hallway behind the bar. "The back."

A muscle works in Jack's jaw as he mutters a curse then looks at the bartender. "Well?" He exhales. "Are we good or not?"

Jonesy eyes him, then me, and a small smile tips the corners of his mouth. "We're good." He nods. "For now."

Jack's shoulders slightly relax as he shifts his stance, throws on a crooked grin, and says, "Then what's a guy got to do to get a beer around here?"

Jonesy chuckles and the tension, still draining from Jack's shoulders, seems to fall away from the crowd as the patrons go back to their chatter and drinks.

Jack steps up to the bar with me in tow and I try to ignore the many pairs of eyes glued on me. Not us. *Me.*

There are only a handful of females in the bar and I'm by far the youngest, which might explain why every guy in the place is looking at me like I'm a walking piece of prime rib. Jack notices this as well and makes no attempt at being covert about the warning glares he stabs at the gawking men. He places his large hand on my lower back, his fingers splayed, and keeps it there. A gesture of ownership, no doubt. But I let it slide because the many sets of greedy eyes slipping over my body make me slightly uncomfortable and Jack's hand quells the shameless hunger of the onlookers, if only a smidge.

"Welcome home, Jack," Jonesy says with a genuine smile as we stand at the counter. "We've missed you."

Jack scoffs. "God, I hope not."

I run my eyes over the shadowed lines of Jack's hard expression and frown. This isn't the same guy I left Arizona with. This is someone else entirely. Someone darker. Someone...dangerous.

I wait for fear to grip me, but none comes. At least none derived of Jack's transformation. I still feel safe with him. Secure. I might not fully know the Jack standing beside me—the one with small scars on his knuckles and burdened eyes when he smokes—but that doesn't seem to change the fact that I absolutely trust him. Which is good, since it looks like having an ally in this place is a must.

"You say that, but you know it wasn't the same after you left," Jonesy says. "We missed your sorry ass. I missed you."

Beneath the teasing tone in Jonesy's voice is a thread of sincerity, and for a brief moment, Jack's eyes crinkle with a sad smile.

"I had to get out, Jonesy," he says. "It was the only way."

"I know." He pulls at his ear. "Doesn't mean I have to like it, though."

"No." Jack shifts. "I guess not."

Jonesy slides his eyes to me. "And who's this pretty young thing?" He looks me over in a way that isn't disgusting but isn't flattering either.

Straightening my shoulders, I wait until his eyes finally make their way back up to my face before smiling sharply. "Did you get a good enough look, or should I strip off my clothes and turn around in circles for you?"

Jack cuts his eyes to me.

Jonesy barks out a loud laugh from the depths of his gut. It's a raking sound, like tumbling stones in a wheel of scrap metal, and heads that weren't already staring turn in our direction.

"Holy hell on ice!" Jonesy chokes out as his laughter wanes. "I like this one, Jack. Pretty *and* mean. I'll bet she keeps you running." He looks me over again, but this time in a more . . . admiring way.

"You have no idea," Jack mutters.

Jonesy nods at me. "This is your girl, I take it?"

"Yeah," Jack says with a single nod. I whip my gaze to him, but he blatantly ignores me and goes on. "Jonesy this is Jenna. Jenna, meet Jonesy."

"Hey, darling." He smiles at me.

"Hey," I say, not sure what to make of this guy. Does he like Jack? Does he hate him?

Jack answers my unasked questions by explaining, "Jonesy is like the grandfather I never wanted."

Jonesy grins at him. "Bullshit. You like me."

"I like you compared to everyone else in this hellhole," he corrects. "But I wouldn't trust you as far as I could throw you."

He winks at me. "And with good reason."

"Case in point," Jack says, then shakes his head at Jonesy. "Sorry about Samson, by the way. I'll pay his tab and get him out of here. Is it cool if we head to the back?"

Jonesy nods. "Go on back. But don't worry about his tab. He's all paid up."

Jack shoves off the bar with a nod of thanks and walks toward the dark hallway. I follow behind him trying to decide on how best to let him know I'm not thrilled with his insta-reply back there about me being his girl.

I finally settle for, "What the fuck was that?" as I come up beside him in the hallway.

He barely glances at me. "I'll explain later."

"I'm sorry, you'll *explain?*"

"Yes. I'll explain," he bites out then stops in the middle of the corridor. "Now hurry so we can get out of here."

He points across the hall to a restroom door and I suddenly remember that I have to pee. With one last scowl angled at him, I turn and head for the bathroom.

When I'm finished washing my hands, I exit the bathroom to find Jack standing just outside the door, facing outward with his arms crossed and blocking the entrance, like he's some kind of bathroom sentry.

I tilt my head. "You're on Potty Patrol now? Wow."

He cocks his head. "Would you rather I ditch you?"

"Well...no."

"Exactly." He says nothing else as we head to the back of the hallway. Following behind him through the darkness, I watch one of his scarred hands push open the red door while the other reaches back for me, and can't help but feel like we're walking into something far more ominous than the storage room of a local bar. Something I should probably fear.

But my eyes trail down the sure lines of the familiar tattoo on the arm reaching back for me—where a large hawk proudly mangles a snake in its deadly talons—and any fear I might have dredged up instantly takes a backseat to the trust I have in Jack. He would never let anything happen to me. To us. I know this in an instinctive and undeniable way. Like it's a built-in truth.

So I slip my hand into his and let the warmth from his grasp wrap around my cold fingers as we enter through the scarlet door, together.

12

JACK

J'm going to kill Samson.

I spy my younger brother the moment I step into the back room, and the sight of his drunk ass sprawled out on the concrete floor has me swallowing curse words as fast as I can conceive them.

I'm going to kill him for putting me in this situation. Jenna wasn't supposed to be exposed to anything regarding my "real" life, aside from my house when she dropped me off, and now she's right in the middle of it. Thanks to Samson.

Vipers? Seriously? Goddamn. What was he thinking coming here?

We're not alone in the back room. Seated at a round table between me and Samson are the "poker players." I know them each by name and contraband, and they know me just the same.

The poker faces eye Jenna, and I can almost hear the wheels turning in their heads. I grip her hand more tightly, feeling like I just walked a gazelle straight into a den of lions.

She's going to bitch at me from here to hell for treating her like she's mine in here, but I had no choice. If she'd just stayed in the car like I said, things would have been fine. But no, the diva had to pee.

All the eyes in the room drift away from Jenna and fall back on me and I relax a bit.

I wasn't sure what was going to meet us on the other side of the red door—I've had such varying experiences it's hard to make an educated guess anymore—but it looks like everyone is playing nice tonight. I glance at a guy seated at the table with a fresh black eye, a bloody lip, and two missing fingers. Nice enough, at least.

"Jack ..." says a familiar voice.

I lock eyes with the owner of Vipers. Alec's never been good at greeting others with any kind of finality to his tone. It's one of the things that make him so unsettling.

I glance at the missing digits on the bloody guy's left hand.

And unpredictable.

Loosening my hold on Jenna, I straighten my shoulders and nod once. "Alec."

Memories I've stuffed in deep dark pockets of my soul start to pull themselves out and slowly unfold within my chest as we eye one another.

He lights a cigarette and takes a painfully slow drag as he watches me. His blue eyes are ice-cold and calculating. The kind of eyes you want on your side, if only to keep from having them against you. He exhales just as slowly as he pulls the smoke into his lungs, and a long wisp of white glides above the table like a sickly cloud.

"Haven't seen you for a while," Alec says. He slowly scratches at the black whiskers on his chin. "I didn't think you'd ever come back. You sticking around this time?"

"Not likely." I look around, my gut crawling with nerves and anxiety. I need to get Samson and Jenna out of here. Fast.

Keeping my composure stern and steady, I gesture to my brother, facedown on the floor behind the poker table. "Did he break anything?"

The poker faces shake their heads in unison. Alec says nothing.

I look at each pair of eyes, one by one. "Does he owe money—or any other type of payment—to anyone here?"

From the corner of my eye, I see Jenna glance at me, but I don't look at her. I can't. I can't believe I let her walk into this. I need to get her out. Now.

More heads shake in response. Still Alec is silent, but his light-blue eyes darken and tension fills the room.

Holy shit. Holy shit.

My eyes dart around, noting the exit door in the back, the rickety wall ladder leading to the roof, and the heavy red door behind me. I'm more familiar with this building than I care to admit, so I know just how cornered we are right now.

Jenna. Oh God. I need to get her out of here.

As if she can sense my thoughts, Jenna steps closer to me, her shoulder pressing into my back like she knows she needs a shield, and lets out a shaky exhale.

Shit, shit, shit.

"No payment is required…" Alec finally says, breaking the silence. His voice is quiet and unresolved. Eerie. "But you know how I feel about…drop-ins."

My pulse rises. "Samson has nothing to do with the business. You know that. He was just…" I glance at my brother's drunk body. So ignorant. So breakable. "Hell, I don't know what he was doing. But he wasn't here to stir shit up."

"Oh, I assure you he was." Alec leans back and gives a subtle nod to the poker faces.

Three guns are immediately pointed at my face, and Jenna sucks in a sharp breath.

Unpredictable Alec.

I know he won't kill me. I know this is just a show. But Jenna doesn't know that. And the trembling hand she has braced against my back certainly doesn't know that.

Goddamn it.

"He was asking a lot of questions this evening," Alec continues, casually. "Probing questions."

Shit. Samson was probably asking around about Drew. The dumbass doesn't know any better, but sniffing around a bar like this—a bar with business outside of just booze—can get a guy killed. It usually does.

I choose my next words carefully. "Samson's intentions were innocent, Alec. He wasn't trying to pry into your business shit. I promise."

"Do you know"—Alec takes another slow drag of his cigarette— "that you're the only person in this…"—he lets out another slow exhale as he gestures around—"industry…whose promises mean anything to me?"

I say nothing.

"And because of that, I have a tendency to trust you." He nods again at his gunmen and they lower their weapons. Alec looks up at me from his seat at the table with a sharp warning in his eyes. "Don't make me regret it, Jack." He stubs out his cigarette, eyes never leaving mine. "I'm serious."

Relief floods my veins and fills my lungs, but holy hell. How am I going to explain all this to Jenna?

Nodding once, I let out a rough exhale. "Are we done here?"

Alec inhales. "I suppose so." He flicks a hand at the dealer and they return to their card game.

Wasting no time, I race toward my brother, directing Jenna along beside me by the small of her back. Samson is several yards behind the poker table, and when we reach him, his head lolls to the side and his hair—the same almost-black shade as mine but slightly shorter and wavier—flops into his bloodshot green eyes as he stares up at me.

"Heh, bro," he slurs. "Please don't punch me."

I hoist him up from the floor and steady his body against mine. He might be my little brother, but he's only an inch shorter and nearly as muscular as I am, so hauling his weight up is no small task.

"You better figure out how to walk on your own, Sam." I prop him upright beside me. "Or I *will* punch you."

Samson rolls his head in a pathetic attempt to nod. "That seems fair."

Jenna steps to Samson's other side and helps steady him until he's on his feet. He's wobbling like a newborn lamb, but standing nonetheless. I point to an exit door in the far corner, where I know just beyond is almost exactly where I parked, and Jenna nods.

"It was good to see you again, Jack," Alec says without looking back at me. "Perhaps we'll meet again soon…"

I try to ignore the sick feeling his words bring to my gut and focus on keeping Samson upright as Jenna and I direct him toward the exit door. Then, pushing it open with more force than necessary, I lead the lamb and gazelle out of the lions' den and into the parking lot.

I unlock the doors of Jenna's car, stuff Samson in the back-seat, and slam the door before climbing into the front. Jenna gets in without a word and clicks her seat belt into place.

She glances at me, fear in her expression, a worry line between her brows, and an angry fleck in her eyes. I've got nothing to say to her, though. Not yet.

Throwing the car in gear, I drive away and wait until there's a few miles between us and the bar before pinning Samson with my eyes in the rearview mirror and biting out, "What the *fuck*, Sam?"

He rubs both hands down his face and groans. "I know, Jack."

"No, you *don't* know. You could have gotten yourself killed back there! Or worse."

My eyes flit to Jenna and guilt wrings my stomach. She's probably terrified.

"I'm sorry. But it's bad." He shakes his head. "It's so bad."

"You're damn right, it's bad." I flex my jaw. "You can't just poke around Alec's business, Sam! The guy thought you were trying to spy on him or some shit. Just because he's not your enemy does *not* mean he's your friend. Understand?" I grimace, my nerves fried from the nonstop adrenaline spiking my veins during that whole encounter. "And what the hell is up with you getting wasted? You're twenty-one, man. Not fifteen. I shouldn't be dragging your ass out of bars."

Samson just keeps shaking his head. "No, Jack. I mean this thing with Drew is bad."

"No shit." I purse my lips. "But getting trashed certainly isn't going to make it better."

"No, man. You don't understand," he says, slurring a bit as he hangs his face between the front seats, seemingly oblivious to Jenna's presence. "I got a call tonight. From one of the Royals. They..." His voice cracks. "They put a bounty out on Drew."

My grip tightens around the steering wheel as I stare ahead, my stomach suddenly feeling hollow and cold.

No.

This can't be happening.

A bounty? My blood ices over with cold black dread.

From the corner of my eye, I see Jenna's mouth fall open and my dread reroutes to other areas of impossible fear. Shit.

Shit, shit, shit. This is *not* how things were supposed to go down. Not with Jenna. Not with Samson. Not with Drew... oh, God.

I draw in a deep breath and glance at Samson. "And the Royals told you that?"

He nods heavily. "That's why I got all messed up tonight. I went to Alec thinking maybe he could help—"

"Dammit, Sam," I mutter.

"But he was just as surprised as me," Samson continues. "He knew nothing about Drew being mixed up with the Royals—or about the Royals putting a price on Drew's head—and I...I just panicked. Jonesy felt bad and poured me a few drinks, and I just kept drinking until it wasn't real anymore." He shakes his head and slurs, "It can't be real."

Angry fear spills into the hollow of my stomach. "I thought you guys were staying out of things, dammit. You said this wouldn't be an issue if I left. You *promised* you wouldn't get involved in Dad's shit—"

"I didn't! I swear," Samson says. "And I didn't know Drew was up to something of this caliber until I got that call tonight." His eyes turn desperate. "The Royals think I know where Drew is—but I don't! I have no fucking clue. And..." He grabs at his hair. "And if they find him, they're going to—"

"I know!" I bark. "Just shut up for a second and let me think."

Samson pulls back and slouches against the seat and I sneak a glimpse at Jenna. I can't risk Samson's drunk mouth spilling any more information about my family's fucked-up situation. Jenna's freaked-out enough as it is.

My drumming pulse roars in my ears as silence fills the car. If Drew's mixed up with the Royals then all of this really is my fault. But how the hell did he manage to contact them without me? The Royals aren't even based in Little Vail.

I slip my eyes to Jenna, who's doing a decent job of pretending like she's totally cool with everything that's happened in the last thirty minutes by picking the purple polish off her fingernails, but I know better. She's scared and she'll surely have a lot of questions for me. I'm just afraid I'm not going to have any answers for her. At least none that she'll like.

"Okay, here's what we're going to do," I say evenly as my gaze shifts to Samson in the rearview mirror. "I'm going to drop you off at Mom's so you can crash and sober up. Then Jenna can take her car and head home"—I nod in her direction and Samson tips his chin at her in greeting—"while I go find out more about Drew's business with the Royals." I stretch my neck. "Then we can get this all sorted out."

Maybe. The Royals putting a price on Drew's head is basically an act of war, so the odds of this turning out well for Drew, or anyone else in my family, aren't very good. But at least Jenna will be safe. She'll be long gone before morning, happily at home with her family, where my troubles can't reach her.

Glancing across the dark car at her profile, fear pricks the back of my neck.

"Are you okay?" I ask quietly.

She thinks for a moment. "Oddly, yes. Considering multiple guns were pointed in our direction just five minutes ago, I think I'm doing pretty damn good."

I scrub a hand down my face. "God, I'm sorry. What happened back there... that wasn't... I shouldn't have—"

Samson groans. "I think I'm going to be sick."

I snap my eyes to him. "Don't you *dare* vomit in the car."

"Then quit taking turns at high speeds," he complains. "Being drunk is hard."

Jenna shakes her head and looks at me. "Let's talk after we drop him off, okay?"

I press my lips together, both grateful and worried that she's taking the night's events so well.

Across the car, she sits cross-legged, with her graceful arms resting against her thighs and her hands tucked in her lap, and the soft glow from the dashboard instruments highlighting the curve of her cheekbone and the length of her neck. She reminds me of good things, happy things.

I can't get her out of this town fast enough.

Looking at the time, however, I start to rethink my plan. It's almost midnight and New Orleans is a good two hours away. Jenna's no doubt exhausted, and her night vision isn't great even when she's well rested. Her driving home alone tonight probably isn't the best idea. Not that she would agree. I inwardly sigh, knowing what's coming.

I clear my throat. "Maybe you should wait until morning before heading home."

She pulls a face. "Why?"

"Because it's late, and dark, and you're probably tired of being on the road—"

"Which is why I want to go home."

"It's a long drive and even with your glasses—"

"Oh my God. What are you, my ophthalmologist now?" She huffs. "My vision is *fine*."

"You're vision is *not* fine, but even if it were I still think it might be a good idea to get some sleep before heading home."

Her jaw shifts in anger. "I'm not wasting another penny on hotel rooms—especially not when my own damn bed is less than two hours away."

I shift my own jaw. "Why does everything have to be a fight with you?"

"Because you keep trying to control me and tell me what to do!"

"For the last time, I'm not trying to control you, Jenna!" I grip the steering wheel. "I'm just suggesting things to keep you safe. *You're* the one who's trying to control everything."

Samson pokes his head between the front seats again and woozily says, "Are you two sleeping together?"

"No!" we shout.

He nods. "Well that explains a lot."

"Shut up, Samson." I turn down the street I grew up on and come to a stop in front of our small house.

It's gray with lopsided porch steps and a square of dead grass in the front yard. Bittersweet memories accompany the sight of the yellow front door and the small wicker table and chair on the porch. Good things happened here. So did bad things. Something thick and hot tugs at my throat as I look over my childhood home.

There were many days I thought I'd never see it again. Days

I was certain I was going to die. On those days, I tried to focus on the good memories of growing up in the little gray house. Wrestling with my brothers. My mom sneaking cookies into my lunch for school. The good outweighs the bad. Now, at least.

Everything about it looks the same as the day I left except the dozens of wind chimes hanging from the porch roof.

I murmur, "What the hell...?"

Samson follows my gaze and groggily explains, "That's Ma's new thing. You know how she's always trying to quit smoking? Well she bought some kind of chime-making kit thingy on one of those late-night TV commercials and now, instead of sucking on a cigarette every two hours, she whittles together a wind chime instead."

"That's..."—I exit the car with a frown—"strange."

He scoffs. "And obnoxious." Tumbling out of the backseat, Samson barely catches himself before glowering at the hanging chimes. "When the wind picks up, it's like living in the bell tower of a thousand churches. I feel like Quasi-fucking-modo up in here."

Jenna gets out and we watch him stagger toward the porch steps.

"Maybe Mom's doing it on purpose," I say. "So you'll move out already."

He spins around and points a wobbly finger at me. "Hey, it's not my fault Trixie kicked me out of her apartment and made me homeless."

"Uh, yeah it is," I say. "You slept with her best friend—"

"I did not *sleep* with her. I just *slept* with her," he says, bumbling over his words. "Why is that so hard for people to understand?"

My mom's voice breaks into the night. "Maybe because you're always spouting off about it when you're hammered." Backlit by the lamplight in the living room, her silhouette stands with a hand on a hip in the doorframe. "People don't care what a drunk man declares, Samson. Now quit crying about Trixie and get inside before I make you sleep in the yard."

I cringe, hoping Jenna doesn't think I was raised by some crazy woman. "Hey, Mom—"

"Trixie, my ass," Mom mutters, her eyes glued to Samson as he trudges inside the house and flops facedown on the couch. "Sleeping outside is probably ten times better than sleeping in that girl's bed."

"Mom—"

"What the hell kind of name is Trixie, anyway? Can't you boys find women with*out* whore names—"

"*Mom!*" I raise my voice and she finally stops talking and turns around. "This is Jenna," I say, inhaling sharply through my nose.

She squints through the darkness and manages to look slightly mortified when she realizes we have company. "Oh, hell."

I gesture from Jenna to the crazy woman standing on the porch. "Jenna, meet my well-meaning, but very tacky, mother."

Amusement sparks in Jenna's eyes as she smiles. "Nice to meet you, Mrs. Oliver."

She gives Jenna a wry smile. "I'm sure it is, darling. Sorry about all that," she says, making her way down the porch steps. "I have no doubt Jack's gonna have some choice words for me later."

She looks good. Healthy. Not too skinny. Not too tired. Her dark brown hair falls in thick waves to the middle of her back and her green eyes—identical in color with Samson's—are clear and bright.

"And please," Mom adds, "call me Lilly." Jenna's arms stick out awkwardly in surprise as my mom wraps her in a hug. "I'm so happy to meet you, Jenna. It's so refreshing to meet a girl with a name that doesn't sound like it belongs to a stripper."

I pinch my lips. "Really, Mom?"

"What?" she says innocently, releasing Jenna from her arms. She places a cool hand on my cheek. "You sad I didn't hug you first?"

I exhale in frustration. "This, among other reasons, is why I don't bring girls home."

She pats my cheek with a grin. "Oh, please. You don't bring girls home for an entirely different reason." Her eyes slide to Jenna then back to me with a wink.

"Mom..." I warn.

She gives me a knowing smile then drops her teasing tone. "Welcome home, baby." She kisses my cheek and, with a quiver in her voice, she whispers, "I'm so glad you're here, Jack. I've missed you."

I kiss her back. "I've missed you too."

Stepping back, she clears her throat and merrily waves us in. "Come on inside, you two. I want to hear how your trip was."

"Actually," Jenna takes a step back and purposely avoids my eyes. "I think I'm going to head out."

The idea of Jenna leaving before I've had a chance to explain, or at least properly apologize, for the intense night she's been through puts me on edge.

"Don't you think you should hang around for a bit?" I say. "So we can, you know...*talk*?" I say that last word through my teeth and narrow my gaze on her.

Her eyes flit from side to side, looking at my mother, looking at Samson. "Oh, no. You and I can talk *anytime*." She shoots me an I-want-to-get-the-hell-out-of-here look. "I should really be on my way. You know, before it gets any later."

Yeah, that's not going to work for me. I can't let Jenna bail on me. Not yet, anyway. I need to make sure she's really okay. More importantly, I need to know if what she saw tonight changed the way she sees me. I put her in a situation where we were held at *gunpoint* for Christ's sake. I'm sure she has questions, or at the very least, concerns.

"Nonsense," I say with a forced smile. "You should stay here tonight. Right, Mom?" I look pointedly at my mother.

"Of course!" Lilly Oliver smiles broadly, obviously thrilled at the prospect of a girl staying in her house. "I would love to have you stay."

Jenna glowers at me before shaking her head with a tight smile. "I really should get home. My mom is probably waiting up and everything." She shakes her phone in an aw-shucks kind of way.

"Great idea," I say, a new, brilliant, foolproof master plan blossoming in my mind. "Let's call your mom."

Her sugar-sweet act drops. "I don't think that's necessary, *Jack*."

"Really? Because I think your mom might have some valuable insight into whether or not you should drive home this late."

She glances at her screen. "Look at that. My battery's almost dead." Dramatic sigh. "I guess I'll have to call her after I charge it in the car."

"No worries," I say. "I have your mom's number in my phone, so I'll just..." Pulling my phone from my pocket, I dial the number and hold it to my ear with a triumphant smile.

Her eyes widen. "How do you have my mom's number?"

"From the last time your grandma was dying, remember? You called me from New Orleans to bitch about your cousin stealing your tattoo idea. Hello, Sherry?" I smile and look away. "Yeah, this is Jack Oliver. I'm..." Jenna glares at me while her mother coos over the phone. "Yep, I'm *that* Jack." I wink at Jenna, who's obviously told her mother more about me than she wants me to know. "So I'm here in Little Vail with Jenna and since it's getting pretty late, I suggested Jenna stay at my mom's house with me. But Jenna's afraid that you might be disappointed since you're waiting up for her and all...uh-huh...uh-huh...I know. I said the exact same thing. And we both know how stubborn she is about wearing her glasses at night..." Jenna sneers at me and my grin grows. "Right... uh-huh...so what do you think? I certainly don't want to take away from precious time with your daughter, but I also want what's best for her safety...uh-huh...I couldn't agree more...Sure. Here she is." I hold the phone out to Jenna.

She stares daggers at me for a few beats then snatches the phone from my hand. "Hi, Mama...uh-huh...uh-huh...okay...bye." Hanging up, she shoves the phone back at me with a tight smile. "Looks like I'm staying here tonight."

"Fantastic," my mom says, grinning from ear to ear. "Now, come on in and I'll get you set up for the night."

As we follow my mother up the porch steps Jenna turns to me with a scowl. "I hate you."

"Yeah." I smile. "I know."

13

JENNA

So tonight has been a little bit crazy. I'd be lying if I said I wasn't completely freaked-out earlier when it looked like every guy in the back room of that bar wanted to kill Jack, but weirdly, I felt safe the whole time. I'm not sure if that's because I trust Jack so much, or because I'm clinically insane. But either way, I was more worried about Jack than I was about myself.

It did raise some questions in my mind, though. Hell, it gave birth to a litter of questions and encouraged them to run around like mad in my head all night. A part of me feels like I don't even know Jack anymore. The guy standing beside me in that bar tonight was a stranger, and I wasn't sure how I felt about that. But the guy sitting beside me right now is the same old Jack I've always known, and I know exactly how I feel about *that*.

Happy.

But it doesn't hurt that Jack's mom is entertaining as hell and keeping a constant smile on my face. Lilly Oliver is a piece of work—and I mean that in the best possible way. I can tell Jack's trying to rein her in, but honestly I kind of want to see her run free.

"You like beer, Jenna? 'Cause we've got beer," she says, swinging around the kitchen from cabinet to cabinet grabbing God knows what. "We don't have wine because none of us can stand the sweet stench. And we don't have champagne because, you know, *ick*. But we've got beer, whiskey, tequila, gin, and beer—shit." She looks at me. "Do you even drink? If you don't, that's totally fine because we've got..."—she opens the fridge and scours the contents with a little hum—"expired milk, half of a Sunny Delight, and tap water." She pulls a six-pack from the fridge and holds it up with a grin. "But we have beer."

Jack rubs his temple. "I'm not sure if Jenna's clear on whether or not there's beer in this house. You might want to reiterate that fact."

She gives him a disparaging look. "I'm just trying to be a good host."

He nods once. "The key word there is 'host,' Mom. Not bartender."

She ignores him and looks at me. "What would you like to drink, darling?"

Biting my cheek to keep from smiling at their exchange, I tap a finger to my mouth. "Hmm. I feel like the right answer here is beer."

"Wait." Jack holds up a hand. "There's *beer* in the house?"

Lilly narrows her eyes as she puts the six-pack back in the fridge. "Do I need to beat you?"

Jack wrinkles his brow. "Why are all the women in my life so prone to violence?"

"Maybe because you drive them to insanity," I quip.

"I can vouch for that." Lilly scoffs. Still standing with the fridge open, she twitches her lips and slides her gaze to me. "So seriously, what'll it be, Jenna? Sunny D? Water?" She winks. "*Beer?*"

I smile. "Uh...can I just have whiskey?"

A moment of silence passes where my stomach clenches in fear that perhaps I've just supremely offended Jack's mom in some way. But then Lilly lets the fridge door fall closed and throws her hands up in glee.

"Finally! A girl with taste! I'm sorry, darling, but I just have to do this." She comes over and kisses the top of my head.

"Mom," Jack groans. "Can you at least try to be normal?"

I laugh as Lilly plants a second quick kiss on my head and pointedly looks at her son. "This *is* my normal. You just brought home a beautiful girl who drinks whiskey. That's cause for celebration." She scurries around the kitchen, collecting three glasses and a bottle of Maker's Mark. "How do you takes yours, Jenna?"

"Just on the rocks," I say.

As she fills the glasses with ice, she looks at Jack and mouths, *I love her.*

He mockingly mouths back, *I can tell.*

My phone buzzes and I see I have four missed calls, all from my cousins. I smile at Lilly. "Will you excuse me for a minute?" She nods as I scoot out my chair. "I'll be right back."

I leave the kitchen and weave down a quiet hallway to the right as I call Callie. No answer. I try Becca. No answer. Checking my texts, I see that they were only calling to make sure I wasn't dead and to know when I thought I would be home.

I text them to let them know I'm safe and that I'll be home tomorrow then start back down the hallway. There's a fairly recent picture on the wall of Jack and Samson, and I squint at Samson. It was hard to get a good look at him tonight, what with all the guns in my face and all the drunk head-lolling he was doing, but looking at him in the photo I realize Samson looks very similar to Jack— tall, dark, and totally hot—but more mischievous and playful. And where Jack's eyes are metallic pools of dark gray with thin rings of hazel green, Samson's eyes are a true green.

Moving on, I round the end of the hallway and see Jack and his mother leaning close together in deep conversation at the table. Not wanting to intrude on their mommy-and-me moment, I quickly duck back into the shadows of the hallway.

"Tell me the truth, Jack," his mom says, sounding worried. "How bad is this thing with Drew?"

Jack sighs heavily. "I really don't know, Mom."

Crap. I need to go somewhere else. I walk into the living room, but I can still hear them talking so I tiptoe to the back of the hallway where I texted my cousins. Dammit, I can still hear them.

Lilly's voice climbs higher in pitch as she grates out, "Is he okay? Is he in trouble? Is he—"

"He's fine." Jack's voice sounds sure. Steady. "He's going to be just fine."

Glancing at the hallway doors, I debate slipping into one of the mystery rooms to avoid listening in on their private dialogue. But sneaking into someone's room in the dark and hiding out there for no apparent reason is like ten times creepier than eavesdropping. So yeah. No mystery doors for me.

She sniffs. "Dammit, Jack. Just tell me so I know. I promise you, everything that I've been imagining is worse. Much worse."

He quietly scoffs. "Yeah, that's probably true."

Screw it. I plaster myself against the side of the hallway and listen as Jack sucks in a deep breath.

"All right, Mom. Here's what it is: Drew got mixed up with some of Dad's associates and now he's trying to get out—but don't freak out. Samson and I have a plan. Everything's going to be fine."

Pressing my back against the cool wall I frown. I know for a fact that Samson and Jack do *not* have a plan, so I can only assume he's lying to keep her calm.

"What associates?" Lilly asks with a bite to her tone.

"Mom..."

"Which ones, Jack?" A beat passes. "Don't make me call Jonesy."

Jack sighs. "The Royals."

"The *Royals*?" A panicked squeak escapes her throat. "Oh, no. Not Drew. No, no, no—"

"Mom. *Mom*. Look at me." Jack quiets his voice to a near whisper. "There is nothing I wouldn't do for this family. For you. For Samson. And especially Drew. So I will find him." He pauses. "No matter what, I will find him and bring him home. Everything will be okay. I promise." His tone is so gentle. So careful.

I've only heard him speak with such tenderness one other time, and that memory clashes terribly with my current situation.

Lilly sighs. "Jack...I'm worried."

"You don't need to worry," Jack says. "I'll take care of Drew."

"No, baby. I'm worried about *you*." I hear the scooting of a chair like she's pulling closer to him. "You've been taking care of this family ever since you were a teenager—even before everything happened with your father. And when you left..." She inhales. "I know I said I didn't want you to go, Jack, but secretly...I was relieved. You needed to get out of this place and away from all the burdens you inherited. And now this thing with Drew has you running back home and I—I'm afraid you're going to slip right back into that burdened role."

"Loving you guys isn't a burden."

"You know what I mean. I've missed you so bad and I'm so glad to see you. But I don't want you to go back to being the Jack you were before you left."

A moment of silence passes before Jack says, "You don't need to worry about the old Jack. I'm different now. Happier."

"I know." I hear the smile in her voice. "I can tell. That's why I'm worried."

"You worry too much, Mom. I'll be fine. And besides, I have you and Sam to keep me in check."

"And Jenna."

He scoffs. "Hardly. She'll be out of here as soon as possible. Not that I blame her. Did you really have to kiss her head?"

She quietly laughs. "Oh, Jack."

"What?"

She lets out a little sigh. "I'm just happy you're home, that's all."

And that's my cue.

Clearing my throat, I make a big production of stomping loudly down the hall before turning into the kitchen with a bright smile. "Sorry about that."

The bottle of Maker's Mark is on the table next to three glasses filled with ice. As I sit down, Lilly pours me a drink then moves to fill the glass in front of Jack.

He shakes his head. "I have to go out later."

Lilly's frown matches my own. "Tonight?" She glances at the clock on the wall. It's almost midnight.

He nods. "I want to catch up with some old friends."

"Can't you wait until morning?" she says.

He shakes his head. "The longer I wait, the more people will know I'm back in town. And I was kind of hoping to...surprise a few people."

I narrow my eyes. After his whole speech about me not driving at night and being so exhausted, Jack wants to go hang out with friends? I call bullshit. He's up to something. And after everything I witnessed at the bar earlier, it's probably something shady.

Lilly shrugs and pulls his empty glass back. "Fine then. More whiskey for me."

"Is it okay if I borrow your car? Just for tonight—" He runs a hand through his dark hair and mutters, "Shit. You don't have your car."

"Nope." She shakes her head. "Samson drove it to Vipers tonight and left it there."

"Dammit. Why did he have to sell his bike? So inconvenient."

"Money," Lilly says. "That Harley was the only thing of value Samson owned." She frowns. "Where is that boy, anyway? Is he asleep on my couch? He better not be drooling on the cushions again." Standing, she plucks her whiskey glass from the table and stalks to the living room, mumbling, "Especially when he's got his own damn bedroom ten feet away..."

Once it's just the two of us in the kitchen, Jack's demeanor changes, like he's slipping back into a well-worn suit as he smiles at me sympathetically. "I bet you're pretty tired."

I eye him as I sip on my drink. "Not really."

He leans back in his seat with a very fake yawn. "It's been a long day."

"Uh-huh." I lift a brow, knowing full well that this is his gearing-up-to-ask-for-a-favor voice.

Wait for it...

He leans forward on his elbows and implores me with his gray eyes. "Is it cool if I borrow your car tonight? Just for an hour or two?"

There it is.

"So you can go catch up with *friends*?"

He nods.

"Sure." I smile sweetly and he perks up. "But only if you tell me why you're *really* going out."

He tries to look innocent, but innocent doesn't really work with the whole unruly-haired, tattoo-covered, bad-boy thing he's got going. "I told you. I'm going to see some old—"

"Friends. Right." I take another drink. "Yeah, you're a big fat liar. And I'm not letting you use my car unless you tell me the truth." His features turn stony so I amend, "Either that, or you have to take me along with you."

His shoulders slump, meaning me coming along isn't an option in the slightest, which in turn means that he's up to no good.

"Whatever," he says.

I shrug. "Whatever."

He sighs and gets serious for a moment. "I know you probably have some questions. About tonight. About—"

"The *bounty* on your brother's head? Uh, yeah."

"Shh!" Fear flashes in his gaze as he snaps his eyes to the living room. "My mom will hear you."

I swallow, feeling guilty, and lower my voice. "Sorry. But… shouldn't your mom know if Drew's in that kind of danger?"

He shakes his head. "No."

"No? These people want him dead, for God's sake."

"I know. But I don't want to tell my mom anything until I do some digging to see if it's a real threat or not."

My mouth falls open. "Are you insane? You should be calling the cops! Not playing detective on your own."

He exhales. "The cops can't help us."

I scoff. "Why? Is Little Vail run by mobsters or something?"

He studies me for a moment. "Something like that."

I blink, waiting for him to correct his statement, but his expression remains serious. Genuine terror races down my spine as my thoughts fly in every direction, all of which lead to Jack dying.

"What the hell is going on, Jack?" I say, my voice on the verge of cracking.

He rubs a hand over his mouth. "You're safe, I promise. And my mom and Samson are safe too. I know you have a ton of questions and I want to answer them—I really do. I just...I need to figure some stuff out tonight and then you and I can talk in the morning."

I purse my lips. "You think I'm going to be able to sleep with all this flying around my head?"

He takes my face in his hands—an act he's only done a few times before—and looks deep into my eyes. "I think you need to trust me." He searches my face and I suddenly want to fall into him and tuck myself in his warmth where everything is familiar and sure; where nothing can hurt us. "I would never let anything happen to you."

I swallow heavily and slowly pull out of his hands. "It's not *me* I'm worried about. It's you, wanting to run off in the middle of the night to visit *friends*. You're not telling me the whole truth."

"You're right." He looks at me sternly. "I'm not."

Lilly suddenly returns to the kitchen, still muttering about Samson, and Jack and I lean away from one another.

"I'm sleepy," she says with a yawn.

Unlike her lying little boy's, Lilly's yawn is authentic and reminds me that this poor woman probably has a real life to attend to in the morning and my penchant for late-night whiskey should probably come to a close.

I quickly finish my drink. "Thanks, Mrs. Oliver."

"Call me Lilly," she reminds me then looks at Jack. "Are you two sleeping in your room tonight or should I..."

She trails off, probably in the hope that one of us will jump right in and prevent any kind of uncomfortable silence from falling over the room like a wet blanket, but alas we do not, so the three of us stand in the soggy awkwardness for a good three seconds before Jack finally says, "Jenna can sleep in my room. I'll take whatever drool-free couch you have left."

Lilly brandishes a smile as fake as Jack's recent yawn. "Perfect. I'll get some fresh sheets and towels."

Ten minutes later, I'm ready for bed. Not wanting to haul in all my luggage, I decide to sleep in the long T-shirt I have on over my leggings. Tomorrow, in the light of day when I'm feeling rested and cheerier, I'll unload some belongings and shower and all that. But tonight, I just want to crash.

"We'll talk in the morning. I promise. Night," Jack says half-heartedly from his bedroom door after I'm all snuggled into his bed.

"Night," I say.

He shuts the door behind him. The latch makes a loud click as it closes and the sound echoes in my ears. I don't know how he expects me to wait until morning to get some answers from him about everything I've seen and heard tonight. I'm not a patient person and he knows it.

A nagging feeling scratches away at me but I can't put a finger on it. Something about tonight. Something about Jack.

I burrow into the clean navy sheets of Jack's bed and inhale. It doesn't smell like him, which disappoints me in a way I'd rather not explore, but the room itself feels like him. Not just the *him* that currently lives in Arizona, or the dark *him* that used to live here, but a combination of the two.

A helmet propped on the simple dresser reminds me that Jack is a motorcycle guy. Whenever I see him on his bike back in Arizona, it always seems strange to me—like he's pretending to be a bad boy—because his personality is always so light and upbeat. But staring at the black helmet in the room, I realize the tortured soul I've seen glimpses of these past few days is the real Jack—or at least the Jack he's trying to outrun. My stomach twists, once again unsure how to feel about this *other* Jack. But then again, it would just be weird to see Jack driving anything other than a motorcycle. Even these last few days, it's been bizarre seeing him drive my car.

The nagging feeling claws at me again and breaks the surface. I sit straight up. My car! Jack drove us here tonight but never gave me back my keys. And when I said no to him borrowing my car he hardly put up a fight, which is so not like him and—

I hear an engine come to life outside and my heart beats almost as fast as my legs jump from the bed and carry me down the hall.

Son of a bitch.

If he took my car, I'm going to be so pissed.

Reaching the living room, I sweep back the yellow curtains on the front window just in time to see the taillights of my little red Charger fade into the night as Jack speeds away from the house.

I drop the curtain with a muttered curse and spin around to glower at the living room furniture.

Well it's official. I'm pissed.

I'm also a little afraid, for Jack, but I'm going to focus on the rage. Let it fester until Jack returns and I unleash my wrath.

I pause for a moment and frown.

Jack might have been right about my violent tendencies. I am rather quick to fury. But that's neither here nor there. *Focus on the anger, Jenna. A boy just stole your car while you were busy smelling his sheets. So really, this is your fault for being so pathetic that a guy's bedding can completely undo you.*

Goddammit, now I'm angry with myself.

Redirect, redirect.

Jack. I'm mad at Jack.

You're also worried about him.

Shut up, you pathetic bed-sniffer.

And…that's how the next twenty minutes go; with me scolding myself like a truly certifiable woman of wrath. But Jack still doesn't return. I take a shower, more to clam my nerves than anything else, and wrap myself in a towel only to remember that all my luggage is locked away in my stolen vehicle. Fantastic.

I look at my discarded shirt and leggings and make a sour face. Putting dirty clothes on after I've scrubbed my body? In the words of Lilly Oliver, *ick*.

Padding my bare feet back into Jack's bedroom, I start riffling through his drawers like a wet raccoon, searching for something that can pass as pajamas. I try on four pairs of basketball shorts and two shirts before finding items small enough to fit me without being obscene.

I'm not a small person—not at all. I'm average height, average weight. It's just that Jack's a giant who, apparently, wears size 100 in everything. Twisting the shirt around my middle so it hangs properly, I absently inhale and smile when I catch Jack's scent.

What? No. Don't *smile* about that, you idiot.

I unclench my fists from his shirt and smooth out the wrinkles I created clutching it to my nose. I'm not like a wet raccoon at all. I'm worse. Raccoons would be ashamed of me.

My inner dialogue—I've just accepted that I'm certifiable, at this point—comes to a halt when I hear an engine in the front yard. My first instinct is to run outside and smack him—you know, violent tendencies and all—but I regain my composure and choose a more mature tactic.

I stand perfectly still in the dark living room and wait for him with a scowl.

Through the window, where the yellow curtain didn't fall back completely, I watch his dark figure stumble out of the car and slowly climb the steps all hunched over. What did he do, go get drunk? Awesome.

I cross my arms, scowl still poised to kill, and wait as he opens the front door and quietly steps inside. He flicks on the living room light and I ready myself for the shit storm I'm about to rain all over his ass. But my words, my anger, my bitter intentions fall away the instant I see his face.

"Jack." It's more a gasp than a word as it leaves my mouth and finds his ears.

He pulls his eyes from his hand, bloody and torn, and sets them on me, just now noticing I'm in the room.

"Jenna. What the hell?" Several emotions cross his eyes. Anger. Fear. Relief. Anger.

I pull a face. "Don't 'what the hell' me. You're the one who took my car and drove off into the night."

He screws his face up. "So you waited up to yell at me?"

"Well…" I pause. *Is* that why I waited up? Well, crap. "Yeah," I finally say, not particularly proud of my answer.

"Typical," he mutters. "Listen. I'm not in the mood to bicker with you right now so if you don't mind rescheduling this bitch-out for tomorrow, that would be great. Thanks."

He marches past me and down the hall. That's when I see

the blood running down his back from a large gash between his shoulder blades and my heart stops.

"Jack?" I say, staring with wide eyes. "What's wrong with your back?"

He looks over his shoulder and frowns. "Oh. That." Turning back around, he continues striding down the hallway. "Knife wound."

14

JACK

*I*n a perfect world, Jenna would shrug the whole thing off and go back to bed without asking any questions. My world is the opposite of perfect.

"*Knife wound?*" Her voice is surprisingly steady for the amount of blood she's probably still gawking at as she follows me into the bathroom.

"Yeah." I avoid her eyes as I pull off my wrecked shirt and toss it in the trash.

"You got *stabbed?*" She circles around me, searching for my eyes as I concentrate on anything but the horror that's surely on her face.

"It's more like a slice." Stretching my neck, I turn on the sink and pull out some bandages and first-aid supplies from the medicine cabinet.

Unfortunately, this isn't the first time I've walked into this bathroom covered in blood. Hopefully it will be the last, though.

"Fine. You got *sliced?*" She has me cornered at the sink with no place else for my eyes to land but on hers.

"Yeah." I reluctantly meet her gaze and brace for the shift that will surely take place in our relationship from this moment on. The guns earlier I might have been able to brush off as local bad-guy antics. But bleeding out from a knife fight? Yeah. She'll never look at me the same.

Good-bye, Arizona Jack. Good-bye, Jenna.

I wait for her eyes to grow wary, but instead I see worry, briefly flecked with pain and quickly replaced with impatience.

"Turn around," she says, twirling her finger. "Let me see if you need stitches."

I eye her carefully then slowly turn around. "I don't need stitches."

She huffs. "I'll be the judge of that."

Finding a cloth, she wets it in the sink and cleans around the cut between my shoulder blades in small circles. She has to wring it out and soak it again several times due to the amount of blood on my skin, but the process is soothing somehow.

I like her hands against my back, her fingertips pressing into me as she softly scrubs the wet washcloth across my skin. The warmth of her exhales brush against my spine as she huffs out in frustration, clearly mad at me and afraid, but doing her best to hold her tongue. I know what a sacrifice that must be for her and I'm not sure I deserve it.

She starts to clean out the actual wound, and while it doesn't especially hurt, the first stinging contact of the cotton swab to my open flesh takes me by surprise and I wince.

Pausing, she murmurs, "Sorry," before gently continuing to disinfect the cut. "You don't need stitches."

I stare at the shower curtain printed with seashells. "Told you."

She doesn't reply and I glance to the side. I watch through the mirror as she carefully draws together my sliced skin with butterfly bandages before covering the full length of the gash with one large one. She tapes it to my shoulder blades with precise fingers and her eyes trail up and down my back, filled with sadness and fear as they trace my tattoos. She takes a shaky breath then, suddenly, her face crumbles.

My chest clenches as, for the second time since I've known her, I watch Jenna come undone. A tear falls down her cheek and she doesn't even move to wipe it away, which is the worst kind of apathy. She's not asking questions. She's not yelling. She's trying not to feel.

Dragging my eyes from her reflection, I hang my head. Jenna considers showing emotion for guys—for anyone, really—a weakness. My bloody body just scared the shit out of her and now she's turning herself off completely.

"Jenn..." I start, not sure where my words want to go. "I'm sorry."

She says nothing. Does nothing. Her instincts will have her pulling away from me before morning so I'll never have a chance to terrify her like this again and she'll never again have to risk caring so much.

I glance back at the mirror and watch the tear fall from her cheek to the floor.

Hell, she might already be gone.

She calmly swipes a hand over her face, then clears her throat and talks to my back. "Want me to clean up your hands too?"

My eyes drop to my bloody knuckles, where my skin is torn and dirty. I don't need help cleaning these wounds, but I still turn around and place my hands in her care.

She doesn't look up at me, not once, as she cleans each cut.

"Are you going to ask?" I say, watching her fingers delicately travel over my hands as she wraps my knuckles. "About where I was tonight? About what happened?"

"I don't think I want to know." Her shoulders rise and fall with small, calculated breaths.

I could let it end here, where Jenna stays in the dark, and nothing unravels. We might even be able to stay friends and pretend like Arizona Jack is the only Jack there is. That's what she wants, after all—to forget about the knife wound in my back and slowly drift away from me.

If I cared only about *her*, I would probably let her have her way. But I care about *us*. And *we* don't have a shot in hell unless one of us gives.

"What if I want you to know?" I say.

She looks up with cautious eyes then goes back to bandaging my hands. "Then I guess I'd listen."

I silently sigh in relief and choose my words carefully. "I went to see a guy named Hedrick who owns a bar downtown and also used to work for the people who called Samson tonight."

"The Royals," she says stoically. "The people who put a price on Drew's head."

I slowly nod. "I wanted to talk to Hedrick and find out what Drew was messed up in. If nothing else, I thought Hedrick could shed some light on why Drew was running so I could narrow down places he'd be running away from, if that makes any sense." Dropping my gaze to the bloody sink, I shake my head. "Hedrick was acting strange, like he was afraid, and claimed he knew nothing about Drew or the Royals. I knew he was lying, but I also knew there was no way he was going to tell me whatever he did know because he was too freaked. So I left. But I noticed that one of the cars in the parking lot belonged to a Royal—and Royals don't interact with Hedrick anymore. At least they're not supposed to. I knew something was up so I drove around the block like I was leaving then returned to Hedrick's bar, parked out of view, and crept to the back window. That's where I saw Hedrick getting the shit beat out of him by two Royals." I inhale. "So I barged in and pulled the guys off. Then we got into it and this happened." I turn my bandaged hands over in Jenna's palms.

She stares at my wounds wordlessly.

Tonight's rumble was severely unmatched, physically at least. Even with two against one, I easily overcame my uncoordinated and sloppy opponents. They weren't skilled fighters, just muscle with a message to send, which made them easy to take down. Had I known there was a knife involved, I could have avoided injury altogether. But the blade blindsided me, and one of the Royals managed to nick me before I had them under my fists. Both men were unconscious in a matter of minutes, but not before putting the hurt on Hedrick.

I shake my head. "Those guys were there to make sure Hedrick didn't talk and when I showed up they must have assumed he did." I curse under my breath. "I'm the reason they messed him up."

Jenna dabs at the last cut with a cotton swab. "Is he okay?"

I frown. "Yeah. His nose is busted and the one guy took a slice out of his leg, but he'll be all right. I took him home and now his girlfriend, Sasha, is taking care of him."

My eyes trail over her dark hair, hanging long and loose over her shoulder, and only then do I realize that she's wearing my shirt. And my shorts. She's dressed entirely in my clothes and something desperate takes root inside me. I don't want to lose her. I can't.

She wraps the final bandage around my knuckle and gently runs her finger along the tape to keep it in place. "And the other guys?" She says quietly, not looking at me. "How did they turn out?"

It takes me a long time to answer as I war with myself over who I am and what she wants. "Not as good as us."

She nods at my hands. "Did you end up finding anything out about Drew?"

"I did." I nod, my jaw tightening.

Anger sparks within me, but beneath the aggression is fear. Thick, black fear. I found out tonight that Drew's mixed up in the exact thing I worked so hard to get my family away from. Just thinking about it boils my blood. Twists my gut. Hurts my soul. God, it hurts. If anything happens to Drew...I immediately force my thoughts elsewhere.

I continue, "I found out who's involved in this mess Drew is in, so now I think I know how to find him."

Running her fingers over my hands, she lightly takes them in her own and looks up at me. "Then I guess it was worth it."

There's no judgment or fear in her golden eyes, but as she scans my face a flash of caginess passes over them and my anger and fear about Drew takes a backseat to the wary look in Jenna's eyes.

"You're freaked-out, aren't you?" I say.

She shakes her head with a frown. "Not freaked-out. Just confused. I feel like I don't even know who you are." Her eyes travel down my chest to my wrapped hands then to the bloody washcloth in the sink. "Like at all."

I nod. "Does that scare you?"

Pulling her eyes back to mine, she sounds both sincere and astonished when she answers, "No." She steps back and scoffs. "But the fact that you showing up with a stab wound *doesn't* freak me the hell out? *That* scares me."

I gesture to the bloody mess I've made in the bathroom and eye her suspiciously. "But all this—the blood, the fighting—this doesn't scare you?"

"Nope." She shrugs like she's mad at herself. "You come home all bloody after a *knife fight* with some 'Royal' bad guys and all I can think about is, oh my God, is Jack okay? Is he in danger? Is he in pain?" she snaps, angrily. "The only thing that scared me tonight was the thought of you being hurt. Or worse." Voice cracking on that last word, she looks away and starts cleaning up the first-aid supplies, angrily thrusting discarded bandages into the trash and shoving unused cotton swabs back into their assigned container.

Stilling her hands with my own, I turn her toward me and run my fingers up her arms until her frustrated, beautiful face is cradled in my palms. She glares at me, but the tear track staining her cheek renders her scowl powerless.

"I'm sorry," I say quietly.

Her eyes fill with conflict as she gazes up at me then scans my face. "You have blood..." she says softly, bringing her finger to a stop just before my lower lip.

I don't remember taking a hit to the face, but as I release her cheeks and press a hand to my mouth, a dull ache swells behind my lip where a small cut has broken the skin. I try to wipe away the blood.

"Stop," Jenna whispers. "You're just smearing it." She carefully cleans the cut with a clean swab before leaning back. She rests a hand on my chest as she searches my face for more injuries, her eyes darting from side to side on a mission to heal me. Her gaze slides over my mouth then back again, lingering on my lips, and the atmosphere changes.

The thick frustration that filled the bathroom just moments

ago thins into a sweet trepidation, curling around us with a daring charge.

Her eyes flick up to mine. "I'm mad at you," she says like she's trying to convince herself.

I nod. "For scaring you?"

"For stealing my car," she says with even less resolve. Then, eyes traveling along my throat and jaw and mouth as I step right up to her, her voice falls to a whisper. "You shouldn't have stolen my car."

I bring my mouth down to hers and hold it at her lips. "You're right. That was a bad thing to do. You should probably stay far away from me." I wait, lips brushing hers.

She whispers, "I really should."

She catches my bottom lip between hers and pulls it into her hot mouth, sucking so hard against the small cut that she's surely tasting my blood. This is the problem with Jenna. She wants me more than she'll admit. And when she wants me, her desire is a feral thing. Wild and strong, and instantly addictive—for both of us. Moments like this prove just how much she's let me get under her skin.

Grabbing her waist, I yank her against me and take control of the kiss. I sink my fingers into her hips and tug at her lips, parting them so my tongue can slip into her mouth.

She moans as I slide my tongue along the tender flesh of her mouth, licking at her teeth then biting at her lip.

Her hands fly into my hair, tugging at it hard as she arches her back, and I squeeze her ass with both hands. She tries to move us away from the bloody sink, but I clutch her to me and lift her onto the bathroom counter. Shoving her legs apart, I press myself between them and right against her hot center as I kiss her jaw and then her ear. I want her like this, against me, always.

She rolls her hips, meeting my erection with her wanting body as she digs her nails into my bare back, and I run my hand up her back and into her hair. Wrapping a handful into my palm, I slowly tug her hair until her head falls back, exposing her long throat to my mouth. I kiss up her windpipe as her panting fills the small room and I suck the edge of her collarbone as my other hand moves under her shirt—my shirt.

The material hangs around her small body like a bedsheet, in lost folds and twisted seams, as I run my fingers over the bare skin of her belly. She sucks in a breath and her belly dips, making me smile against her collarbone as I move my hand higher.

Releasing her hair, I bring my mouth back to hers as I trail my fingertips over the swells of her breasts and the hard tips of her nipples. She kisses me back hungrily, and slides her hands down to grip my erection through my jeans. I groan into her mouth, wanting her so badly, hating that I've had to restrain myself these past few months when all I've wanted was this perfect, wild body in my arms.

I kiss her again before leaning back and pulling the shirt off of her completely. It falls to the floor as my eyes take in her beautiful naked breasts. Tattoos curl around them, flowing up to her shoulders and down to her stomach, as I lean down and pull one tight nipple into my mouth, rolling my tongue over its textured surface.

Jenna grabs the back of my head and whimpers as she holds me to her chest. Pulling back and tugging the other nipple into my mouth, I trace my fingers down her belly to cup the center of her open legs with my hand. She writhes against me as I lightly rub at her core. Kissing a trail down her chest and stomach to the sensitive skin just below her belly button, my eyes fall on the colorful phoenix tattoo that spans her hipbone and lower rib cage. Wings spread and feathers on fire, the mythical bird seems to be mid-flight on Jenna's torso. Enticing and fierce, like Jenna herself.

I start to pull her shorts down, but her hand slaps over mine, holding the shorts in place, and she snaps her head up to look at me. We stare at each other, both out of breath and flushed, for a long moment.

"We can't. I can't." Jenna shakes her head.

I slip my hands around her body so I'm holding her in my arms. We're still pressed against one another with my hard body screaming at me for relief and her soft body so wet I can feel it through the shorts, but she closes her eyes, refusing to look at me, and the passion sweeping around us starts to fall.

She's so afraid of feeling something that she tortures herself— and me—and tries to deny that this is something she wants, and maybe even needs.

I gently stroke my thumb over her cheek. "Please look at me."

She shakes her head.

"Jenna," I say.

"Don't. Please don't," she whispers.

Her face curls up like she's going to cry and my focus instantly shifts. "What's wrong?" I kiss her forehead. "Please look at me."

She scoffs, her eyes still closed. "What's *wrong* is that you say my name and kiss my forehead and hold me like you care."

I pull back. "I do care."

"I know," she snaps, finally opening her eyes. "And that's the problem. Can we just—I'm sorry." She shakes her head again. "I can't do this. Not with you. Not right now."

I clench my jaw, feeling slightly offended and a whole hell of a lot of frustration. "Not with me. Not right now. But with someone else maybe?"

She sighs. "That's not what I meant."

"I think it *is* what you meant," I say, letting my arms slide away from her as I step back. "I think if I was some douche bag who didn't give a damn about you, you'd probably be on top of me right now."

Her eyes sharpen. "That's not fair."

"You're right," I say, my chest pounding with the weight of her rejection. "It's *not* fair."

She sits up straight and doesn't move to cover her bare chest. "I'm trying to save what we have, Jack. Sex nearly destroyed us before and I don't want to risk it again. I can't lose you."

"*Bullshit.*"

Her mouth falls open. "Bullshit?"

"Yes. Bull. Shit," I say, overpronouncing each syllable. "Having sex didn't destroy anything. You just can't handle the fact that you felt something with me—that you connected with me." I smack a hand against my chest. "It scared the hell out of you because you couldn't *control* it. And now you're freaking out because, once again, you're losing control."

She slides off the counter so I'm no longer between her legs and stands in front of me with amber fury in her eyes. "This"—she waves a hand between our naked chests—"isn't about control."

"Yes, Jenna, it is." I nod. "That's why you stopped us just now. You're trying to control what you feel by controlling what you do— or don't do."

"No, I stopped because I don't want to lose y—"

"You won't lose me!" I growl. "And you know it." Looking down at her pretty face, struggling to keep me close without wanting me closer, my chest aches as I soften my voice. "You're not scared of losing me, Jenna. You're scared of having me."

She blinks a few times, her eyes drifting around my face like lost puppies searching for a place to hide. But she says nothing and I know there won't be any resolution for us tonight. We could argue until dawn, but it wouldn't matter because Jenna still believes she can outwit her heart. And until she thinks otherwise, I'm just a bloody guy in a bathroom waiting for the girl of my dreams to realize that she's in love with me.

15

JENNA

I wake up to a pillow being thrown in my face and a male voice yelling, "What the fuck happened in the bathroom? It looks like someone performed surgery in there."

I sleepily sit up and squint at the doorway. "Wha...?"

"Shit. Sorry," Samson says, making a face. "I thought you were Jack."

I rub my eyes. "Not Jack."

"Right." He nods once. "You're...Jenna? Is that right?"

I nod with a yawn.

"Sorry about last night," he says. "I swear I'm not usually a lush."

"No worries."

"You don't happen to know where Jack is, do you?"

After our interlude in the bathroom last night, Jack and I parted ways; him sleeping on the couch while I slept in his bed. I haven't seen or heard from him since.

"No." I rub my eyes. "Is he not on the couch?"

Samson sighs. "Nope."

"Samson!" Jack calls from somewhere down the hallway. "What are you doing? Let Jenna sleep."

Samson turns his head. "Where've you been, man?"

"I got breakfast. Leave her alone."

Samson looks back at me with an apologetic smile. "Sorry I woke you up. Later." He pulls the door closed and I stare at it for several long seconds.

Last night spins around my mind like a carousel horse, up and down, around and around, replaying every critical moment. Scary *bar mobsters* held us at *gunpoint* before Jack *stole my car* and got into a *brawl with some gangsters* then came home all *bloody* and I patched up his *knife wound* before we started *kissing* and almost got down and dirty. Such a bizarre chain of events.

But more than the bloody gangster madness, my mind turns with the things Jack said about me wanting to be in control and being afraid of having him. He made it sound like I'm some sort of crazy person who has feelings for him, but thinks that if I keep my hands off him then those feelings will just disappear. But that's not the case.

Or is it?

The reason I stopped our kissing session was because he was about to pull my shorts off and see all the tattoos on my lower pelvis, which wouldn't be a big deal except there's a new tattoo that wasn't there the last time he saw me naked. And I didn't feel like explaining it to him so I panicked.

Then I realized that having sex with Jack on the bloody bathroom countertop was probably a bad idea anyway, especially since we're stuck with each other later this week when we drive back to Arizona together. So yeah. I cut off our little make-out frenzy.

I expected Jack to argue with me, but then he put his arms around me and held me. He *held* me. Like a goddamn doll. Then he kissed my forehead and said my name, and it was all I could do not to sob in his arms.

When Jack said my name, my whole world came undone. My insides turned to goo and my strength to mush. Just that single word "Jenna" on his lips made me wish for things I have no business wanting. Things like love and romance and babies and forever. Things that have no place in my future.

Stopping was the right thing to do.

Hanging over the side of the bed, I reach for my purse and do what all girls do when they start to question their life choices. I call my best friend.

Pixie answers on the second ring. "Jenna!" she squeals happily. "How are you doing? How's the road trip going? Are you there yet? How are things with Jack?"

Righting myself back into a sitting position, I smile at the bedspread. "Good. Fine. No. Weird."

She clucks her tongue. "I knew it. I knew things were going to go down if you and Jack spent an excessive amount of time together—hey, what are you—" She giggles through the phone. "Levi, come on…baby…" More giggling. "Stop, Leaves…I'm trying to talk… to Jenna…"

It's funny to think that just a few weeks ago, Pixie was just a shadow of her real self and now, after finding Levi, it's like she's come back to life. Smiling, laughing, loving. I will forever love Levi for giving my best friend her soul back—even if he's stealing all her attention away right now on the phone.

I clear my throat. "Should I call back?"

"Hmm? What…oh! No. I'm fine," she says, stifling a laugh. "Let me just get out of bed." I hear Levi protest in the background along with some shuffling, then Pixie exhales triumphantly. "Okay! We're good now. Sorry about that. I'm listening. So what's going on with Jack?"

I quickly fill her in on the Jack-and-Jenna events of the last few days, leaving out the guns, stab wounds, and other bloody details, and sticking with just the sexy kissing stuff.

"And...that brings us to today," I say. "I don't know what to do, Pix. Or what to say to him. Like, do I apologize or do I just play it off, or what?" I start picking at the bedspread.

"Huh." She's quiet for a long second. "Jenna...is there something you're not telling me?"

I drop the bedspread, adrenaline spiking my veins. "What? What do you mean?"

"I mean...I know I said you and Jack have weird sexual tension, but it's more than that. You and Jack seem to be close. *Really* close. Like, closer than your typical girl-boy friendship."

"So?" I snap. And shit, I said that too quickly and way too forcefully. She's going to know.

"*So?*" she mocks, then starts laughing. "Oh my God. Jenna Lacombe, you slept with Jack, didn't you?"

I sigh into the phone. "Yeah."

More laughter. "Holy wow. When?"

I frown. "Last winter."

Her voice rises in pitch. "And you never told me?!"

"No," I say, then quickly add, "but only because I wanted to pretend like it never happened. And I knew if I told you, you would make a big deal about it and then I'd have to address it with Jack and blah, blah, blah. I just wanted to avoid all that. I swear it wasn't because I was trying to hide it from you."

"No, no. I get it." I can almost hear the wheels turning in her head. "But...why did you want to pretend it never happened?"

I pause, debating if I should tell her the ugly truth. But then I think about all the ugly truths Pixie has let me in on—and she's had some *ugly* truths in her past—and I realize there's no way I *can't* confide in her.

I take a deep breath. "Because . . . I cried."

"You cried?" She pauses. "Like, afterward in the bathroom because you forgot to use a condom and thought you might be pregnant?"

"What—no!" I stare at the phone. "Sounds like you did, though."

"Don't change the subject. When did you cry?"

I run a hand through my hair. "Uh, during sex. Like right in the middle of it. When I was on top of him."

"Whoa."

"I know."

"So why did—how come—what made—?" She's lost for words. I know the feeling.

"I don't know, Pixie." I tip my head back and groan at the ceiling. "We were having this hot delicious sex, and then Jack said my name, and I suddenly got all emotional. I started thinking about how great Jack is and how he always makes me laugh and never lets me down, and how I trust him more than anyone else in the world . . . God, it was sappy in my head. But I couldn't stop caring about him, you know? I was looking down at him and thinking about how great he is. Then I just started crying like a weirdo, tears running down my face—and *I kept riding him.*"

"Whoa."

"I *know.*"

"Did he totally freak out?"

"No!" I say. "That's the weirdest part. He just went with it. He pulled me down and kissed me and stroked my hair and whispered in my ear and shit, until I was all turned on again."

"Damn," she says with a heavy exhale. "Well this changes everything."

"What? No. It shouldn't change anything. Nothing is changed."

"Okay, calm down. I wasn't talking about your life. I was talking about your issues with Jack. This changes what I think about your conversation with him."

"Oh. Okay." I relax on the bed. "Carry on, then. What do you think about what Jack said last night?"

"I think he's right about you trying to control things."

I gasp. "Traitor."

"Think about it. You are pretty weird about your future. I mean, you couldn't even handle me saying 'this changes everything' a second ago. Change is not your friend, Jenna. And as far as him saying you're afraid to have him, well...I think he's right about that too."

"Maybe you should be besties with *Jack* then."

"Listen. You're the one who told me not to be afraid to love when everything was happening with Levi. Remember that? You said love isn't safe and life isn't guaranteed, and that I needed to let Levi in?"

I wrinkle my nose. "*Did* I say all that? Crap."

"I'm just saying that maybe you should give Jack a chance. See where it goes."

"I know where it goes," I snap. "It goes from love to marriage to babies to divorce to loneliness to poverty to death."

"Wow," she says blandly. "That might be the most depressing thing I've ever heard."

"That's the truth, Pix." I pick at the bedspread again. "Happily ever after is for romantic comedies and fairy tale books."

She huffs. "Is that what you think is going to happen to me and Levi?"

"What? Of course not," I say. "You guys are going to be together forever. Levi loves you madly."

"And who's to say you won't be loved like that someday?" she says. "Maybe even by Jack?"

I grumble into the pillow. "Stop twisting my words around."

"Stop being a baby."

"I'm not a baby."

"Yes, you are," Pixie says. "You're a big fat chubby baby with control issues."

I snort. "Oh yeah? Well you're a big fat meanie."

"Fine. But I'm a meanie who loves you and knows that some great guy is going to love you madly and give you the happily ever after you never wanted."

I scoff. "This conversation is *not* going the way I'd imagined."

I can hear the smile in her voice. "I love you too."

After hanging up with Pixie, I exit Jack's room and head for the kitchen. On my way there, I pass the bathroom and glance inside. The trash can is brimming with bloody cotton swabs and bandages, and there are smudges of blood on the floor. I understand now why Samson was freaked-out.

Rounding the hallway, I walk into the kitchen where Lilly and Samson are sitting at the table, eating bacon and omelets, while Jack has his back to me at the stove where he's cooking something I can't see. He has a shirt on this morning so I can't see the bandage on his back, but hopefully I did a decent job of cleaning him up last night.

"Good morning, darling." Lilly smiles at me brightly.

Jack glances over his shoulder and our eyes meet in a silent truce. We don't want to be awkward around one another. We don't want there to be uncomfortable tension. Our friendship is more important than our disagreement on whether or not we should be getting naked with each other whenever we feel like it. So as we lock gazes across the kitchen, there's a peaceful understanding between us. No hard feelings or repressed anger. We're good, like usual. We're always good.

I smile. He smiles. Then he goes back to cooking.

That's the thing about Jack and me. We're always good. Even when we're fighting, we're still friends. I wasn't lying last night when I said I didn't want to lose him. Jack's friendship is one of the most important things in my life. But after all the bloody madness of last night, I have a feeling I'm going to lose him anyway, one way or another.

I honestly don't know what to think. His family is clearly tied up in some shady undertakings, but oddly enough that doesn't frighten me—beyond Jack getting hurt, of course. If anything, it just makes me more curious about who the real Jack is.

"Morning." I smile back at Lilly and nod at Samson.

"You want an omelet?" Lilly asks.

I pull out a chair. "Uh…"

"Jenna doesn't like eggs," Jack says, his eyes still on the frying pan.

"Oh." Lilly looks surprised. "I thought that's why you were making breakfast for us, because we have a guest."

"No, Mom." He flips something in the frying pan. "I'm making breakfast because no one in this house cooks and I thought you needed a hot meal for a change."

Lilly winks at me. "Jack's always trying to take care of me. You'd think he was the parent with all the fussing he does." She takes a sip of coffee. "But he's right. I'm a lousy cook. Samson and I live off of microwave dinners and takeout."

"The picture of health," Jack mutters from the stove.

Then he comes to sit at the table with a plate of pancakes—my favorite—and slides one onto a plate for me before putting one on a plate for himself.

"Thanks," I say quietly, appreciating the fact that he knows me so well and cares about me even more.

"Nice knuckles," Lilly says, eyeing Jack's bandaged hands. "Do I want to know?"

He stabs a bite of pancake. "Probably not."

Lilly considers this for a minute. "Did anything helpful come of it at least?"

It's interesting that Lilly seems to be in on everything, or at least aware that her boys are involved in some seriously shady activities, and isn't fazed. This must be the norm for the Oliver family.

Jack shrugs. "I guess so."

She sets her mug down and goes back to her omelet. "Then I guess it was worth it."

At her words—an exact repeat of my words last night—Jack and I lock gazes. I can't explain what I see in their gray depths. Maybe trust. Maybe fear. It's hard to tell with my heart beating so fast. But it seems that Lilly and I feel the same way about Jack beating bad guys to a pulp, and I'm not sure what that says about me.

"Trixie called me this morning," Samson says, taking a bit of bacon. "And said that Sasha called her last night after you dropped Hedrick off all black-and-blue at their house."

"Ugh." Lilly shakes her head. "Trixie. Sasha. Hedrick...It's like you find all your friends at brothels."

Samson glares at her then turns to Jack. "You wanna tell me what the hell happened to Hedrick? And maybe why the bathroom looks like a vampire's pantry?"

Lilly nods at her omelet. "Hedrick would be a *great* vampire name."

Samson flashes his mother a fake smile. "And Lilly sounds like it should belong to a four-year-old girl with blonde pigtails who lives under a rainbow."

Lilly grins at him. "I know."

Jack interrupts with a dark look. "I went to talk to Hedrick last night and tussled with some Royals. Long story short, the Royals were taken care of and I found out that Drew made a deal with Clancy."

Samson sucks in through his teeth and Lilly's happy countenance falls completely.

"Don't worry," Jack says, more to his mom than to Samson. "I've got a plan."

His eyes steel over, fear and anger marring their silver depths. But something else shines inside too. Something that looks a lot like sadness. And worry.

I have the sudden urge to throw my arms around Jack and wish the sadness away, especially since I have no idea what's going on or why Jack looks so—so defeated.

Lilly squeezes Jack's arm. A comforting gesture. Meant to console. An action that would make total sense—if it were Jack trying to console his mother, and not the other way around. But Lilly seems to feel the need to comfort *Jack*.

Samson shakes his head and mutters, "Shit," as he stares at the table.

Jack pats his mother's hand before gently shrugging away from her reach and loosening his shoulders. "Don't worry. I know Clancy and I know Drew, so this whole thing is going to work out. Okay?" His voice is lighter now, optimistic; probably more for his family's sake than for his, but it replaces the heaviness in the kitchen with hopefulness and the shift is so palpable I almost feel lighter.

"Okay, baby." Lilly smiles.

Samson goes back to eating bacon as a breeze blows in through the open front door, and through the screen door I watch the many wind chimes strung from the roof sway with the wind that carries their happy lilt into the kitchen.

Lilly inhales. "I need a smoke." She gets up from her chair and Jack lifts a brow.

"I thought you quit smoking?" he says.

"I did." She nods and starts for the porch. "Which is why I need to make another wind chime." The screen door squeaks as she pushes through it and sits down at a small table on the porch, where her wind chime supplies are laid out.

Jack gives Samson a questioning glance and Samson explains, "When she hears the wind chimes clink together, it reminds her that she wants a cigarette, and when she wants a cigarette, she decides to make a new wind chime instead. It's a vicious cycle, really." His phone rings and he pulls it out if his pocket and checks the screen. "Be right back."

He leaves the kitchen and then it's just me, Jack, and a pile of pancakes.

I break the silence first. "Are you mad at me?"

He frowns. "Why would I be mad at you?"

I cock an eyebrow. "Because I'm a tease."

He smiles at his fork. "You're not a tease. Not at all. But to answer your question, no. I'm not mad at you. I would never be mad about you not wanting me." He winks, but the remark still stings.

"That's not why I stopped us, and you know it," I say.

"I do." He nods. "The question is, do you?"

Not wanting to travel down this path again, I finish my breakfast and take my plate to the sink. "Got any more coffee?"

Jack nods to the coffeepot as he puts away his own dish. I pour us each a mug and follow Jack into the living room where Samson is just now getting off the phone.

Samson sighs. "That was my boss. Apparently, calling in sick because you get a call that your brother is being hunted by the Royals is frowned upon. I'm on my third strike now at work. We need to find Drew, man. What's your plan?"

Jack takes a deep breath. "Since we know Drew is mixed up with Clancy, and Clancy is the leader of the Royals based in the French Quarter, I think our next move is to go down to New Orleans and talk to Clancy. If we can figure out what happened, maybe we'll get a lead on where Drew is."

Samson shakes his head. "I don't know. The NOLA Royals are bad news. And Clancy?" He lets out a low whistle. "He's not going to give you shit on Drew. You know that."

He nods. "I know Clancy won't talk, but he might bitch. And if he starts complaining about whatever the hell Drew did or didn't do then maybe I can figure out what we're dealing with. So hurry and get dressed so we can grab Mom's car from Vipers and head down to New Orleans."

"Uh, this isn't Mommy's Rent-A-Car," Lilly says through the screen door, holding an unfinished wind chime. "You boys aren't taking my car to NOLA. I have things to do today."

"Yeah, and I have work this afternoon," Samson says with a frown, holding up his phone. "I can't risk ditching out again. But we can leave tomorrow."

Jack mutters a curse, clearly impatient to get on the road and find Drew.

"Or Jack can just head down with me today," I say with a shrug.

His eyes snap to mine, two gray irises filled with hope and relief. "Really?"

"Of course." I nod.

Samson says, "And I can come down later this week, and in the meantime you can stay with Uncle Brent. He stills lives in NOLA, right?"

"Yeah, but he's away for the summer," Lilly says from the porch as she adds another chime to the project in her hand.

"Then I'll stay with friends or something," Jack says. "Hopefully I can find Drew today and won't need to stay at all." He turns to me. "Are you sure you're okay driving me down? It would be great to get there as soon as possible, but I can hitch a ride or borrow a car if you'd rather be done with all this and go straight home."

"I'm sure," I say. "I'd have to come back here to Little Vail on my way back to Arizona anyway. This way, you'll already by in NOLA by the time I'm ready to leave and we can just leave from there. And the sooner you find Drew the better, right?"

I smile, like my reasoning is totally selfless and has nothing to do with how giddy the prospect of more Jack time makes me.

I'm so full of shit.

"All right then." Jack scans my face. "Thanks."

Samson's phone rings and his eyes light up. "Trixie!"

"Oh dear Lord…" I can almost see Lilly's eyes rolling as she shakes her head on the porch.

Samson leaves the living room as he answers his phone and I look up at Jack. "We can leave whenever you're ready. I just need to get my suitcases out of the car and change out of these." I gesture to the large clothes I'm wearing that belong to Jack.

His eyes fall over me in an endearing way and my heart squeezes.

"I like you in my clothes," he says. "You look cute. Little."

I roll my eyes. "Any girl would look little in your giant clothes."

He shrugs. "But I've never seen a girl in my clothes before."

"Really?" I eye him suspiciously.

He nods and the moment suddenly feels intimate. The very clothes on my body feel intimate. I almost feel bad for helping myself to his wardrobe, but at the same time I feel powerful for being the only girl to ever do so.

Wow. I really do have power issues.

Desperate to change the subject and get his eyes to stop looking at me in that loveable way, I say, "So it's morning. Are you ready to tell me what's going on with your brother and why he has a price on his head? Who are these Royals? And why is everyone freaked-out about this Clancy guy?"

Jack's whole body stiffens as he scans my face. "The short answer is that the Royals are enemies of my father's, in a way. The long answer is a bit more complicated than that. To tell you everything, I'd probably have to start at the beginning—which isn't pretty."

I sit down on the couch and cross my legs under me. "Pretty is overrated."

16

JACK

When I was eight years old, I went camping with some friends and fell into the campfire. We were messing around, shoving each other and laughing, and I lost my footing and tumbled into the raging flames beside us.

I remember the heat snaking up my face and into my nostrils and eyes, suffocating me with smoke. I thought I was going to die. It was terrifying and immobilizing. And I truly thought my life was over.

One of my friends' dads immediately pulled me out of the fire and, thanks to the thick coat and scarf I had on, I didn't suffer any burns other than a few on my hands.

My coat and scarf were singed through and trashed, and my hair was brittle and carried the stench of smoke for days, but I was fine. I was alive.

The burns on my hands healed quickly, but the fear of fire—of death by hot, licking flames—wasn't so quickly soothed. Even to this day, bonfires or any other type of large, open fire unsettle me.

But standing here, in my living room, with Jenna's eyes waiting for all my dirty truths to muck up everything I could ever hope to have between us, is worse than any wild flames. I'd rather walk through a thousand fires than tell Jenna the truth about my past.

But there's no escaping these flames. Not now. Not after everything she already knows about, everything she's already seen.

Pulling in a long inhale, I lean forward and say, "Well, here goes nothing." With a slow, bracing inhale, I quietly clear my throat and step into the fires of honesty. "When I was a kid, my dad had this business. But he wanted to make it a family business by having me work for him full-time, and I just wasn't all that into it. We had a disagreement, which led to a blowout, of sorts, and then he split and left my mom and us kids with…well, nothing. He had some old business debts—which I paid off—but then we were free and clear of the whole industry and had a fresh start." I pause and glance down the hallway where Samson is on the phone and pacing. "At least, I thought so."

"And what kind of 'business' are we talking about here?" Jenna asks.

I drag my eyes back to hers and try to gage how much I can salvage here. Her perception of me is clearly shot to hell, but that's not necessarily a bad thing. So I'm edgier than she thought; more dangerous. If her past sexual partners are any indication, that just makes me more her type.

If I spin all this so it looks like my family's involved in some sort of competitive market—something cutthroat but legal—she'll have no reason to write me off forever. I might not be suitable for her to consider as more than a friend, but fuck it. I wasn't really making progress in that department anyway.

"Here's the deal…" I say, drawing in a breath and hoping she doesn't see through me. "The best way to sum up what my dad used to do is…Okay, you know how some industries are more competitive than others and they…Okay, my family used to be involved in—"

"Drug dealing," Samson says, shoving his phone back in his pocket as he enters the living room and plops onto the couch beside Jenna.

And there it goes.

Years of hard work in Arizona, crafting a different lifestyle, a different reputation—hell, a whole different personality for myself—down the drain. Just like that.

Jenna will never look at me the same.

I glare at my brother with the cold fingers of betrayal walking up my spine. I know he was completely oblivious of my plan to *not* tell Jenna about our family's illegal activity, but I can't help feeling like he's a traitor.

He sees my scowl and shrugs. "What? You were taking forever to spit it out." He leans forward. "*Drug running.* It's not that hard to explain, Jack."

I blink. "I cannot believe you."

Jenna's eyes are wider than usual but other than that she doesn't seem to be freaking out. Yet.

"So you guys sell drugs?" She points back and forth between Samson and me.

"No," we say at the same time. Even my mom chimes in with an echoed "No."

Jenna glances at Lilly and furrows her brow. "You're drug dealers that don't sell drugs?"

I scrub a hand down my face. This was a bad idea. Such a very bad idea. "No."

"Just tell her, Jack." Finished with her wind chime, Mom enters the living room and sits in the rocking chair beside the couch.

I lift a brow at her. "Tell her?"

She nods. "Jenna can handle it."

I hesitate, not sure how to start, then slowly nod as I look back at Jenna. "Okay. It all started with my dad. He started working with the Vipers, which isn't just a bar. It's a drug gang, of sorts, run by Alec, the guy you met last night. And the Royals—the gang that put a bounty out on Drew's head—are rivals of the Vipers." I pause and make a face. "Which I realize sounds ridiculous, like I'm making all this up—and God, I wish I were—but I'm not. So just... just go with it. Okay?"

She nods. "I'm listening."

I exhale. "I have no idea what the Royals want with Drew, but based on their history with the Vipers, it's safe to assume that Drew's involvement at this point has something to do with my father's ties to the drug world. My dad got in with the Vipers years ago, running cocaine shipments back and forth for them. Mom didn't know anything about it until my dad was too far in. When she found out what he was involved with, she tried to leave him, but he threatened to take us boys away from her. He had money and powerful friends—dangerous friends—and her hopes of getting out of the marriage with us kids went down in flames. So she stayed. For our safety."

I watch my mom's eyes drop to the ground and I want to reassure her that she did what she could. That she was trying to do what she thought was best. There's no handbook for how to be married to a drug dealer. No guide to raising kids with a powerful psychopath who'll blackmail you at every turn. She did well with what she had. I've told her that a thousand times, but I don't know if guilt like hers ever goes away.

She looks up and our eyes meet. I give her a small smile. Something that says, *Look at me. I'm okay. You did a good job with me.*

Then I swallow and carry on. "It wasn't until a few years after my mom found out about my dad's drug business, that Sam, Drew, and I found out as well. But by that time he couldn't have gotten out without getting shot—not that he wanted out." I shift my jaw. "Tommy Oliver was a greedy guy and selfish too. He liked the money too much to abandon the life so he towed our family into it. I can't even count the number of times he's put our family in danger because of his enemies. Death threats, robberies, drive-by shootings. The Vipers have enemies—enemies like the Royals— who are ruthless. It's amazing any of us are alive." I pause, remembering how horrible my teenage years were, when our house getting shot at was a common occurrence.

"When I was seventeen, the Vipers wanted to bring me on and show me the ropes of dealing. My dad was ecstatic, but I wanted nothing to do with it. I wanted out, completely, but Dad wouldn't let me."

Mom shifts in the rocking chair, hating this part of the story, as Jenna's expression goes from concerned to curious then back to concerned.

I look at my hands. "When I refused to join in with criminal activity, he beat the shit out of me. Every day. Thinking I would cave if he kept hurting me. I was never going to give in. Never. But then he threatened to hurt Mom. She didn't know—no one knew—but that was it for me. I couldn't risk her being hurt. So I gave in and agreed to be part of the Vipers. For the next three years, they owned me." I let out a long sigh. "I'm not proud of the things I did for them, but I kept telling myself I was doing it to protect my mother. My family. The whole time, I kept trying to find a way out, but it was next to impossible. Until Dad finally slipped up and I saw my opportunity.

"I found a safe hidden in my dad's shed out back and figured out that he was stealing money from the Vipers, slowly siphoning out of their profits and shoveling it away for himself. The gang knew they were bleeding out, but couldn't pinpoint how. So I made a deal with Alec. I would turn over the thief—and the money—but only if the gang let me and my family go free. My dad would be busted, I could walk away without any threat on my life, and no one would bother my mom or brothers again.

"Alec wasn't thrilled about my proposal because he wanted me to stay on. He even threatened to kill me if I didn't just tell him who the thief was. But I still refused and told him he was free to kill me if he wanted that more than saving his gang from going broke. He was bluffing, of course, and couldn't bring himself to kill me. So instead he agreed to our deal."

I glance at my mom, who gives me a small smile, silently encouraging me to continue. We've never told anyone about our family skeletons before so this is new territory for us. Trusting someone outside of our fucked-up little clan doesn't come naturally for my mom, probably because of all the guilt my dad's dirty business put her through. She blames herself for not catching on sooner, for not being able to stop him and protect us boys from the dealing scene, and I've watched that guilt form defensive walls around her ability to trust others. But Jenna...

There must be something about Jenna that my mom instinctively trusts. Or maybe it's not Jenna at all, but me. Maybe the fact that *I* trust Jenna is enough for my mom to trust her too.

"So what happened?" Jenna asks. Her voice is quiet but her eyes are alert, absorbing every word as she leans forward and scans my face, searching for answers she may or may not want.

But once you have an answer, it's yours forever. You can't give it back. Can't return it. Answers are a bitch like that. They're a gift that, once opened, can never be wrapped again. A naked present in your hands with nowhere to go. Nowhere to hide.

And Jenna's eyes are asking for all of mine. All my carefully wrapped truths. And all I want to do is jump into the nearest fire.

Rubbing the back of my neck, I take a breath. "I knew handing my dad over to the Vipers could cost him his life, but every day I stayed in the drug game was a day I was risking the lives of everyone else in my family. So I ratted my dad out."

Jenna's eyes widen in horror, but only for a split second.

I swallow. I shift. I blink.

Then I continue. "The Vipers messed him up pretty bad, but they let him live. Sent him running away with his tail between his legs, but he survived. He was shunned by all his shady acquaintances so he fled town and went into hiding. With twenty warrants out in his name, a fistful of enemies out for his blood, and no friends left to protect him, he had no choice but to disappear.

"But after that, the rest of us"—I gesture at Mom and Samson—"were off the hook. Alec got his money back from the safe and I moved to Arizona for a fresh start." I shake my head. "So there it is. I used to be involved in illegal drug running and I've probably committed more crimes than I can count." I look at Jenna.

She says nothing.

A breeze flutters across the porch and the singing wind chimes fill the silence in the living room. My mom concentrates on a spot on the floor, her features soft despite the tightness in her gaze, while Samson studies his hands.

Jenna keeps looking at me, her eyes roving over my face, my body, my face. Her lips part then press together.

My pulse rises. "Please say something," I say, wondering if burning alive would be as frightening as this moment.

Blinking a few times, Jenna comes back to life and glances at my mom and Samson before holding her mug out to me with an arched eyebrow. "I'm gonna need more coffee."

17

JENNA

*W*hoa my God.

After everything Jack just told me I don't know what to say. Drug dealing? Jack Oliver was a drug dealer? It just doesn't...fit.

I look him over as Lilly takes my mug to get me more coffee, and I bite my lip. Shaggy dark hair, big muscles, tattoos, scars everywhere. I guess he does kind of look like a bad guy. It's just odd because he's *not* a bad guy.

That's just it. He's not a bad guy.

I might not know him as well as I thought, but I know that he's good. What happened in his past doesn't change the way I think of him now.

"What are you thinking?" Jack says with total worry in his eyes.

Oh God. He thinks I'm about to lose it. He's waiting for me to bail and curse him and all his dark sins.

He should know me better than that.

Lilly returns and hands a hot mug of coffee to me before returning to her seat in the rocking chair. I take the mug and wrap my hands around its warmth before looking up at Jack.

"I think..."—I look him dead in the eyes—"that we need to

get to New Orleans as soon as possible so you can find Drew. If these Royals are anything like the Vipers then Drew's in a lot of trouble and could really use his big brother's help." I casually take a sip of coffee and watch Jack's surprised eyes slide from me to Samson and then to his mom.

"See?" Lilly says. "Told you so."

He eyes me carefully. "And you're sure you still want to drive me down?"

I nod. "I'm ready when you are."

He visibly relaxes his shoulders. "All right. Let's get moving then."

After packing up our things, Jack and I say good-bye to his mom and brother. He and Samson make a plan to call each other later to see if Samson's presence will be required in New Orleans, while Jack tries to comfort his concerned mother.

"Please don't make that face, Mom," Jack says softly. "Drew's going to be fine. He's probably just laying low for a few days. You know the biz. Things get hectic and Drew doesn't handle stress well. He's probably just taking it easy."

She shakes her head. "You always were the best bullshitter in the family."

"I'm not bullshitting you."

"Sure you are, baby." She kisses his cheek. "But I like it. Just bring our Drew home, okay?"

"I will." His eyes harden. "I promise."

I turn my eyes away, not wanting to intrude on their moment. I can't imagine how worried they both must be.

The four of us file out of the house and down the porch steps to my car, where Jack throws our bags in the vehicle.

"Stay safe," Lilly says, as he closes the trunk.

"We will," Jack says.

She grabs his arm and waits until he meets her eyes. "I'm serious, Jack. None of this is worth anything if you go missing too." She cocks an eyebrow. "Understand?"

He nods. "I'm going to find Drew and bring him back home. Everything will be okay."

She crosses her arms. "I need you to be smart about this. Don't do anything risky."

"Mom—"

"I'm not kidding." Her eyes flit to me then back to Jack. "And take care of Jenna too."

He seems genuinely offended. "Jenna's safety won't ever be in question. I would never—"

"I know." She smiles and pats his cheek before giving me a sly wink. "Just checking."

He rolls his eyes and mutters, "Damn women."

"I heard that," Lilly says with mocking sternness. "I'm just making sure everyone comes home safely."

"I'll take good care of him, Mrs. Oliv—I mean Lilly," I say, throwing a grin her way.

"I know." She takes my face in her hands and bores her eyes into mine, like she sees me, like she knows my fears and wants, and the conflict they constantly create. "I know you will." With a quick kiss to my cheek, she releases my face and steps back. "Okay, does anyone need condoms?"

Jack juts his jaw. "Really, Mom? God."

Lilly frowns. "I seriously doubt God needs any condoms."

I can't help but smile as Jack rubs both hands down his face in frustration.

"What?" she says. "I have a bulk supply in the house and—"

"No. Uh-uh." Jack plugs his ears.

"Oh, come on. It's a practical question to ask." Lilly raises her voice and overenunciates each word as she repeats, "DOES ANYONE NEED ANY CONDOMS?"

Jack looks horrified. "Kill me now."

"I do!" Samson raises his hand with a smile.

Lilly lifts her chin and says to Jack, "See? At least someone appreciates my offer."

"Oh my God. You're the most embarrassing mother ever." Jack turns away and snaps at me, "What's so funny?"

My grin grows so wide my face hurts. "Everything."

"Just get in the car."

"I love you," Lilly sings out cheerfully as we climb into my car.

"Right. Yeah. Love you too," Jack says, not looking at her.

"Bye!" I wave happily at Lilly and Samson before starting the engine and pulling out of their driveway. Navigating the small-town streets of Little Vail, I soon exit the city limits and turn onto the freeway, heading south for New Orleans.

God, I love Jack's family. I always assumed I'd like them—if ever I met his brothers or mom—but I never imagined liking them so *much*. They feel real to me. Honest. Loving.

In a lot of ways, they remind me of my own family. Maybe that's why their family history—as unconventional as it may be—doesn't rattle me. They clearly love each other, and family does fierce things for love.

I think about the many risks Jack took to protect his mom and brothers. Dealing drugs, risking prison, ratting out his father. He did so much to keep them safe, and all at the cost of his own freedom and safety.

After everything Jack did, I can understand why he'd be upset about Drew being involved in all this. It makes sense now, why Jack seemed to take the Drew thing personally. Why Lilly was comforting him this morning when he told everyone about Clancy. Jack fought to keep his brothers safe from the very thing Drew is now endangered by.

I glance at the beautiful guy sitting beside me and my stomach clenches. It's just all so... personal. It couldn't have been easy for him to tell me everything earlier.

"Thanks for telling me about your family stuff," I say, looking forward again. "I'm sure that wasn't easy."

He scoffs. "Thanks for listening to all that without hating me."

I frown. "You know I could never hate you."

He scratches his cheek. "Well, drug dealing tends to be a deal breaker, so I was kind of nervous about how you'd take it."

I grin. "I make you nervous?"

He shakes his head and bites back a smile. "You make me a lot of things."

Something flutters in my chest, like a swarm of butterflies looking for a way out.

I clear my throat. "I'm sorry that Drew is caught up with the Royals, especially after all you did to keep your family out of it."

His shoulders tense. "Yeah. I was pretty pissed. Pissed and scared." He shakes his head and mutters "Fuck" so softly I hardly catch it. Scrubbing a hand down his face, he turns to me and shakes his head. "It's just crazy. Drew was always the good one, you know? He was the little mama's boy who was always happy and nice. I don't understand why he would get mixed up in all this. It's not like him. I mean, I love the guy, but he's not cut out for the drug business. He's not cold, or hard, or ruthless—"

"Neither are you."

He smiles sadly. "I can't tell you how much it means to me that you think I'm not those things."

"You're not."

"But I am," he says. "Or I was. I don't know. My point is just that Drew is not, and has never been, those things. So his involvement with Clancy makes zero sense. How did he even get connected?" He shakes his head again as he stares out the window, confusion marking every one of his features.

I smile reassuringly. "Maybe you'll find him the moment we get to New Orleans and you can ask him yourself."

"God, I hope so."

"Speaking of which, where should I go once we get to NOLA?"

"Clancy owns a bar in the French Quarter called Crowns. You can just drop me off there." He looks at me sincerely. "I really appreciate all this, Jenn. I know this wasn't what you had planned for your visit back home."

I scoff. "The only plan I had for coming home was to scold my grandmother for dragging my ass out here *again*."

He smiles. "Don't act like you don't love having an excuse to be back."

"Please."

"You do," he says. "You get all antsy and nervous, but I see the excitement in your eyes. Admit it."

I bite back a grin. "Never."

I don't like how costly it can be, but Jack's right. I *do* like having a reason to come home. I miss my family, but it's hard for me to justify spending lots of money to come home just because I miss them.

A short while later, we arrive in New Orleans. The French Quarter is cramped with tourists and traffic once we reach the district, so we crawl along from street to street as Jack directs me where to go.

"I've never heard of Crowns before," I say. "Which is weird, because I used to party down here. A lot."

He stares out the window with hard eyes. "Clancy has a very specific type of clientele and you're not it."

I lift my eyebrows. "But you are?"

He keeps staring out the window. "Yes."

The way he says it makes a shiver run through me.

"This is it," he says, pointing to a black building with only one door.

I pull in front and stop the car, squinting at the windows of the bar. "It doesn't look open."

Jack examines the windows as well, scratching his jaw. "I know...Hang on."

Getting out, he paces to the back of the bar, disappearing around a corner for a few moments, then returns to the entrance of the bar and cocks his head at the small lettering on the door. He walks back to the car and leans on the car door.

"I tried the back door, but no one answered, and the sign out front says they don't open for another four hours," he says with a frustrated exhale.

He *tried the back door.* Of course.

"Okay, well." I look around. "Why don't you come back to my house? My mom called earlier so I know she made a disgusting amount of food for my homecoming. My whole family will be there, which might be a tad overwhelming, but at least you can kill some time and eat your heart out. Then I'll drive you back here after they open."

He looks out at the street, fidgeting with the car door as he deliberates. "Yeah. Okay. That's probably better than me loitering the streets down here. I don't want Clancy to know I'm here yet and his guys are probably all over the place." He gets back in and shuts himself inside. Then turns to me with a grin. "And besides, I've always wanted to meet your mom."

I roll my eyes as we drive away. "Don't make me regret inviting you over."

———

Twenty minutes later, I already do.

"OH MY GOODNESS! A boy is in the house!" My six-year-old sister, Raine, runs up the moment Jack and I step inside my house and throws her arms around Jack, a guy she's never met before. Taken aback, he stands frozen with his arms out and looks down at her with a tentative smile.

"Ooh! He's pretty!" Shyla runs up to us as well, climbing her four-year-old body into my arms for a big hug while at the same time staring openmouthed at Jack. She whispers in my ear, "He gots big muscles."

"Hi there," Penny, my sixteen-year-old sister, says in a silky voice as she holds out her hand. "I'm Penny. It's so nice to meet you."

Jack hesitantly shakes her hand. "I'm Jack."

"Oh, I know," she says, still shaking his hand.

"Is this Jack?" my mother calls out as she enters the front room with my grandmother. "It is so nice to meet you!" Mom approaches and kisses him on the cheek, leaving a lipstick kiss mark on his face.

"You're such a handsome young man," Grandma coos as she walks up to us with the energy of a teenager and the healthy glow of a yoga instructor.

Dying, my ass.

"So handsome," Mom repeats, rubbing the lipstick mark off Jack's cheek before patting it like he's a chubby baby in a high chair and not a grown man standing in her living room.

Jack's big gray eyes look slightly terrified at all the attention he's getting. Raine is sitting on his right foot with her limbs wrapped around his left as she stares up at him in awe, while Shyla has reached out from my arms and is now petting his shoulder and chanting, "Big muscles. Big muscles." Penny is *still* shaking his hand, refusing to release it as she bats her lashes, and my mom keeps grinning while Grandma goes on about how attractive he is.

He glances at me, his eyes crying for help, and I call the dogs off.

"Okay, everyone, step away from the boy!" I say. "Step away. From the boy. That includes you too, Penny." I shoot her a look as Jack delicately pulls his hand from her grasp.

Mom and Grandma back up a few feet, still smiling at Jack like he's some kind of celebrity, while Raine scoots off of his foot, but remains on the floor next to him.

I shake my head. "You'd think no one in this house had ever seen a guy before. God. Isn't anyone in this house happy to see *me*?" I tease, and my sisters instantly start babbling their hello's.

I make the rounds, greeting each of my family members with kisses and hugs, and my mom beams as my sisters and I hug.

"Look at all my little peacocks, together in one place," she says. "Ooh, I just love my girls!" She brings us all into a gripping hug and I laugh.

It's good to be home.

When my mom releases us from her hold, I walk over to my grandmother and look her up and down with a grimace. Given that she's supposedly on her deathbed, I expected her to be all hunched over and missing a few teeth, or at least have a walking cane and a shawl on. But no.

Her hair is in perfect curls, her chocolate skin looks radiant, her amber-brown eyes are rich and sharp, and the purple silk dress she has on matches her fingernail polish and glittering earrings.

"Hi, Grams," I say, kissing both her cheeks before lifting a brow at her fashionable attire. "You look quite put together," I say. "And astonishingly *healthy*."

She grins. "Well, death comes like a thief in the night."

"Mm-hmm." I nod. "A thief that makes yearly house calls?"

"Hush, Jenna," Mom says, sashaying over to Jack. "We're sorry for overwhelming you, Jack." She throws him a smile that says just the opposite. "We're just so happy to meet you."

"A king's welcome," Jack says merrily. "I like it."

"Well if you like that, hopefully you'll like a king's feast as well." She waves us into the kitchen where the table is literally covered with food.

Jack's eyes widen. "This looks amazing."

I swear food turns men on just as much as boobs.

Chatter sails in from the front door, where my cousins enter the house and file into the kitchen, where they immediately come at me.

"Oh thank God, you're safe."

"Did anyone try to eat you?"

"You totally didn't call as often as you said you would."

I stare at them. "Wow. It's good to see you too."

Jack leans over and says, "*Eat* you?"

I wave a hand. "It's a long story."

"Okay, come on now. Let's eat." My mom ushers everyone into seats.

I sit next to Grandma with Jack on my other side, while my younger sisters fight over who gets the chair next to Jack. Penny wins and smiles brightly at Jack—too brightly, if you ask me—as she sits down. And lunch begins.

The first thirty minutes of the meal, everyone asks Jack questions. Where he's from. What he likes. What his tattoos mean. Like mine, Jack's tattoos melt into one another like one big mural, there are so many. But as I look more closely at the hawk on his arm, with the snake tangled in its talons, I wonder if the hawk represents Jack and the snake represents the Vipers. It would make sense.

He tells my family that there's very little meaning behind his ink, but I know better.

I know about the midnight bird of hope.

I frown. Knowing more about Jack's history, I can only imagine he got that tattoo when he was involved with the Vipers. A symbol of hope. Hope to be free. Hope to be safe.

Looking at him now, I bite down on a smile. It was a lucky tattoo after all.

My family members eventually stop interrogating Jack and turn their inquiring minds to me. I catch them up on all things Jenna, but their eyes keep drifting to the handsome guy at my side.

I guess I can't blame them. My family is all girls, all the time. It's a rare occurrence, having a guy at the table, let alone a very attractive one.

"So Grandma," I say, leaning over. "You still don't look like you're dying to me."

She shrugs with keen eyes. "Looks can be deceiving, child."

I snort. "You know what else can be deceiving? Grandmas who cry death."

She smiles. "If that's what I need to do to get you to come home, then I'll keep dying every year."

"Ha. I know you will," I say, kissing her on the cheek. "But seriously, it's good to see you. I've missed you so much."

"You too, child. You're my star." Her gaze slips to Jack. "And he seems to be yours."

I roll my eyes. "Not even close. You know me, Grams. I don't need a man."

She huffs. "Who said anything about need? I'm talking about desire. I'm talking about the *heart*."

Oh God. I come from a long line of hopeless romantics, and they seem to think it's their job to make sure I fall in love and breed at some point.

Pushing food around my plate, I scoff. "Mom had desire and heart, and look where that got her."

"I am looking at it," Grams says, looking at me. "And it's the best thing that ever happened to her."

I draw in a breath. "Well you'll have to excuse me if I don't want to end up a broke single mother."

She *tsks* at me. "Your mother chose her path. Besides, what is it you *do* want to be? A rich childless woman?"

I chew my food and think about that. Sure, I never wanted to get married. And I never wanted to be poor. But do I want to be childless? I guess I could always foster kids, like my mom. I'm her only biological child but Penny, Raine, and Shyla have lived with us since they were babies and it's been awesome. But is that what I want? To raise kids on my own? Or to live forever without being a mother?

Ugh. I don't like where this train of thought is going. Leave it to Grandma to stir me up.

I playfully wink at her. "Who doesn't want to be rich?"

She tuts and looks away. "All I'm saying is that sometimes getting what you want is the worst fate of all. Most of the time, actually." She takes a graceful sip of her sweet tea. "I like your new ring, by the way." She nods at my left hand, where the red-stoned ring Jack bought for me at the art festival the other day sits two fingers away from the gris-gris ring she gave me when I moved to Arizona. "It looks rather special."

I stare at my fingers, adorned with various rings of all shapes and sizes. "How could you tell I got a new one?"

She daintily sets her tea glass down. "Your fingers didn't tell me, love. Your eyes did." A shrewd smile curls her lips. "Is it a gift from your young man?"

I shake my head. How does she always know things?

"You're crazy, Grams," I say.

She keeps smiling. "But am I wrong?"

I tuck my hands away with a defeated sigh. "No. You're not wrong. The ring was a gift from Jack."

She goes back to her lunch with a triumphant gleam in her eyes. "That's what I thought."

I roll my eyes, but my heart beams in my chest. I still can't believe Jack bought me a ring. I chance a glance in his direction and he catches me. A bright smile lights up his face, his storm-cloud eyes sparkling beneath thick dark eyebrows, and he winks at me. My beaming heart leaps like I'm some giddy schoolgirl and I quickly look away.

Jack.

He makes me feel things—things I wish I didn't want to feel.

When lunch is over and I go help with the dishes, my youngest sisters whisk Jack away with happy giggles.

Forty-five minutes later, I wander through the house looking for him. Entering the playroom, I find my cousins and Grandma watching something with adoring smiles and follow their gaze to where Jack is surrounded by a gaggle of girls. Again.

He's sitting at a children's table that's so small compared to his giant body it's laughable. His long legs are bent and tucked awkwardly in front of him as he sits in a chair designed for a two-year-old, but the quirkiest part of the scene is the fact that he has a sheet tied around him like a dress, a large hat with flowers on his head, and white gloves that barely fit around his hands. And he's wearing makeup. Bright-pink blush stains his cheeks and purple eye shadow is scribbled below his brows, while neon-red lipstick marks up his mouth and sticks to the stubble on his chin and jaw. Shyla and Raine are also dressed up and lathered in makeup, and the three of them are sitting at the table with stuffed animals having a tea party.

"I see my gris-gris bag is working," Grandma says, startling me.

It's only then I realize I'm grinning from ear to ear as I stare at Jack with my sisters. I try to get my beaming smile under control.

"I don't know what you're talking about." I shift my weight.

She rolls her eyes like she's sixteen years old and not, you know, a hundred. "Please. I know love when I see it and that boy is in love with you." She sighs. "It seems my superstitious beliefs are paying off."

Now *I* roll my eyes. "Of course you would take credit for this."

She smiles. "So you admit he's in love with you, I like that." She winks. "Progress."

I glare at her. "You're insufferable, you know that?"

Her smile turns more knowing. "You're welcome."

Jack sees me and a giant grin spreads across his face. "Hello, Jenna. Would you care to join us for some tea?" He lifts a tiny teacup in the air.

"No, no, no, Mr. Jack." Shyla points a scolding finger at him. "You have to lift your pinkie finger when you drink. Like this." She demonstrates with her tiny pinkie, wearing a very serious face as she does so.

"Oh, I'm so very sorry." He flicks up his pinkie. "Is that better, Ms. Shyla?"

She nods. "Much better."

"Come join us!" Raine says, smiling as she tugs on my arm. "We're doing makeovers."

"I can see that." I sit on one of the small chairs and Raine and Shyla immediately start fussing with my hair and clothes. They put a tiara on my head and drape dozens of pearl necklaces around my neck, then take turns painting my face with their junior makeup kits.

"Ta-da!" Shyla smiles when they're finished.

I feel like ten pounds of clay are on my face as I turn to Jack and smile. "How do I look, Mr. Jack?"

He bows his head. "Absolutely marvelous, Ms. Jenna."

I laugh at the ridiculousness of the floppy flowered hat on his head when it tips off with his bow, then I pick it up and place it back on. Even covered in my little sisters' makeup and dressed like a gaudy gypsy he manages to look masculine. But more than that, his gray eyes are the same, piercing me with his joy and easiness with my family, sinking into me with the heaviness of the life he's trying to fix and the lightness of what he sees in me, and I want to get lost in them.

Gris-gris bag aside, there is something growing inside me. Something born of passion and nourished with time. Something Jack's known about for God knows how long and isn't afraid of.

Something that feels a lot like love.

He's like a drug, this man. And if I'm not careful, I might get addicted.

This is, if I'm not already.

18

JACK

*T*he black building that was completely deserted earlier is now bouncing with music and people as Jenna rolls to a stop down the street.

Her three cousins are overdressed in the backseat, plotting their evening with text messages and nonstop chatter. When they found out Jenna was driving me to the French Quarter, they insisted on making a night of it and forced Jenna into a very sexy outfit—a skintight top with no straps and matching skintight jeans with heels. The sight of which makes me wish I were invited to stay, but Callie made it clear this was a "girls" night only.

"Thanks for the lift," I say, turning to Jenna.

"No problem." She frowns. "And you're sure you have a place to stay for the night?"

The honest answer is no. I know a few people in New Orleans, but none well enough to crash on their couch. But Jenna needs a break from all my chaos and I'd hate to ruin her night out by bunking up with her family.

God, I can't believe I pulled her into all my drama. I've walked her into one crazy situation after another—and all the poor girl wanted to do was drive to New Orleans to visit her sick grandma.

I'm an asshole.

Jenna deserves way better than me, on all levels. So my plan is to check into one of the many hotels in the Quarter after I've talked to Clancy.

"Yep. I'm good." I smile and get out of the car before ducking my head back in. "Are you still planning to leave on Saturday?"

She nods. "I was, but if you don't find Drew by then—"

"I will," I say with more confidence than I feel.

"Okay," she says slowly. "I'll text you later this week and we'll figure out a meeting place. Sound good?" I nod and she lowers her voice. "Text me when you find Drew, okay? Just so I know he's okay and that... that you're okay too."

The concern in her eyes pulls at my gut. I like that she cares— that she's not *afraid* to care—about my safety. If only she were fearless enough to admit she cares about more than just my well-being, then maybe she and I could finally be on the same page about *us*.

"I will," I say.

With a quick wave, she drives away with her cousins.

Turning around, I stare up at the flashing lights surrounding Crowns and crack my knuckles. Time to face my latest opponent.

The Royals.

Clancy.

My one shot at finding Drew.

————

In his purple suit and alligator boots, Clancy looks like a comic book villain, complete with a polished black cane and a white fedora crowning his head. He's more colorful than a grown man should ever be, especially one who should be keeping a low profile. But I learned the hard way not to underestimate the outlandish stylings of Clancy.

I absently run a finger down the very thin and very faded white scar trailing from the back of my jaw to the top of my collarbone. The business end of a steak knife left me branded by the man long ago. Someday I hope to return the favor.

"Jack Oliver," Clancy says, rising from his seat in the back room of Crowns. A single gold tooth glints among his other white ones as a slow grin curls up the corners of his mouth. "I certainly wasn't expecting to see you anytime soon. Or ever, for that matter. To what do I owe this pleasure?"

As I step farther into the room, two of his watchdog minions casually reach for the guns in their belts. "Trust me, Clancy. Nothing about visiting you is pleasurable."

He cocks his head, his smile still in place but growing sharp. "All business then? Funny. I thought you no longer wanted anything to do with our line of work."

"I didn't," I say. "Until my brother went missing."

He eyes me for a long moment. "So you don't know where he is either?" A loud sigh blows out his lips. "And here I thought you'd come to negotiate."

I cross my arms. "I try not to negotiate with enemies."

He grates out a dark laugh. "Now, we both know that's not true."

"We had a deal, Clancy. You agreed to stay away from my family."

"And I did."

"Then why is there a price on Drew's head?" I grit out.

"Because he's done some irrevocable damage to the Royals." He steeples his fingers. "The kind of damage that cannot be repaired."

"Damage he wouldn't have caused if you'd just left him alone," I bark. "What did you get him mixed up in?"

His nostrils flare. "*I* didn't get him mixed up in anything. If you want to blame someone for your brother's sins, I would suggest you track down your father."

My blood instantly boils—not just with anger, but also with gut-wrenching fear—as I narrow my eyes. "My father? What does he have to do with any of this?"

"Everything," Clancy says. "He's the one who brought Drew into the fold. Do you know where your brother is?"

I jut my chin. "I already told you. No."

"Do you know where your father is?"

"No."

"Then this conversation is over."

"I don't understand—"

"And you don't need to," Clancy snaps, walking toward me. "You came into my bar, my place of business, demanding answers, and you have nothing to give me in return. So this conversation is over." He waves a hand at the watchdogs, who in turn crowd in on me until I start backing up.

"If anything happens to Drew," I say, sinking my eyes into Clancy, "I will find you and then you'll know what real damage looks like." Walking backward, I step out into the balmy Louisiana night with the watchdogs still in my face.

"If you see your father," Clancy says with cold eyes, "tell him I'm looking forward to the next time we meet."

If I see my father…

He's supposed to be on the run. He's supposed to be in hiding—or even dead.

He's supposed to be gone from our lives forever.

Jabbing emotions cut through me at what my father being back in the picture might mean. So many things. None of them good.

Clancy's watchdogs slam the door in my face and I'm left standing in a dark alleyway with one thought racing through my mind.

I'm going to kill my father.

19

JENNA

*S*hockingly, Grandma decided not to join my cousins and me for a rough and rowdy night of terrible-song karaoke. Not because she wasn't feeling well, but because she already had plans to play bingo with some of her book club friends.

I swear that old woman has more of a social life than I do.

So here I am, wedged between Callie and Alyssa at a sticky bar table as a very drunk Becca wobbles up to the stage in her five-inch heels and takes the microphone.

The four of us wore matching strapless shirts—per Becca's request—and each one is a different color. My mom said it was perfect because it made us look like a flock of peacocks. I informed her that colorful peacocks are always males and are notoriously mean and obnoxious, to which she responded, "So what's your point?"

Alyssa chose a blue top. Becca chose yellow. Callie, green. And I went with red. Because it matched my newest piece of jewelry.

Glancing down at the red-stoned ring shining on my left hand, I can't help but smile.

Jack loves me. No question.

How is it that I can *accept* that Jack loves me, but not *trust* that he does? No wonder the guy gets so frustrated with me.

The opening notes of "I Will Survive" play through the cheap speakers propped up in the corners of the smoky room and everyone cheers. Becca takes her stance on the stage and dramatically gears up to sing her heart out—and maybe our ears.

If I were drunk right now, I'd probably be having more fun. But my stomach has been unsettled all night, so sick with worry about Jack and Drew that I haven't been able to consume any alcohol.

My cousins, on the other hand, haven't had any trouble tossing 'em back. They're still going hard, while all I want to do is check in on Jack and see if he found out anything from that Clancy guy.

Excusing myself from the horrible performance Becca is subjecting the bar to, I slip out onto Bourbon Street and call Jack.

He answers immediately. "Is everything okay?"

I blink. "What? Yeah. I was calling to see how things were going with you."

A horse-drawn carriage goes by with a drunk couple inside holding a megaphone. Through the megaphone they shout, "HELLO, BOURBON STREET!" and fall back laughing.

I wouldn't think much of it, except I heard the couple's craziness through my phone, and not just my ear, which means Jack is somewhere nearby.

"Where are you?" I ask, searching the street.

"I'm headed to a friend's house for the night."

Spying him through the window of a hotel lobby across the street I frown. "Oh yeah? You're not checking into a hotel?" I hurry across the street and slip through the hotel's front doors.

He heads for the elevators. "What? No. That would be silly."

I duck inside the elevator, just as the doors close us inside. "Gotcha."

He sees me and looks startled. "What are you doing here?"

The elevator starts heading up.

"Well, I saw you lying to me from across the street so I thought I'd come catch you in that lie. Busted." I scowl and gesture at the elevator. "Why would you stay at a hotel? Why not just stay with my family?"

He sighs and runs a hand through his disheveled hair, pieces falling into his face and across his cheekbones. "Because you need a break from all my craziness, Jenn."

I furrow my brow. "No, I don't. That's why I was calling you."

The elevator *dings* and the doors open. I follow him out and walk beside him down the hotel corridor, passing one red door after another.

"You might not think you do, but trust me," he says, coming to a stop in front of red door number 2323, "you need a break from me."

He won't look at me and a sliver of rejection pierces my heart.

"Well at least tell me if you found anything out about Drew," I say. "I'm dying over here."

"Go home, Jenna. You don't need to be mixed up in this." He slips his key inside the door and enters the room.

He doesn't invite me in, but I follow after him anyway. I don't like this not-being-wanted feeling. I know we've spent a lot of nonstop time together these past few days, and it would make sense that maybe Jack wants some space, but *I* don't want space.

And hell, that's new for me.

I always want space. Freedom. I always want to get *away*.

Until now.

"No," I say. "I want to know what you found out."

The door closes behind us with a loud *click* and I stare at him with pleading eyes. The idea that Jack might be getting sick of me is...well, it's heartbreaking. I want him to keep me around. To let me in. To want me—to *trust* me.

"Please?" I say.

He studies me for a moment then scrubs a hand across his jaw with a heavy sigh. "I found out that my father is in on all this."

I stand with my mouth open for several long seconds. "Oh my God. I'm so sorry, Jack."

He laughs bitterly. "Me too. All this time, I thought I'd saved my brothers from my dad and his mess but here I am, trying to clean up after him again."

I place a hand on his shoulder, my heart sinking with all he's probably feeling. "I really am sorry, Jack."

He looks at me with broken, gray eyes. "I'm sorry I dragged you into all this, but I'm glad I have you at the same time, you know?"

I nod, energized by the affirmation of his words. "Of course."

He wants me. He trusts me.

Am I crazy not to give him those very same things in return? Am I insane to continue pushing him and us and the possibility of love away?

I have my reasons, my future. But there's a fine line between sticking to your guns and shooting yourself in the foot. And sometimes I feel like I'm trying to outrun myself. Like I'm fighting against my own heart. Not my dreams. Not my fears. My *heart*.

I'm racing in circles—fleeing a storm of my own making—while Jack waits patiently, ready to catch me when I collapse of exhaustion.

I glance at his beautiful face and bite my lip. "Jack, I..."

What if I gave in? What if I let the storm consume me? What if I braved the wild torrents and crashing waves that come when Jack and I collide and just let go?

I try again, "I…"

Sensing the shift inside me, he leans over and kisses me on the forehead. It's an innocent kiss, but my eyes fall shut at the touch and I realize I want nothing else than to just let go.

I want to drown in the unknown. Flail in unruly winds.

I want to surrender to the storm until I'm a piece of it. A willing tempest.

I want—

I want—

I want to just…let…go…

I lift up on my tiptoes and press my lips to his. Pulling back, Jack looks down at me with desire in his eyes and then takes my mouth in his. It's rough and sudden and I claw at his back for more as he yanks me against him and holds my tongue hostage. Our kiss is savage and hungry, and I moan and whimper because he tastes so good and being away from him for even a few hours was too long.

I want him, I realize. I want him and he's taking me. This is different than last night. *I'm* different. He pulls away, giving me a chance to change my mind but I don't move.

My eyes fix on his mouth, tracing the curves of his full lips as hot breath flows in and out. His broad chest rises and falls with the rhythm, the wide collar of his shirt shows the thick muscles that wrap and layer around and beneath his collarbone.

In the dim light of the room, every shadow is exaggerated along the lines of his shoulders and throat, seducing me silently as my gaze travels up and over his jaw and to his piercing eyes. Gunmetal gray rimmed with pale green and cut with sharp silver fills my vision, slowly pulling me in and taking me captive. And I, the willing prisoner, absently lean closer as if he's a magnet and I'm helpless metal pieces.

The tips of my breasts brush against his hard chest, sparking a white-hot flame deep inside me at the touch and causing my eyes to flutter as I tip my chin up to see him more fully. My lips part of their own accord, the pieces of me coming even more undone than they already are as I stare up at Jack in desperate want.

All feeling leaves my fingers as I give in to the great weight of desire I've been pushing back all this time and press my lips to the base of his chin. Heat washes over my body as I kiss him gently then move my mouth to his bottom lip and set my lips there as well. I want him against me.

I want to play at his mouth and slide against his skin. I want to draw pleasure from his body and look down on him as ecstasy ignites in us both. I want to conquer him until I'm exhausted and sated.

But I know better.

This is Jack and he will not be conquered. Jack will not be owned. Jack will not be taken. He is the victor and king. With him, I am not the hurricane. *He* is the storm and I am the ravaged.

His force will destroy me; wrap me up in the fierce wind of his passion and the heavy water of his love. And that's what it is: love. Undeniable and irrevocable love. And it is his stormy love that terrifies me most of all.

The storm will come, flatten me completely, and I will never be the same.

But I've been lying to myself all along. The storm hit me last winter and I've been a fledgling in his unsettled waters, pointlessly thrashing against the wind and rain, all the while knowing I've already lost.

Jack pulled me under last year. The only thing left to do now is throw myself into the tempest and let the chaos that is Jack take me where it will.

His large hands go to my legs, laying against the sides of my upper thighs as my mouth stays softly against his lower lip; not kissing, not moving, just waiting. He moves his palms up the sides of my hips, rolling along my curves until they reach my waist. He grips me there and pulls me against him, clutching me to his body in a possessive way that leaves no question as to who's in charge. This is it. If I don't slink out of his embrace now there's no going back.

But I'm already in the storm, wet and undone, lost and sailing.

I gently set my teeth around his bottom lip and softly tug him into my mouth.

There's a split second where his fingertips sink into my waist and a deep sound rumbles in the back of his throat but then all sanity is lost and his chaos sweeps me away.

One hand snaps to my back to keep me in place against him as the other grabs my face and brings my mouth to his more fully. He kisses me without reserve, crushing his lips against mine just once before parting them with his strong tongue, which he slips inside with hot entitlement. Like the very flesh of my mouth is his, and his alone, to touch and taste. And that he does.

I meet his tongue with equal aggression and desire. Our mouths work against each other for the same cause and with the same greedy desperation. I curl my hands around his upper arms, unable to clasp him as fully as I'd like due to his large muscles. I sink my nails into his skin, scratching him briefly before moving my hands to a more satisfying grip around his neck.

In response to my clawing, he grabs my hips and roughly yanks me against him as he bites the corner of my lip.

"If you're going to scratch me like a feline," he says between ragged breaths, "I might have to handle you like a tiger." He spins us around and shoves me up against the wall, towering over me like a hungry shadow as his hands squeeze my ass.

I nip his tongue and undo his pants, tearing the fly open. His erection is still hidden in his jeans but since he has no underwear on I get a healthy view of his bare pelvis. I pull back from his hungry mouth just long enough to sharpen my eyes on his silver irises.

"I'll scratch you where I damn well please," I say, tucking my hand into his open jeans and setting my fingernails against the hot skin far below his belly, where I slowly scrape them up to his treasure trail.

A low noise tumbles from his throat as he kisses me again, his hands slipping over the tight material of my shirt and the curves of my breasts. He sucks my earlobe into his mouth, twisting it around his tongue before running his teeth down my jaw. My eyes roll back as I tip my head, exposing my throat to his claiming kisses as he sucks at my skin.

He tucks his fingers inside the top of my strapless shirt before tugging it down to bare my breasts. My nipples tighten in the cool air then harden even more under his gaze. His eyes rove over my naked curves as his hands cup my breasts and his thumbs flick over the erect peaks. I gasp, watching the pads of his large thumbs continue to run back and forth over my aching nipples as I arch my hips further into him.

I go to pull my shirt off and he stops my hands, gripping my wrists tightly before knocking them away. A reminder that Jack is the hurricane. I let my hands fall away, feeling oddly safe in my powerlessness.

He runs his palms over my chest and squeezes my breasts. Lightly at first then more firmly until my breaths are quick and short. He lifts them, tugging my left nipple into his warm mouth, groaning, then doing the same to my right.

My core begins to tighten along with my hard nipples, growing wet and achy as I grind against him. My nails sink into the back of his neck in need. He pulls back and the wet tips of my breasts chill in the cool air of the room, causing a shiver to run through my body as Jack slips his fingers through the belt loops on my jeans and uses his hold there to pull me from the wall.

Walking backward, he tugs me along until he reaches the bed and sits on the edge. He pulls my hips up to his face, me standing above where he sits, and undoes the button of my jeans. He pulls the zipper down, only an inch, and looks up at me darkly. His gaze lingers on my bare breasts, spilling free from where my shirt is tucked beneath their masses, then moves up to my throat, my mouth, my eyes.

For a moment, standing above him like the queen I usually am in the bedroom, I feel confident and sure. I could shove him back and straddle his big body, riding him until I feel powerful and pleased, then climb off of his undone mess. But the powerful feeling is fleeting.

As I try to push him onto his back, he grabs my wrists and pins them to my side, locking them there and eyeing me darkly until I relax my shoulders. Releasing me, his hands move down the sides of my legs, trailing down the fabric of my jeans and then back up my legs to the bottom of my open zipper.

He pulls my pants even farther apart so my jeans are still loosely around my hips but my red thong is completely visible. Even with my shirt and pants still technically on my body I feel more naked than I've ever been. Not in an uncomfortable way, certainly not—I trust Jack more than I trust myself, which is nearly as frightening as the love I see in his eyes even amidst the lust—but in a vulnerable way. Because I'm not in control.

He leans in and kisses the top of my panties, his hot breath warming the center of the red triangle of material separating us. I want his mouth lower but he doesn't move his lips as he yanks my jeans down to my knees and runs his hands up the back of my thighs.

A tremor runs through me and I feel myself grow wetter. I squeeze my legs together to give myself some relief but none comes as Jack's hands glide up and over my naked ass and drives me even more wild.

I shove my hands into his black hair, tangling them in his locks and trying to guide his mouth to where I need him. His fingers slip under the waistband of my red thong and pull it down and I freeze.

"This is new," he says quietly, his eyes zeroing in on the tattoo I got just after the last time he and I were naked together. A moon, right above my pubic bone, with the silhouette of a flying bird.

A midnight bird of hope, identical to the one over his heart.

Jack realizes this. No question.

He had told me it represented hope. Hope for something to come, hope for something more. And that night last year with Jack made me hope for something I didn't know I ever wanted. And while I wasn't ready to admit it, my soul couldn't deny it.

Jack had changed me and he'd done so through sex, so I had the midnight bird inked along my most private of places because what we shared that night was intimate, and no one else needed to know about it. Ever.

He runs his fingers over the tattoo, brushing the sensitive skin there with reverence. Then he leans over and gently kisses the bird.

Like he's honored. Like he's grateful. He looks up at me with a million lost emotions in his eyes, and my heart tumbles over. What I feel for this man—for his heart, his bones, his stormy eyes and raspy voice—is beyond words. I would tattoo his name across every bare inch of my skin just to see him gaze at me this way. It's bigger than me, this thing I feel. Stronger. More powerful.

And it has overthrown my ruling completely and fallen head over heels in love with Jack Oliver.

His eyes drop to the special tattoo again and he traces it with the pad of his thumb. "Jenna."

Oh God. My name. That voice.

He looks up at me beneath long, dark lashes, still brushing my tattoo. "You love me."

I don't deny his words and a devilish smile curls up the ends up his mouth. With one final kiss of my inked skin, he returns to my panties with a whole new fervor.

His fingers still inside the waistband, he slides them to the center of my back, where the thin red string disappears between my cheeks. Flattening his palms over the round globes of my butt, he pulls his hands out from the waistband and carefully sets his fingertips along the center string and slowly runs them down the crease where my cheeks meet.

The featherlight touch, running down the sensitive skin of my backside, makes my stomach clench and my thighs tremble. Until he reaches the bottom where the red string meets the triangle that wraps up and around to my front and finds me completely wet.

He slips his fingers back under my panties, gently touching me between my legs, and I quietly gasp and grip his hair tightly in my hands.

As his naughty fingers begin to stroke my slippery skin, I

squirm in my imprisoning jeans, wishing for release as I try to move his stubborn mouth once again.

With hazy vision, I look down to see him smile against my panties.

In a raspy voice I say, "Bastard."

His smile grows as his fingers glide out of my panties and move around my thigh to the front of the red triangle.

He quietly says, "Do you want me to stop?" then slips his thumb under the material again and strokes me up...and up...and right to my clit.

I jerk at the touch, clutching his hair like a handlebar on a wild roller coaster as he gently rolls his thumb over me in small wet circles.

"Do you?" he asks, placing kisses along the seam of my panties where they meet my thighs. Then he takes the seam between his teeth and lifts it from my skin. With the edge of my panties in his mouth, his hot exhales drift inside the material and blow across my wet folds and needy clit. A shudder races through me.

I swallow, my legs shaking on the verge of orgasm and my eyes blind with desire as I whisper, "N-no."

He pulls my panties to the side with his mouth, exposing my most sensitive flesh, now glossy with my own wetness, and holds them there with his free hand as his sweet thumb falls away from my clit. I whimper, protesting the lack of contact. I was so close!

He takes a good look at my wanting nakedness, his pupils dilating with pleasure and hunger. I hold his head with both hands, bracing myself as his long tongue slips out from his mouth.

I watch as he slowly licks one long stroke up my center and I let out a small cry. My body trembles even more as he replaces his thumb with his hot tongue, rolling the textured pad of his tongue over my soft cluster of nerves. I hold his head against my V, moaning in ecstasy as more wetness leaks from my core and drips down my inner thighs. I tug his hair, feeling powerful as I guide his head between my legs.

The pleasure suddenly stops as he pulls away and lets my panties shift back into place.

I blink in confusion. "What are you—?"

Taking my hips, he throws me to the bed on my back. Then he pulls my jeans off the rest of the way and yanks my shirt off completely, his eyes sharp and dark as he climbs over my body and pins my arms above my head on the pillow with one hand.

I arch my back in protest and longing, not sure what to do without my hands as I breathe out, "I want to be on top."

His eyes pierce mine. "I know." He slips his free hand inside the only piece of clothing I still have on—my panties—cupping the place his mouth just pleased. "But I want you *my* way."

He pushes a finger inside me, sliding it between the achy, wet muscles of my core as I whimper again and my eyes fall shut.

"I want you to trust me." He kisses me lightly, gently, on the lips and whispers, "Do you trust me?"

I nod, unable to speak or open my eyes against the fierce pleasure inside me.

He pulls his finger out and my muscles try to grab at him as he does, desperate to have something to cling to and pulse around. He bends his head to tug one of my nipples into his mouth, and as he does, he pushes into me again and I exhale as his finger dives deeper than before. With my arms locked above my head and his hand inside my wet panties, pushing his fingers in and out of me while at the same time sucking on my nipples, I feel completely helpless. And it's incredibly arousing. Being at his mercy. Trusting him completely with my body.

He pulses in and out of me again but this time with a second finger added to the first to give me even more satisfaction. It's such extreme pleasure, wicked and sweet. But it's still not enough as I moan and wiggle under the crook of his fingers. His hands pull away from me then he lifts my hips and pulls off my soaking red panties before tossing them to the floor.

He spreads my thighs apart and lowers his mouth to my center, the tiny textures of his tongue rubbing against the needy nerves of my clit once again and I cry out in bliss.

I've been pleased by a guy's mouth before but never while on my back. I keep my position above guys. I sit above their mouths or ride atop their bodies. I don't lie beneath them and let them shove my thighs apart with their large hands—until now. Jack has me completely spread open for him and has his lips and tongue against me to do whatever he wishes. And all I can do is gasp and moan and beg for more as I tangle my fingers in his wild hair.

He licks at me mercilessly, his hot tongue rolling over and over the bundle of nerves at my center as I grab him by the hair and hold him to me. I start to see stars as his lapping increases and soon it's too much. A wonderful orgasm drives me to the peak and I whimper breathlessly as he licks me over the edge.

My thighs begin to quake, destroyed by such pleasure, and my lower belly spasms in time with my aching core. I arch my back, wanting relief for my tight center, but not yet able to move my arms or open my eyes under the weight of such delicious bliss.

I hear Jack hastily grab a condom and open my eyes just as he slips it on. Hovering over me, he pins my arms above my head again, forcing my breasts to stick out, swollen with need and nipples taut, and with my thighs fallen open from the climax and my core dripping with want and tightness, he pushes his thick cock into my body and pleasure darts through my limbs as he fills the aching need inside me.

Open and completely at his mercy, I cry out for more, begging in pants and rejoicing in gasps as he thrusts into me again and again. The friction between our bodies flicks against my swollen clit and sends me over the edge again as I buck.

He moves within me, filling me completely, driving into me again and again. My body is a wet glove, grasping at him, trying to hold him deep inside, but failing to keep him from pulsing in and out. In and out.

Arching my back as far as my spine will allow me, I bow up to him, tipping my head back and closing my eyes against the blissful sensations his thick hardness sends through my nerves.

With my hands trapped in his above my head, I'm completely without control. I'm his to touch. To do with what he will. A thought that lights my desire even more.

Hot exhales escape my mouth as I watch the taut muscles of his chest and shoulders work for his satisfaction and mine, straining against one another. He pushes deep inside me and slips his hands away from mine, freeing my wrists as he traces his fingers down my arms and over my breasts. The rough skin of his palms catches on the tenderness of my needy nipples, shooting pleasure straight to my core.

His hands slide lower and he lays them against my belly, his fingers brushing over the hollows of my pelvis as shaky breaths jump from my lips. Then, with his erection still buried deep inside me, he takes my hips in his hands and slowly begins to pump in and out of me again, this time with my hands free to roam his sweaty body. To grip his ass. To claw at his back.

And I do all three as he plunges into my wanting body over and over. The tiny muscles of my core grip his hard erection inside me, milking him for dear life as I come undone beneath him and soon the tendons in his throat pull taut and his shoulders go rigid as he climaxes inside me and we both become a liquid mess.

It's the most pleasure I've ever experienced and yet my body lies open and bare beneath his. I don't know how such a position could bring me such bliss. All I know is I want to experience it—experience Jack—again.

20

JACK

Running a finger down her spine, I watch the morning light fall over Jenna's face as she lies in my arms and slowly opens her eyes. It takes her a moment to register where she is and the events of last night, and when she does, her eyes dart around the hotel room until landing on the door.

I trace my finger up her back. "You want to run, don't you?"

She snaps her eyes to me and quietly says, "No."

I inhale slowly and smile. "Yes, you do."

She drops her eyes to my chest. "I don't want to run. I've just never slept with a guy until morning before and it's..." She traces a small circle on my stomach. "It's weird."

I tuck a strand of her dark hair behind her ear, wishing she would look back up at me. "What's weird about it?"

Keeping her eyes downcast, she lifts a naked shoulder. "I don't know. It feels all domestic."

My fingers trickle down her spine again as I nod. "And Jenna will not be tamed."

She cuts her eyes to me. "That's not what I'm saying."

"That *is* what you're saying." When my fingers reach her waist, I wrap my arms around her more fully and prop her on top of me completely. "But you could have left anytime you wanted last night. You didn't have to sleep beside me."

"I know."

"Then why did you stay?"

Her eyes flick to the tattoos on my collarbone. "Because I liked being in your arms. And I liked how warm you were. And the soothing the sound of your heartbeat when I laid on your chest." She scowls. "Ugh. Listen to me. I sound like one of those lovesick lunatic girls who think sex equals love and happily ever after—"

"No you don't," I say sharply, growing impatient with her endless efforts to not want me. "You sound like a woman who cares about the guy she woke up with."

She blinks up at me and bites her lip then rolls onto her side to face me. "Jack . . ."

"Shh . . ." I kiss her, softly, slowly.

It doesn't matter what she says. I saw the tattoo. I know she has feelings for me. I knew how she felt long before seeing her newest tattoo, but the fact that she permanently drew a reminder of me— of us—on her skin means that she knew it too. And she's known it all along.

Pulling back from her sweet mouth, I glide my hand over the curve of her shoulder, her elbow, the dip of her waist and the flare of her hips. God, she's breathtaking.

I gently nudge her onto her back and trail my fingers across her belly. "You don't want to be caged. I get it, Jenna. But this thing between us isn't going away. Because it's *real*." I slide my hand down her body and she sucks in a breath as I softly caress the moon tattoo. "I know you have feelings for me," I say, so quietly it's almost a whisper. "And I'm crazy about you."

She watches my fingers trace the lines of the design. "Midnight bird of hope," she says quietly. "That's what I call it."

I look down at the matching tattoo on my chest and repeat, "Midnight bird of hope." I smile. "What were you hoping for?"

She hesitates. "You, I think." She looks up and our gazes lock.

This girl.

I love her more than life itself.

My heart starts to pound. "I think we should give it a shot."

Her eyes fill with warring emotions as she opens her mouth to respond. But then the phone rings.

"Oh, crap," she says, whipping her head to where her phone sticks out of her purse. "I bet that's my mom freaking out because I didn't come home last night." She clambers over me and answers with a rushed, "Hello?...Oh, hi Becca...Yeah, I'm not sure if I'm going to make it...I know...Okay, maybe next time...Love you too." She hangs up and flops back on the bed. "I forgot that my aunt wanted everyone to come over for breakfast this morning, but I know it's really just a ploy to get everyone to help set up for a family barbeque this afternoon." She sighs. "It's never-ending with them and their family activities."

I smile. "My uncle Brent used to have barbeques all the time. My brothers and I loved going over there because he had this cool attic and Drew always wanted to play hide-and-seek in there—" I freeze as a thought hits me.

"What?" Jenna perks up.

"Drew loved my uncle's house," I say distractedly. "I wonder if he went there to hide out." I start nodding, my adrenaline spiking. "I bet he did." I look at Jenna. "I bet he did."

"Do you really think so?"

I keep nodding, feeling optimistic about my hunch.

"Okay." She smiles. "Then let's go."

"Yeah?" I smile.

She nods. "Let's go check it out."

We hurriedly get out of bed and get dressed. Every few minutes, I look over at Jenna, trying to figure her out. But her lack of response to my asking her to give us a shot is telling enough. She doesn't want a relationship with me and that's something I can't change.

I can't help but feel disappointed, though. I don't know how to convince her that caring about me—or even loving me—isn't a mistake. Especially now that she knows all about my crazy family and probably wants nothing to do with me.

Could that be part of her hesitation? My family's fucked-up drama? I guess it's possible. And if that were the case, I wouldn't blame her. Because that would make sense. This whole afraid-of-being-in-love shit is total nonsense.

Ten minutes later, we're checked out of the hotel and on our way to my uncle's house. My theory about Drew being there could be wrong, but my gut says otherwise. My gut says that once we get to Uncle Brent's house, my brother will no longer be missing. But my gut also says that finding Drew is only the beginning.

21

JENNA

*L*ast night was out of control.

I had hot, rocking sex with Jack, where I was definitely not in charge, and I liked it. I liked it a lot. But more than that, I felt connected to Jack the entire time. He wasn't just a warm body giving me pleasure. He was Jack. And somehow that made every touch, every kiss, every heavy breath and heartbeat so much sexier.

Even thinking about it has my heart pounding like a drum. Jack and I drive along the streets of New Orleans toward his uncle's house as my mind races with a tangle of unfamiliar emotions and desires.

Did Jack ask me to be his girlfriend? Is that what he meant this morning while we were lying in bed? I inwardly scoff. I don't do boyfriends—and he knows that. I do sex, not relationships. And yes, I know that makes me sounds like a douchey frat boy but whatever. Relationships aren't my thing—and certainly not with Jack. If I started dating Jack, then I'd start sleeping with him all the time, and if I started having nonstop sex with Jack, I'd keep feeling connected to him and get all emotionally mushy, and if that happened, well...I'd be a goner. I'd be hopelessly stupidly in love.

And I can't afford to be in love.

I have a future all mapped out for myself. I'm going to finish college and get a great job. I'm going to make good money and never rely on anyone else for anything. I'm going to have my own house, my own car, my own everything. And no man will ever knock me up and break my heart and leave me high and dry. No man!

Glancing over at Jack, I try to envision what it would be like to have him leave me. The pain. The heartache. The angry bitterness.

But none of those emotions come because all I see when I look at him is loyalty and love and safety. I can't picture Jack leaving anyone he loved—ever. And *that* puts an ache in my heart like no other.

Here's this great guy who would do anything for the people he loves—even deal drugs and make scary pacts with gangsters—and all he wants is for me to admit that I care about him and give him a chance.

What is wrong with me?

We pull up to a small house in a quiet neighborhood and exit the car. Jack's shoulders are tense so I don't say a word as I follow him to the front door. He knocks three times. No answer. He knocks again. Still no answer.

My hope starts to deflate as we stand on the front porch, but Jack keeps his chin held high as he waits. Just when I'm starting to think it's time to give up, the door cracks open a few inches and an eyeball looks out at us.

"Jack?" says the eyeball.

"Drew!" Jack sighs in relief. "Thank God. We've been looking everywhere for you."

Opening the door all the way, Drew glances at me before looking back at Jack and yanking him inside. "Hurry and get in here, before anyone sees you."

We rush inside and Drew quickly locks the door behind us.

He's a completely different version of an Oliver brother. Jack and Samson are both tall and broad, with shaggy dark hair and pale skin, and muscles creating curves all over their bodies, while Drew is shorter and more clean-cut. His dark hair is short, matching a set of perfect arched eyebrows over a pair of baby blue eyes, and he's built like a surfer—and has a tan like one too.

He says, "Am I glad to see you," before throwing his arms around his brother, then pulls back in a panic. "I'm in a lot of shit, Jack. I don't know what to do."

"It's okay," Jack says. "We're going to figure everything out."

Drew nods and gestures for us to follow him into the living room, where none of us take a seat, probably because we're all too nervous.

"God, Jack. I'm so sorry. So sorry." Drew runs his hands through his hair and starts pacing. "It's such a mess."

Jack nods. "Just start at the beginning and tell me what happened."

Drew swallows a few times then wrings his hands together. "Well...Dad called me a few months ago, out of the blue. I thought he was dead. I mean, we all thought he was dead, right? After everything went down, he just disappeared and I was sure he was taken down by some gangster or something. So when he called I was—I was just so surprised. And then he said he wanted to make things right with me. He said that he'd made a lot of mistakes and hated losing you and Mom and Sam, but that he didn't want to lose me too. Dad never paid attention to me, you know? Even when he was around, he didn't make time for me. You were his favorite. You know, firstborn son and all. Jack the smart kid. Jack the strong kid. Jack the kid who made Dad proud. And Samson was a mini version of you. But I—I was different. Weaker. I was the son that Dad didn't give a damn about, so when he called and said he wanted to make things right..." He shakes his head. "I just gave in. I wanted to believe him so badly that I just didn't care what it cost." He sighs.

"So we started meeting up every now and then. I never told you guys or Mom because he told me not to and, honestly, I liked having Dad all to myself." He snorts. "God I'm an idiot."

Jack crosses his arms. "What happened?"

"Dad asked me to get him back in the business. When you broke things off and got the family out, Dad lost all his ties and loyalty. And he wanted me to help him rebuild. At first I refused. I saw the shit you went through to get us out and I didn't want to betray you and Mom. But Dad...he got under my skin, you know? He started promising me things. Money. Power. He said he and I would start up our own syndicate, just the two of us, and he wanted me to be in charge." He looks at Jack desperately. "I've never been in charge, Jack. I'm the baby. The reckless kid. I've never been trusted like that before. I couldn't say no." He runs his hands through his hair and stares at the ground. "I should have said no but I couldn't."

Jack quiets his voice. "What did Dad make you do?"

Drew's eyes are wide with panic when he looks up. "He had me set up a deal between the Royals and the Northmen. You know the Royals have been wanting to buy product off the Northmen for years, but after you busted Dad a few years ago the Northmen refused to keep working with the Royals." He shakes his head again. "But I guess Dad worked his way back into the Northmen's good graces and made some contacts there, which is how he was able to set this whole thing up. He knew the Royals would never meet the Northmen in person for an exchange because they're afraid of being taken out. So Dad's solution was me. The deal was, I would go pick up the drugs from the Northmen, deliver them to the Royals, pick up payment from the Royals, and then deliver the payment back to the Northmen. Everyone would get what they wanted and no one would have to risk their life—"

"Except you," Jack says, his eyebrows knitting together.

Drew slowly nods. "Yeah, but *only* me. I'd be the only person in danger. It was low risk for everyone else. Dad thought it was the best way to open a truce—and the Royals and the Northmen agreed."

"Of course they did," Jack mutters darkly. "So what went wrong?"

Drew blinks a few times. "Nothing—at first. I picked up the drugs and threw them in the trunk of my car then headed to Crowns for payment. When I got there, Dad was waiting with Clancy to check out the product. They were both beyond pleased. Clancy even laughed about how much profit they were going to make on such high quality cocaine. He handed the drugs off to Dad and told him to put them away, then handed me the cash to drive back to the Northmen. Halfway there, I get a call from Dad and he's all stressed-out and panicked. He starts going on about how he's afraid the Northmen are setting me up and want to kill me. I was so confused. Why would the Northmen have a beef with me? It made no sense. But Dad was freaked and kept saying how he didn't want to lose me and he couldn't live with himself if something happened to me. So he tells me to pull over and wait for him at this run-down rest stop. A few minutes later he shows up, still flustered, and begs me to let him finish the delivery. He said the Northmen wouldn't hurt him so it was the best plan, you know, to keep me safe. So I gave him my keys and we switched vehicles." Drew looks to Jack with wild eyes. "He just kept talking about how he wanted to keep me safe..."

Jack nods understandingly. "And then he stole the money."

Standing silent in the corner, I choke on my own breath.

"Yeah," Drew says in disbelief. "He got in my car with all the Royals' cash in the back and drove away."

Jack's jaw is clenched so tight I can hear his teeth grind against one another. "That son of a bitch. I can't believe he would do that to you. Leave you indebted to the Northmen like that."

"And that's not all," Drew adds. "He stole the drugs too! When Clancy handed them off at the bar, Dad didn't put them in the safe. He must have stashed the coke somewhere else."

Horror fills Jack's face. "Dad took off with the drugs *and* the money?"

Drew nods. "So now the Royals and the Northmen are at war with one another and—"

"They blame you for their losses and both want you dead," Jack says in a low voice. "There's not just a price on your head. There's a fucking race to cash it in."

Silence falls over the room. I swallow and the sound echoes in my ears along with my pounding heart.

"That's why I took off and didn't call you guys. I couldn't have them thinking you were hiding me. I couldn't risk either side hurting you or Sam or Mom to get to me," Drew says, his voice rising in panic. "But now it's only a matter of time before they find me and kill me. And they *will* find me. I'm going to die, Jack."

"No, you're not," Jack says, clenching his fists at his side.

"Yes, I am!" Drew cries. "Oh my God. I should never have trusted Dad. I'm going to die. I'm going to die—"

"You are *not* going to die!" Jack shouts, and Drew jumps back. Jack stalks over to his little brother, looks him in the eye, and quietly says, "There is nothing in this world that I won't do to protect you. Do you understand?"

Drew slowly nods.

Jack continues, "I know Dad treated you like you weren't important, but you are. To Mom. To Samson. You're important to *me*." His voice is steady but his eyes are a silver storm. "And I won't let anyone hurt you. Ever." They stay like that, eye to eye in tense silence for several long seconds before Drew nods.

Jack leans back. "We need a plan."

"I've been trying to think of a plan nonstop since I took off," Drew says. "But I've got nothing. There's no way out."

"There's always a way out." Then the storm in Jack's eyes fades away as he paces the room in thought. "If Dad had taken just the money, that would be one thing, but he took the money and the drugs, which means he plans on selling. This is a good thing."

Drew frowns. "How is that possibly a good thing?"

"Because it means he needs a buyer."

I watch him rub his mouth in thought and my nerves stand on end. I fidget with the rings on my fingers and shift my weight. This new Jack...or I guess it's the old Jack—whatever, this Jack that I just recently discovered is so fierce...and kind of a badass. And while that's very, very incredibly hot, it also scares the crap out of me.

I don't want Jack to take any unnecessary risks. I don't want him to get any more wrapped up in all this danger than he already is.

His eyes dart from side to side, the wheels in his head clearly turning at Mach speeds, and I know I've already lost him to whatever he's cooking up in his mind.

Jack stops pacing. "As far as I know, there are only two buyers in the area that are greedy enough to buy a hot shipment from a guy who no longer has any ties. The first is Raymond Lotts, but he's currently in prison. There's no way Dad would risk all the time and middlemen it would take to complete a transaction with Raymond." Jack drops his eyes to the floor with a frown.

"Then who's the second person?" Drew asks.

Jack looks up and a shadow crosses his face. "Alec."

22

JACK

*M*otherfucker.

My father is the lamest asshole to ever walk the earth. I can't believe he did this to Drew. How dare he come back into his son's life and manipulate him like this? Mother. Fucker.

"No way." Drew shakes his head. "Dad stole money from the Vipers. Alec would never do business with him."

I clench my jaw. "He would if it meant lots of money. And I'm willing to bet the profit on Northmen coke is pretty hefty. The Northmen are picky about their coke. They only move the pure stuff. And Alec knows that."

Pulling out my phone, I dial a number and hold it to my ear.

"Who are you calling?" Drew asks.

"Alec," I say, though that's not strictly true.

Jonesy answers on the second ring. "Vipers."

"Jonesy," I say, trying to keep my voice steady.

"Jack?"

It never fails to surprise me, Jonesy's knack for identifying people's voices with just one word.

"What's wrong?" he says in a tone I know is typically reserved for drug runs gone bad.

He's not entirely off track.

"Nothing's wrong," I say, then pause. "Not really. I just have to talk to Alec about something and I need him to be in a ... conversational mood when I do."

Jonesy curses under his breath. "He's still pissed about Samson coming in here the other night. He's not gonna want to talk to you."

"I know," I say, my tone unflinching. "But this is business."

He scoffs. "That's even worse."

"It doesn't have to be—as long as Alec's in the right frame of mind when I talk to him."

A pause.

"Let me guess," Jonesy says. "You want me to rile him up?"

"Exactly."

I can almost picture Jonesy nodding as he says, "All right. Who do you want Alec pissed at?"

I clench and unclench my fist. "My father."

Silence meets my ears for a long moment. "Shit, Jack ..." he murmurs. "What the hell is going on?"

Taking a deep breath, I feel a sense of justice seep into my lungs. "Payback."

I hear him take a breath. "All right."

Jonesy doesn't ask for any more details before leaving the line quiet to go to talk to Alec. I can only imagine how their conversation is going. Jonesy is a decent guy. A good bad guy, if you will. But his forte, aside from tending bar, is running interference—or stirring it up, if need be.

Several minutes pass before I hear rustling on the other line and then a heavy sigh. "What?"

"Alec," I say.

"Hello, Jack ..."

Goddamn his greetings.

Alec huffs. "If you're looking for a drunk sibling of yours, I'm fresh out."

"I'm actually looking for my father," I say.

"Tommy?" He scoffs. "Haven't seen him in years."

"Cut the shit, Alec. I know you're buying some product from him."

Alec pauses. "What do you want, Jack?"

I inhale. "I thought you might want to make a deal with me instead of my old man."

"And what makes you think I'd want to make a deal with *you*?"

"Because unlike my father, I'm good for it," I say. "And because I know you hate my dad for stealing from you and would rather watch him go down in flames than turn a profit on some coke."

Alec pauses for a moment. "Okay, you have my attention. What do you propose?"

I quickly go over my plan with Alec and, after hashing out a few details, we come to an agreement.

"This better work, Jack..." Alec says, in that damn unresolved tone of his.

"It will," I snap darkly, and end our call before looking at Drew and Jenna. "Okay, the first thing we need to do is get the hell out of this place. Drew." I turn to my little brother. "Do you have a car?"

He shakes his head.

I exhale. "Okay. Pack up all your stuff as quickly as possible. Jenna, can Drew use your phone?" She nods. "Perfect. Drew, call Samson and have him come to New Orleans as fast as possible. We'll need a car three hours from now. I'll fill him in on all the details later."

Jenna pulls out her phone and Drew dials Samson's number before stepping out of the room when he answers. I hear Drew smile when he says, "Yes. Yes, I'm fine. I'm sorry, bro. I didn't mean to freak you out. No really. I'm okay. But hey, listen. Jack needs your help..."

I look at Jenna's big eyes and my heart stops for a split second. Why do I keep allowing her to be dragged into all this?

"Drew and I are going to drop you off at home and find a ride with someone else," I say to her. "Maybe Samson, if he gets here in time."

"What? No." She puts a hand on her hip. "You're not dropping me off at home so you can go off on some vague drug mission."

I blink, frustrated and terrified. "Why do you always argue with me?"

"Because you're always trying to keep me out of things."

"For your *safety*," I snap. "You can't come with me. It's too dangerous."

She shrugs. "If it's too dangerous for me then it's too dangerous for you."

I stare at her. "That's not even remotely logical."

"Yes, it is—"

"No, it's not, Jenna! These are *real* bad guys. Professional criminals and drug lords. I'm not going to let you tag along simply because your pride won't let you stay at home."

"Uh...Jack?" Drew steps back into the room and holds up his phone with a frown. "She might have to."

"What?" I say. "Why?"

Drew bites his lip. "Because Samson might not be here in time. He says he's going to hurry, but he's not sure if he'll make it before everything goes down."

I bite back a string of curse words and curl my hands into fists.

"I guess I'm *tagging along* after all," Jenna quips.

I look at her and my heart hurts. Physically aches. This—this crazy overwhelming sensation I have every time I look at her is exactly why I don't want her to come along. But I also can't stay here, by her side, and risk missing an opportunity to clear Drew's name.

"Fine," I bark. "But you have to do exactly what I say."

She lifts a smug eyebrow and I want to growl.

Doesn't she know I'm only trying to protect her? Doesn't she understand that if anything were to happen to her I would never—ever—recover?

"This isn't about me trying to control you," I say.

She looks annoyed. "Right."

"Jenna." I say her name quietly and her whole demeanor changes. "This is me caring about you. Protecting you. Worrying about you."

She meets my eyes and seems to understand the importance of what I'm saying.

"I know." She nods. She swallows. "I really do."

I start to reach for her, then drop my hand. Now's not the time to get into it with her.

I turn to Drew and say, "I'm going to need your contact with the Northmen."

Drew's eyes grow wide. "Garrett? No way." He starts shaking his head. "That guy doesn't mess around. And if he finds out where I am—"

"He won't."

"He'll kill me!"

"He *won't*," I say sternly. "You have to trust me, Drew. I know what I'm doing."

He looks at me like I'm crazy, and maybe I am, but he hands me the number for Garrett anyway.

I call and explain to Garrett that Drew is innocent and my father is the real culprit, and ask the bounty on Drew to be recalled. Of course Garrett is skeptical, but when I let him in on my plan with Alec—and remind him that the Northmen have nothing to lose by trusting me—he eventually agrees to it and promises to spare Drew from the Northmen.

Next, I call Clancy and have a similar conversation. He also agrees to call off the price on Drew's head—as long as my plan works—and save Drew from the Royals.

It's a tricky business, negotiating with scoundrels, but it's a business I have a talent for.

When my phone calls are complete, I turn back to Drew and Jenna with a deep breath, my palms sweaty and my heart pounding. "Okay, the plan is in motion."

My stomach drops to the floor for a moment. People might get hurt. Things could turn sour. My plan is risky.

But then I remember what's at stake—Drew's life—and I pick my guts up and stuff them back inside.

This is life and death. This is love.

I look at Jenna first, then Drew, and take a deep breath. "Here goes nothing."

23

JENNA

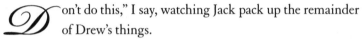on't do this," I say, watching Jack pack up the remainder of Drew's things.

Drew's outside on the phone with their mom, assuring Lilly that he's safe, so Jack and I are alone for the first time since Jack went all Mobster Boss and started making shady phone calls and deals with the devil.

"Don't do what?" he says, not looking at me.

I bite my lip. "Don't use yourself as bait. Just...don't."

Had I known what his full plan was, I certainly wouldn't have pushed so hard to stay. But he let me in on his scheme a few minutes ago and my pulse has been racing ever since. Not because I don't want to come along—I do, and there's nothing Jack can do to change my mind—but I don't want Jack to go through with it at all.

He stares at me for a long moment. "Why?"

I open my mouth. Close it. "What do you mean?"

He scratches the back of his neck. "Why don't you want me to do this?"

"Because it's dangerous."

He waits. "And?"

"And there are no guarantees." I know that's not the answer he wants, but it's just as valid.

"And?" He arches an eyebrow.

"And—and—and it could backfire and Drew could die." I'm desperate now. Reaching for answers that don't involve me caring about him. *Loving* him.

He deserves to hear the truth, but my mouth is a coward, and my heart is even worse. So I stay in silence and watch the hopefulness in his eyes drain away.

Stepping up to me, he slides his hands over my shoulders and down my back and around my waist. Not really going anywhere, just caressing me all over with slow, liquid movements. He bows his head and warms my neck with his hot breath as he places a single kiss against my pulse.

Pulling back just far enough to see my face, a pained expression pulls his features together and he quietly says, "What you're feeling right now? That fear, that driving sense of urgency and protectiveness? That's love, Jenna." I look down and he tilts my chin back up to see into my eyes. "You know how I know?" He scans my face. "Because that's exactly how I feel about Drew. Fear. Urgency. Protectiveness." A small smile tugs up his lips and he kisses the tip of my nose. "So I'm going to do this—this dangerous thing—because I love my little brother. And I don't expect you to understand or approve. Hell, I'm glad you don't. But I do expect you to admit to yourself that what you feel right now, in here"—he touches a finger to my chest—"is very, very real."

Then he presses his lips to mine in a kiss so soft and gentle I'm not sure it's even there. Like a whisper against my mouth, his lips softly touch mine before walking away. Headed to danger. To possible death.

Because of love.

24

JACK

Shortly after the sun sets, I sit in Jenna's car with her and Drew outside an abandoned industrial complex. Handoffs don't always go down the way you see in the movies, but they do always occur in shady-ass places such as this.

The surrounding buildings are old and vandalized. Cracked mortar and peeling paint mar every wall and door, and scattered bits of trash litter the concrete of the parking lot.

The three of us sit in anxious silence. Drew keeps checking over his shoulder, while Jenna keeps fidgeting and biting her lip.

I've assured her that everything will be fine but she's still antsy. Drew's just as worried, but his worries stem from fear that someone will find him and turn him in to either the Royals or the Northmen. I've assured him that won't happen either.

All the key players are in place and everyone crucial to the evening's events has been clued in. If everything goes according to plan, all of my assurances will be justified.

A dark car rolls up to a nearby deserted warehouse and kills its headlights. A lone figure emerges from the driver's door carrying a duffle bag most likely filled with cocaine.

My father.

Tommy Oliver is dressed in a suit and tie like he's some legit businessman, and I have to refrain myself from sneering at the sight. He can't see our car from where we're parked, so he stands beside his, waiting.

His posture is confident. His expression sure. The ease with which he stands and breathes makes me sick to my stomach. He practically signed Drew's death certificate, yet here he is, unfazed. Eager to go about his selfish business without remorse.

I'm ashamed to call him blood. And worse, looking at him is like looking at an older version of who I would have been, had I not bowed out of the drug game. The smugness, the ratlike desperation, the constant underbelly dealings. I was almost everything he is. Everything I hate.

My stomach churns even more and I scrub a hand down my face.

I look back at Drew. "Remember, make the call when I give you the signal." Then I look at Jenna. "Don't worry. Everything's going to be fine."

She shakes her head. "Jack—"

I lean in and kiss her, pulling her face into my hands as I press my mouth against hers and coax her lips open with mine until my tongue can slide against hers. She quietly whimpers, shoving her hands in my hair and pulling me closer, like she can't get enough of me. I break the kiss, but keep her face in my hands as I look into her eyes.

She's been a rock through all of this. Steady. Non-flinching. It's crazy that I had to go all the way across the country to meet the girl of my dreams, when my entire life that girl lived just a few hours away.

"I love you, Jenna," I confess without hesitation or debate. I don't care that Drew's here or that we're at a drug meet. I need her to know, without a doubt, that I love her.

Her mouth falls open in shock, but I get out of the car before she can respond. She's not ready to say she loves me yet—I know that—but one of us needed to say it out loud.

Closing the car door, I walk around the corner and approach my dad casually. His dark hair is cut short and graying at the temples, but it's still thick and wavy. His eyes are an unsettling shade of gray. My mother used to say they were captivating. I always found them icy and unfriendly, but then again, my encounters with that particular set of gray eyes have been more negative than not. He's shorter than me, by just an inch or two, but far slimmer.

His build is the only thing that we don't have in common, as far as looks go. Everything else—his eyes, his hair, his smile...there's no denying I'm his son. I used to be proud of that fact.

I'm not anymore.

When he sees me, a deep wrinkle creases his brow.

"Jack?" he says, looking shocked, nervous, and angry. "What are you doing here? Alec called and said *he* was meeting me here."

"To buy your coke?" I nod. "I know. He sent me instead. I'm working for him again," I say, trying my best to act pleasant.

He looks me over. "Alec didn't mention that."

I scoff. "Of course he didn't. The guy hates you, remember? But that doesn't really matter anymore, because I'm sick of working for him, anyway." I pause, letting my words sink in, then add, "I want to make a deal. With you."

He eyes me suspiciously "What kind of deal?"

"The kind where you and I screw Alec over and work together," I bluff, knowing full well that my father's greatest wish was that he and I would work hand in hand. Even after I screwed him over, he begged and pleaded with me to bail with him and start our own business. He said he understood why I did what I did—why I betrayed him—and he would forgive me if I followed him to a new life of crime.

He cocks his head, a grin pulling up the sides of his mouth. "I like the sound of that."

I smile. "Drew told me you were back in the game and let me know what happened—"

"Now that was a misunderstanding," he quickly says, holding up a hand. "I was just trying to protect your brother."

"I don't care. All I want is the money." I lift my brows. "Did you really get away with it? Because I'm not giving up my gig with Alec unless I know you can support the start-up of you and I working together."

"Of course." He scoffs and nods at his car. "It's in the trunk right now. I'm headed out of state after this." He studies me. "You finally ready to uproot?"

I nod proudly. "Absolutely," I lie, then nod at a large work truck pulling up to the industrial park. Right on time. "But first I have a few associates I'd like you to meet."

The truck comes to a slow stop and Garrett, Drew's Northmen contact, exits the vehicle. I've only met Garrett one other time, under friendlier circumstances, and even then I thought he was scary as hell. He's tall and bald, with muscles that look out of place on his narrow frame, and eyes so dark they look like black holes. He's known for torturing his enemies by plucking out their fingernails—a fate I wouldn't wish on anyone, even my father. Hopefully, tonight's transaction won't come to that.

Garrett walks around the corner to meet us along with five Northmen guys. All armed and ready to shoot.

My dad's face falls in horror. "Jack. What is this?"

I step back so Garrett and his men can close in on him and say,

"This is me clearing Drew's name since, thanks to you, there's currently a price on his head."

"Hello, Tommy," Garrett says, an evil smile curling up his lips. "It seems you have something that belongs to me."

My father takes a step back and visibly begins to shake. "I—what? No. No—I—there's been a misunderstanding."

As Garrett's men grab my father, I give Drew the signal to call the cops.

Garrett holds a gun under my dad's chin and reaches for the duffle bag. "I'll be taking this back."

He tosses the duffle bag to another one of his goons, who quickly verifies its contents. Bricks of cocaine fill the bag and the goon nods in affirmation.

I head to my dad's car and pop the trunk. Inside, just like he said, is the money. Grabbing it, I nod to Garrett and he quickly has his guys tie my dad to the nearest parking-lot lamppost.

"You know, Tommy," Garrett says, jabbing the gun roughly against my dad's jawbone as the goons secure his bindings, "I would enjoy killing you. Slowly. And painfully." He lowers his voice. "You deserve that much."

Tommy whimpers. "P—please, don't."

Garrett growls and lowers his gun. "I won't. But only because your son requested I not kill you. It seems he has a different plan for you."

"Time to get moving, Garrett," I say.

He nods at me. "Good doing business with you, Jack. Best of luck with that one." He gestures at my father before loading his guys back into their truck.

I look at Tommy Oliver in disgust. "You're pathetic."

"Jack, don't do this—whatever you're planning to do with me," he begs. "I can make things right."

I stare at him. "You almost had Drew killed." I shake my head. "There's no making that right."

Garrett and his Northmen pull away from the parking lot and drive off with their reclaimed drugs as I run back to Jenna's car and hop inside.

"Are we good?" Drew asks nervously. "Did that go well?"

"Is everyone in the clear?" Jenna adds, as I start the car and drive us to a darker spot where we can park and be completely hidden in shadows.

"Almost." I stare out the windshield, where I still have a view of my father tied to the lamppost. "Did you tip off the cops?" I ask Drew.

"Yep. I told them that a known felon would be unarmed and waiting for them at this address right about..." He looks at the time. "Now."

Police vehicles suddenly pour into the area and officers jump from their patrol cars and surround my father. With numerous warrants out in his name, they arrest Tommy Oliver and drag him into the back of one of the patrol cars and peel away from the scene, their sirens blaring.

"So what now?" Drew asks.

I exhale. "Alec agreed to let me meet Dad in place of him, as long Dad got arrested, which we did. So our business with Alec and the Vipers is finished. The only person left to deal with now is Clancy." I start the car. "Just one more stop, then we're done."

We drive to the French Quarter and I park us outside of Crowns. While Jenna and Drew wait in the car, I slip inside the bar with the briefcase of money from my dad's trunk and find Clancy. Throwing the briefcase down in front of him I say, "Here it is. Every last penny."

He laughs as he counts it and shakes his head. "You sure know how to close a deal, Jack. I'll give you that."

"Are we good then?" I say, crossing my arms.

"Oh, we're good." Clancy nods with a grin. "We're all good."

I nod once then hurry back outside and into the car. Once inside, I turn in my seat to look at Drew and smile. "You're free and clear, bro."

"Really?" Drew's eyes light up.

I nod. "The Northmen got their drugs back and Clancy got his money back, so there's no longer a price on your head." I lower my voice. "But promise me, Drew—promise me—that you will never get involved with any of this shit again."

He swallows and nods. "I promise."

"Good." I nod. "But hey."

He looks up at me.

"You did good tonight, Drew," I say. "This couldn't have happened without your help."

He presses his lips together and nods once. "Want me to call Samson? He's probably still on the road, but I can tell him to meet us in the French Quarter if you want."

"Yeah," I say. "Good idea."

Drew slouches back in his seat and makes the call.

I stare out the windshield at the parking lot of Crowns, thinking about the evening's events, specifically my father being hauled away by the police, and a great weight lifts from my shoulders. Jenna must sense this because she squeezes my hand.

"You did good too, Jack," she says.

I turn to her and smile sadly. "I just facilitated a drug deal and had my father arrested. Good is relative."

She lifts my hand in hers. "You saved your brother's life," she says, kissing the inside of my palm. "You did good."

We stare at each other in the dark car, our gazes locked and filled with emotion.

"Sam's on his way," Drew says, and Jenna releases my hand.

We drive through the French Quarter and I park beside a familiar green car on one of the neighborhood streets. Two figures clamber out of the green car: my mom and Samson. They rush over as the three of us get out of Jenna's car and my mother throws her arms around Drew.

"Oh, baby! I was so scared," she says. "I'm so glad you're safe."

Drew sighs into her hair. "I'm so sorry, Mom. I totally messed up. I'm so sor—"

"Shh. I don't care. You're safe. That's all that matters." She hugs him again and a tear falls down her cheek.

Samson hugs him next, pounding him on the back with a fist. "You scared the shit out of me, man." Pulling back, he claps him on the shoulder. "I love you, Drew. But don't ever do that again. Or I'll kill you myself."

Drew grins. "It's good to see you too, asshole."

Samson smiles, relief rolling off of him in waves. "Thanks, Jack."

"Yeah," Drew says. "Thank you."

I frown at them. "For what?"

"Uh...for everything?" Drew says.

I shake my head. "No, don't thank me. If I hadn't bowed out of your lives, none of this would have happened."

"No, dude. You needed to leave, for your own good," Samson says.

"But I didn't need to check out completely, the way I did." I inhale slowly. "I'm going to be better about it, from now on. I'm going to come out here more often. Be a part of your lives like a real family member."

Mom kisses my cheek. "No arguments here. I love you so much, baby. I'm so happy you're safe." She looks at each of us with a scolding gaze. "Now can we all agree that none of you will ever, *ever* get involved in this nonsense again?"

We all nod.

"What's that?" She puts a hand to her ear sternly.

"Yes, ma'am," we say almost in unison.

Mom turns to me. "Is it over, then?"

"Yeah," I say. "It's over."

After arranging for Drew to go back home with Mom and Samson, and saying good-bye to each of them on the street, I turn back around and look at Jenna.

"Let's go home," I say.

25

JENNA

*A*nd here I packed all my best black dresses, thinking I'd be attending some kind of Voodoo funeral," I say with a mock frown as I stare at my overstuffed purple suitcase and cluck my tongue.

Grandma chuckles from her seat in the living room's rocking chair. "I'm sorry to disappoint you, dear. I'll try harder to die next time."

I scoff. "I'll believe that when I see it."

I sit on my suitcase and try to zip it shut, without success. I dragged it out to the living room in the hopes that having more space would increase my chances of sealing the damn thing up more efficiently.

How is it that suitcases are always harder to close at the end of your trip than they are at the beginning? It's not like I bought a bunch of crap and tried to squeeze more stuff inside. The exact same amount of clothes are in this piece of luggage as when I left Arizona. So what the hell?

"So where's your gentleman caller at the moment?" Grandma asks, with the subtlety of a morning rooster.

"'Gentleman caller.' 'Traveling companion.' Are you and Mom

watching only black-and-white movies again? We need to update your vocabulary. Better yet, I'll introduce you to the Urban Dictionary and blow your mind. You can thank me later."

Her eyes smile. "Interesting how you changed the subject so quickly when I asked about your beau."

"He's changing the oil in Mom's car. And he's not my beau, Grams. He's my...friend." I plop down on the purple luggage again. Still the zipper does not cooperate.

She *tsks* and shakes her head. "And you think I'm the liar."

I whip my eyes to her. "What's that supposed to mean?"

"You're clearly in love with the boy," she says. "And yet you deny having feelings for him."

I roll my eyes. "Please don't start—"

"Love is the most important thing in life," she says, nodding. "Why would you deny it?"

"Uh, because it's the twenty-first century and women don't need men to take care of them anymore. Oh and also, I have goals that I plan on accomplishing before I die. I don't want anything to stall my dreams."

"Stall yours dreams? Jenna. Listen to yourself."

I inhale slowly, trying to compose my frustration. "Don't take this the wrong way, Grams, but I want more than what you and Mom ever had. And I have a plan to make that happen. Love is a nice thought." I think about being in Jack's arms. Watching him drink tea with my sisters. The way he protects his family and sacrifices for them. "A very nice thought." My voice cracks and I clear my throat. "But it's completely unpredictable and reckless. Bottom line? I can't control love. And I made a promise to myself a long time ago that I would control everything about my future." I shrug.

I swallow. I give up on the suitcase and stand upright. "So love just isn't in the cards for me."

She eyes me knowingly. "Ah, but it's in your stars."

"Grams—"

"I've seen it, Jenna. A great love. A true love. A love that needs you just as much as you need him." She stands up, her aging eyes sharp and serious, as she walks up to me. "You won't be settled until you understand something, my little star." She watches me closely. "Love is the absence of control and the presence of faith. And you won't truly be happy until you surrender to it."

An uncanny chill tickles my arms and cheeks as I let her words float between us. This is the part of my grandmother that no one dares to question. The part that deals out advice with love, and warnings with conviction.

The hard edge of her words dissipates as she tips her mouth into a crooked smile and shrugs. "And I can't die until you're happy."

I snort. "Well I guess I'll never allow myself to be truly happy then, because I don't want you to die." I raise my chin. "Not ever."

"But wouldn't it be a shame if I died anyway?" She grins. "And I never got to see you happy?"

I narrow my eyes. "Well played, Grams. Well played."

She shrugs again and returns to her rocker. "I try."

———

Saying good-bye to my mom and sisters was harder than ever before. I'm not sure why. Maybe because of how life-and-death this trip was for Jack's family members. Or maybe because, for the first time in years, I really appreciated just how lucky I am to have a family. To have so much love.

Either way, it was rough to say farewell. I kissed my sisters more than necessary. I clung to my mother when she went to hug me, and babbled in her ear about how great a job she did raising me. We didn't have much and, sure, I'm shooting for a life far different than hers. But she gave me everything she had, and that sacrifice isn't something I take lightly.

But now it's time to say good-bye to Grandma and I'm just falling apart. Not in tears, but in heartbreak.

"I love you so much," I say as I wrap my arms around my grandmother's small frame. "I really do. And I'm going to miss you more than you know."

She chuckles softly. "I bet I'll miss you more."

I sniff. "Why do you always have to one-up me?"

She laughs again and pulls back to look me in the eyes. "Be brave, my little star." She holds my face in her hands. "Be brave. It's worth it. I swear."

I blink, not exactly sure what she means, but nod anyway. "I will."

Jack endures a few rounds of hugs and kisses from all the many females in the house and, before I know it, we're on the road and headed home.

Jack takes the keys and drives and I don't argue. When we pull onto the freeway, he turns on the radio and hands me a tissue. Only then do I realize I'm crying.

"Since I want to be more involved with my brothers, I told my mom I'd come visit her this winter," Jack says. "So I was thinking, maybe you could come with me. We could road-trip it again and visit both our families. What do you think?"

My sad heart immediately bursts with hope and joy. "Seriously?"

He nods. "I figure, we'd both save some money that way. I know my mom would love to see you again and since your grandma will probably be gearing up for another near-death experience—"

I reach over the center console and throw my arms around him, squeezing him so tight I hear him suck in a breath.

"Yes," I mumble into his shirt.

He quietly laughs. "Okay."

I release him and pull back, composing myself as much as possible after something as embarrassing as side-hugging someone while they're driving down a massive freeway.

But wow. Just the idea that I'll be coming back soon unbreaks my heart. And Jack knew, damn him. He knew that's what I needed to hear.

God. These past few days have been a total whirlwind. And last night was the craziest of all.

Jack had his own father arrested and Drew was able to come out of hiding. But the craziest thing of all was Jack saying he loved me.

We haven't talked about it, so there's a slight tension in the air—a tension that seems to grow with every mile that passes. By the time we're halfway through Texas, it's downright awkward in the car.

Jack eventually breaks the silence. "Are you okay?"

I look at him. "I'm okay. Are you okay?"

He nods. "I'm okay. You just seem a little...weird, that's all."

I shrug and lie. "It's hard to leave home."

He nods once. "Right."

Suddenly feeling defensive, I say, "You seem a little weird too, you know."

He raises his brow. "Do I?"

"Yep."

"Well, you know." He flexes his jaw and looks at me pointedly. *"It's hard to leave home."*

I cock an eyebrow. "Do you have something you want to say, Jack?"

"Yes, as a matter of fact I do," he says. "Is there a reason you haven't said anything about me saying I love you?"

I clear my throat, not expecting him to just blurt that out like that. "Uh...well, I don't know. But maybe it's better if we don't talk about it. I mean, I'm not girlfriend material, Jack," I say, then start listing off some of my more obnoxious qualities. "I never check my voice mails. I leave cabinets open in the kitchen. I'm messy. Like inexcusably messy. And I hate motorcycles. *Hate* them." I shrug dramatically. "I don't even know why the hell you want to be with me."

I instantly feel like a bitch. Why do I always do this? Make things difficult?

He scoffs and sits in silence for a moment, his eyes hard and sharp as he processes my words, but then his expression softens and he clears his throat.

"I want to be with you," he says. "Because I hurt when you hurt. And I'm happy when you're happy—and not because you have control over me, but because I love you. And I *like* loving you."

I take a shaky breath, suddenly on the verge of tears. "But you want me to be your girlfriend, or something."

"Yeah, so?"

"So...what if that's a mistake?"

"Why would we be a mistake—why would *I* be a mistake?" he says bitterly. "Because I don't fit into your *plan*?"

"It's not about you fitting into my plan."

"Yes, it is. You and your fucking 'plan' are what this *whole thing* is about," he says. "And that hurts, Jenn! Do you honestly think I'd ever keep you from your dreams? Of course not! I would support you forever. Follow you anywhere. I would never stand in the way of your goals. If anything, I'd rearrange my dreams to make yours come true."

"But that's the problem!" I shout. "I don't want you to give up on your dreams for me! I want us both to get exactly what we want."

"I didn't say 'give up,' I said 'rearrange.'"

I scoff. "Like there's a difference."

"There's a *huge* difference!" he says. "And dreams mean nothing to me if I don't have you."

I blink, stunned by that confession.

"Yeah," he says sharply. "That's how serious I am about us. That's how important making *this*"—he gestures back and forth between us—"is to me."

I swallow, upset and confused and afraid and desperate. "Well excuse me for caring about the future—"

"The future." He rolls his eyes. "Fine. Then what about caring about right now? Or do you not give a damn about you and me right now?"

"You and me just aren't the right plan," I snap, trying to shut him down. Trying to keep away the powerful emotions taking over inside me.

He laughs darkly. "And tell me about this 'right' plan of yours. Tell me how you've got the future all figured out and how perfect your life is going to be as long as you stay away from me. Because it sounds pretty ridiculous to me," he snaps.

My jaw clenches. "Finish school. Get a kick-ass job. Live by myself in a rock star apartment and open my own art gallery. And maybe get a pet pig. *That* is the right plan." I shout. "You...you and your big heart and caring about me...that's the WRONG plan. *You* are the wrong plan!" I cry.

The pain in his eyes is palpable and I immediately regret my words. But it's too late. I've already crushed him and he whips his beautiful gray eyes away from me and stares out the window.

"Good to know," he says in a low voice. Defeated. Hurt.

It takes all the willpower I have not to scream or beg or cry. God, this man has me all screwed up! This is why I can't get involved with him. If he can have this kind of power over me when we're not even together, I can't imagine how helpless I would be if we were a *thing*.

We stop at a motel in San Antonio for the night and get two separate rooms. In silence. We unload our luggage from the trunk of the car. In silence. Then we go to our separate rooms and shut ourselves away from each other. In silence.

I throw my luggage in the corner with a curse and fall onto the bed with my heart flip-flopping in my chest. I'm so undone, so broken, when it comes to love. Why can't I just be normal?

No. This isn't *my* fault.

Jack's the one who keeps pushing.

Yeah. This is all Jack's doing.

I'm just trying to do what's best for me—for us.

I stare at the wall, where Jack's room is on the other side, and let out a long, sad sigh. I wish there was a broken door between us again. Swinging and screeching and making things uncomfortable. I wish I could stare across the space between us and see him. Make sure he's okay.

Ugh. I'm a basket case.

Rolling over, I turn my back to the wall and wrestle with my screaming heart.

In silence.

———

The next day, we drive without speaking more than necessary. We stop for lunch and exchange words about the weather and which hotels are the best to stay at, but it's obvious our friendship is strained. And honestly, it feels like we've broken up. My heart hurts. His jaw is in a constant state of being locked and flexed. And nothing between us feels right.

As we cross the border from Texas into New Mexico, I try my hardest not to care about Jack. Hot sex is fine. But a relationship? Love? No. I don't want that...do I?

Regardless of all the current unease between us, Jack makes me happy. Truly happy. Happy in a way no one else ever has. Would accepting that I love him—telling him that I love him—make me just as happy? I think about my grandma's words to me when I said good-bye and my heart squeezes.

Wouldn't it be a shame if I died anyway? And I never got to see you happy?

She shamelessly threw that classic Lacombe family guilt in my face. The nerve. I promised her I'd be brave before I left. But for some reason, every mile that passes where Jack and I don't talk, I feel like I'm letting her down.

Looking over at Jack, I think about how hard it's been for him to keep his family safe and away from trouble his whole life. Maybe when he's asking me to give him a chance, he's not asking for me to give up any part of myself, but to accept him for who he is. Maybe it's not about me and my fears at all.

But fears are funny that way. They live and creep around inside you despite any logic that might say otherwise. And I can't help but fear that getting too close to Jack might change my entire future—and that's a fear I'm not ready to face.

Right?

26

JACK

*W*ould you just pull over already?" I plead, clenching my jaw as I look at her across the dark car.

Determined to get home as soon as possible, Jenna tried to drive all the way through from San Antonio, without stopping in Las Cruces for rest. Now we're both exhausted, it's nearly midnight, and we're still two hundred miles from Tempe.

"I think we can make it," she says, yawning.

"No way. You're going to fall asleep and get us killed. Just pull over."

"Why? So you can drive?" She frowns. "You've had less sleep than me."

She's right. I didn't sleep well last night and I didn't take two catnaps today like she did.

"Yeah, but at least my vision works at nighttime." I look out at the road signs and mutter, "We aren't going to make it. We have to stop for the night."

She looks around. "Where are we going to stop? The only hotel place between here and home is…" She thinks for a second. "Willow Inn."

I sit up. "The place where Pixie works?"

She nods. "But I don't think Ellen would want us rolling up in the middle of the night—"

"We're doing it. I bet Ellen would rather have you alive and bothering her in the middle of the night than dead on the side of the road."

She sighs and concedes. "Fine."

Twenty minutes later, we're pulling off the freeway and back into the parking lot of the quaint little inn. The porch lights are still on.

"See?" I say, nodding at the light. "She's probably still awake."

"If she's even here," Jenna mutters.

Getting out of the car, we trudge up to the front door and carefully open it. Dim lights shine in the lobby to where Ellen is behind the front desk with a pair of glasses on, typing furiously. She looks up when she hears the door and lifts a brow.

"Jenna?" Her expression turns panicked. "Is everything okay?"

"Yes. Everything is fine. We've just been on the road all day and we're exhausted, and this guy here didn't want me to drive any farther so he asked me to pull in here but I told him you were probably booked so I'm really sorry to bother you but—"

"Of course." She smiles. "You guys should stay here for the night. In fact, I have a free room. Let me just make sure no one is checking into it first thing in the morning." She goes back to typing.

"We're very sorry to bother you so late," I say quietly, standing behind Jenna.

Ellen waves me off. "You're not bothering me at all. I was just doing some inventory stuff so you've actually given me a nice little break." She squints at the screen. "Okay. Looks like room four is open tomorrow too. Are you guys okay sharing?" She looks at Jenna knowingly and my heart stops for a brief moment.

I wait to let Jenna answer, fully expecting her to make me sleep in the car or something, but instead Jenna says, "Yeah, that's fine." I turn to look at her.

She holds my gaze for a beat. I'm not sure if what I see in her golden eyes is acceptance or weariness, but either way she's okay sleeping by me and I can't help but take that as a victory.

Ellen gives Jenna the room key and directs her where to go and we head upstairs. I follow after Jenna, carrying most of our luggage, and watch her hips sway with each step. God, she's sexy. My eyes trail up to her shoulders and then her profile as we reach the top of the stairs and she turns. She's beautiful too. Her long eyelashes, her full lips, her elegant throat…her fighting spirit, her strength, her silent acceptance of my ugly past and my crazy family. She's everything I've ever wanted.

And she won't let me love her.

The ache in my chest grows uncomfortably tight as we enter the small room down the hall and shut ourselves inside. There's a king-size bed in the center of the room and a full bathroom off to the side. The only light in the room comes from the single lamp on one of the nightstands that flank the bed, and it gives off a soft glow so everything looks calm and hazy.

Setting our bags down, we walk farther into the room and I say, "Are you sure you're okay with us sharing a bed?"

She nods. "I'm sure. Are *you* okay with it?"

I start to nod, but then realize that would be a lie. "No, actually," I say. "I'm not."

Her eyebrows hitch up. "What?"

I shake my head. "I get that you don't want to be with me and

I respect that. But I can't keep acting like we're just friends. That's bullshit. I love you, Jenna—I *love* you," I repeat when she starts to look away. Stepping closer to her, I tip her chin up so her eyes lift back to mine. "And I know that scares the shit out of you. But I can't change the way I feel, and I wouldn't want to anyway. You're the best thing that ever happened to me. So I'd rather sleep on the floor or in the car than in that bed." I point to the bed beside us and swallow. "Because I don't want to sleep in a bed with you unless you *want* me there. To hold you. Be with you."

Her eyes search mine in the soft bedroom glow as she slowly lifts up on her toes and places her hands on my chest. Leaning in, she presses her lips to mine, kissing me, softly at first then more aggressively as I kiss her back. At first, I'm thrilled, thinking maybe Jenna has changed her mind and wants to let me in.

But as she pulls off my clothes and bites at my mouth and claws at my back with urgency, I realize she's using sex as a distraction. She's so terrified of what I just said—so scared to respond—that she'd rather surrender her body to me than admit that she might feel something too.

The sadness that floods into me at this thought is dark and cold, sinking through me like a weight in water. I've been so patient, so understanding all this time and she can't even give me a damn sentence?

Stripping her clothes off, she walks our naked bodies back to the bed and tries to push me to the mattress. I don't budge, waiting until she looks up at me before staring down at her with my dark heartache pouring from my eyes. She looks startled for a moment, not expecting to see such anger after she'd just kissed her way up and down my body and peeled off all my clothes, but I don't relent. She quickly turns her eyes away, which only adds to my hurt.

Grabbing her chin, I turn her face back to mine so she has no choice but to see my pain. She blinks several times, as if trying not to cry, and it's too much for me to handle.

Sliding my hands down her body, I grasp her hips and turn us around so I can push her onto the bed. Her eyes flash with excitement, grateful that I'm giving in to what she wants: sex instead of truth. My anger spikes for a moment only to plummet back into sadness at the eagerness on her face.

I roughly flip her over and she gasps. Then I run my hands down her body so she's lying flat on her stomach, her head turned to the side and her dark hair fanning out on the pillow. Her breathing is uneven, unsure, as she eyes me from the pillow. Gliding my hands up the sides of her rib cage, I brush her arms out from where they're tucked against her body and slide them up to the pillow. Then I gather her long hair and twist it up before laying it to the side of her head so the back of her neck is exposed. She lets me do these things without a sound. She simply watches me from the corner of her eye and waits with nervous breaths.

My eyes slip over the naked backside of her body, now laid out before me, and follow the curve of her ass and the dip of her spine. The soft skin of her thighs and the swell of her breasts, smashed beneath her and spilling out on the sides. I grow thick and hard as I look her over.

Jenna wanted just sex. Emotionless, simple, impersonal sex. And that's what she'll get.

Crawling up her body, I bring my mouth to the base of her head and breathe on the tiny hairs that stand on end there. She squirms beneath me. I set my mouth against the back of her neck and gently sink my teeth into her skin. Her squirming continues as I lightly nip at her neck then run my teeth to her ear before scraping them down her jaw. She twists her head to meet my mouth with a kiss but I pull away from her and refuse her lips. A small cry escapes her throat as I bite into her shoulder, hard enough to pinch her skin but not hard enough to leave a mark, and her head snaps back. She tries raise up on her arms to arch herself away from me, but I trap her arms above her head and pin them there as I bite her other shoulder, more gently this time.

She buries her head in the pillow and moans as I lick the spots that I just bit then kiss a trail between her shoulder blades. Sliding my hands down her arms, I tangle one hand into her hair while the other travels down over her round ass and between her thighs, where she's already hot and wet.

She jerks as I tap my fingers against her wetness and I tug at her hair so she has to bring her face out of the pillow. Turning her head to the side, facing away from me, she pants as I touch the wet place between her legs.

I whisper, "This is what you wanted, right?" as I tease her tight, wet entrance with my finger. "For me to take control of your body?"

She begins to squirm again, trying to coax my finger inside her by angling her hips just right, and pants, "Yes."

I push my big finger into her wanting core and she lets out a blissful whimper. I slowly pull my finger from the grip of her inner muscles and roll her wetness over the sensitive nub of her clit again and again as she squirms and jerks and gasps beneath me. I don't stop sliding over that special spot until her fingers dig into the sheets. Then I start to pluck at her tiny clit and she cries out.

The sound of her pleasure makes my cock grow painfully hard. Her hips jerk back and forth with her orgasm, causing her backside to jiggle with the movement and my body to scream for release.

I push two fingers back into her core, where she pulses around me, and another satisfying whimper leaves her mouth. My need for release claws at my every muscle.

"Total control?" I whisper, sucking on her earlobe.

She nods desperately, a gasp leaving her mouth as I withdraw my fingers from her tightness.

Pulling back, I yank her up onto her knees and elbows so her beautiful ass is bent over before me. Her inner thighs glisten with her arousal, driving me wild as I scramble to pull a condom from my discarded jeans and roll it on.

Without my hands on her, Jenna arches her back, presenting herself to me more fully and my pulse hammers. Positioning myself behind her, I grab her hips again and she looks over her shoulder at me. Considering that, by her own admission, she's never had sex in this position, I expect to see nervousness or hesitation in her eyes, but instead there is only lust and desire. I slide my hard erection into the warm, tight grip of her core and let out a groan as her flesh wraps around me like a tight fist.

Jenna moans loudly, an animalistic sound, as I fill her completely and it's all I can do not to moan as well. As I pull out, she arches her back in wanting, crying out as I thrust back into her. Gripping her left hip, I slide my other hand up her back and around to her right breast, cupping it in my hand as I pump in and out of her hot body. Running my thumb over her nipple, I glide my hand down her belly to the warmth below and slip a finger over and around her clit until she climaxes again. The tiny muscles of her core tighten and pulse, drawing pleasure from me as pressure builds from her orgasm.

Not yet wanting to finish, I slide out of her heavenly body. More arousal spills from her core and down her thighs and the sight makes me want to pound into her again and again until I'm fully satisfied. But then I see her face, eyes closed and tilted back in bliss, and I remember what my mission is here.

I turn Jenna over, so she's on her back, and gently spread her legs to accommodate my large body between them as I crawl on top of her and turn off the lamp on the nightstand.

The only light now is the moonlight from the window, making the room feel quieter, kinder, and Jenna's eyes snap open to see me on my elbows above her open body.

Still out of breath from her orgasm, she stares up at me with questions in her eyes. My only answer is to bend down and softly kiss her lips as I run a hand up her leg, where her knees are bent and her thighs are open for me. She kisses me back with breathless desire, liquid in my arms, pleased and willing, sated and safe.

I set my still-wanting erection at her entrance and gently push into her as I trace my fingers up her breasts and to her cheek. Cupping her face, I softly pump in and out of her as we kiss. She whimpers into my mouth as our bodies dance against one another until I feel something hot run down my hand.

Pulling back just barely, I see a tear escaping her closed eyelids and I brush it away with my thumb. This girl. So full of passion and fight that she can't contain her love for me. Not like this. Not when she feels my love in return. It kills her to fall apart with me, but she can't help it, and it's this single tear running over my thumb that is the truth.

She chose sex over truth, but truth won. Truth always wins.

"Jenna," I say quietly. "Do you want me to stop?"

She opens her eyes and another tear falls as she shakes her head. "No. Never."

I slowly continue moving in and out of her, kissing her cheeks and forehead and collarbone. "I love you."

She nods as more tears fall down her cheeks. "I know." She moans as I thrust into her again and she arches her back. Her tears dry up as another orgasm ripples through her and her thighs begin to tremble.

Hammering in and out of her tight body, I draw my own release as I climax inside her hot, wet core and we're swept away in a whirlwind of blinding pleasure. When my heart begins to pound less violently, I lean down and roll Jenna into my arms as we lie beside each other.

She sniffs and wipes her cheek. "I'm sorry I'm so weak."

My heart clenches at her words.

"Jenna," I quietly say, "love isn't a weakness. It's the strongest part of the heart. It's the part that tells you that being with someone else makes you better." I run a hand over her hip. "And whether you like it or not, you are in love with me, and I know it."

I hear a hitch in her breath, a hesitation, and I kiss her shoulder.

"You don't have to say it," I say, "because I feel it."

I take a slow breath, wishing I could wrap her heart in my hands and make her feel safe enough to trust me with it forever. We lie in silence for the rest of the night, but I'm almost certain another tear rolls down her cheek before we fall asleep.

27

JENNA

I wake up in Jack's arms feeling happier than I've ever felt before. Which terrifies me. My plan is falling apart.

I stare at Jack, sleeping peacefully beside me, and think about how much I ached for him—emotionally needed him—last night. I was desperate for him. And I wanted to surrender everything I was just to be with him.

And that's what I did. I surrendered.

Jack, who has quietly pulled me apart for the past year, silently keeping in my presence all these months until my head and heart were so filled with his essence that there was hardly any room left for me and my resolve, finally won.

And the crazy part? Giving in to him, giving up my control, felt liberating. Completely freeing.

Last night wasn't just sex with a guy I really like. It was connecting with a man who loves me and cares for me. It was... It was *making love*. And I *liked* it.

Ugh. This is *not* how things were supposed to go. I know what happens next. Jack and I start dating and then my heart is forever at his mercy.

But then again, isn't my heart at his mercy already? If last night proved anything, it was that my feelings for Jack aren't going away, despite my best efforts. If anything, they've grown stronger. I might have kept my mouth from professing my love for him, but I sure as hell haven't kept my heart from latching onto his.

I'm in so much trouble. I need air. Or a minute to think for myself away from Jack. Slipping out of his arms, I quietly pull on some clothes and creep downstairs.

The inn is already bustling with people having breakfast in the dining room. Kayla, the pretty blonde I ran into when we stopped here on our way out of Arizona, is apparently working here now as a waitress. I watch her laugh as she takes a couple's order before swinging into the kitchen. She looks a hundred times lighter than she did the last time I saw her. In fact she looks downright happy.

Her eyes catch on mine through the dining room doors and she smiles broadly. I give her a little wave and she says something to the couple at her table before exiting the dining room and hurrying through the lobby toward me.

"Good morning." Her smile is genuine and bright as she approaches.

Up close, it's hard to look at her without staring. She's just so pretty. Her blonde hair is perfect. Her sun-kissed skin is flawless. Her curvy body is beyond sexy.

I really want to hate the girl, but I can't. Because she's actually a really sweet person.

It's so annoying when pretty girls are sweet *and* kind. All nice hot girls should pluck at least one eye out, just to make it fair for the rest of us trying to rock our normalcy.

"Jenna?" she says, tilting her head in concern. "You okay?"

"What?" I stop gawking at her lovely golden hair and blink a few times. "Oh yeah. I'm fine."

I just got so caught up in your Barbie-like beauty that I forgot to speak. You know, like a creepy stalker.

A pair of tan, muscular forearms slips around Kayla's waist, and suddenly Daren Ackwood is nuzzling her neck.

Nuzzling. The guy is actually *nuzzling* her neck. Like he loves her or something.

Which doesn't exactly fall in line with my initial impression of Daren.

When I first met him, I thought he was a giant douche bag. A ridiculously hot douche bag—because holy hell, he's just as beautiful as Kayla—but a douche bag nonetheless. But Pixie claims that he's not really a bad guy, just a severely misunderstood one. And Kayla must feel the same way. She is, after all, letting the guy play with her hair and whisper in her ear.

"Daren, come on…Daren…" Kayla giggles in his arms as he tries to kiss her neck. "I'm trying to say hi to Jenna."

Her giggle remind me of Pixie's giggle and I find myself wondering what it would be like to be so happy I giggled.

Daren sees me watching them like an unwanted third wheel and immediately stops smooching Kayla's throat. "Oh. Sorry," he says, giving me a small smile as he nods. "Hey, Jenna."

I lift an eyebrow. "Hello, Random Kisser."

Earlier this year, he planted an unsolicited kiss on Pixie in front of Levi, just to make Levi jealous. I'm not really pissed at Daren for his brazen act, because it did, after all, get Levi to make a move on Pixie. But I still feel like it's my responsibility, as Pixie's dear friend, to hold him to it.

Kayla lifts her own eyebrow at Daren and he blushes—he actually blushes. "Yeah, not my proudest moment."

She nods. "Is this the stealing-a-kiss-from-Pixie thing?"

Daren sighs. "Yeah."

I just wanted to bust Daren's balls, but wow. He already told Kayla about the Pixie kiss? And he's all ooey-gooey in love with Kayla? So he's not a total douche bag anymore?

Well damn. I can't hate him now that he's a good guy.

Why must these two supermodel lovebirds make it so freaking impossible to hate them?

He turns to me. "But I apologized to Pixie. I swear. We're good. And you don't have to hate me anymore, Jenna, because I'm completely crazy about Kayla." He points to the stunning blonde beside him, who's now blushing worse than he was a moment ago, and smiles. "I don't want to kiss anyone else. Ever."

Kayla's lips part. "Aw…"

They exchange a heartfelt look and I'm suddenly a raging sea of sorrow and jealously.

What is happening to me?

"I just wanted to give you another good-morning kiss," Daren says, pressing his lips to her temple, "before I go to work for the day."

Looking him over, I realize he's dressed in a Willow Inn chef's coat. "You work here?"

He nods proudly. "Ellen just hired me to replace Pixie."

I nod. "Congratulations."

"Thanks." He smiles at Kayla. "I gotta go. Love you!" Turning to me he calls, "Nice seeing you, Jenna," before disappearing into the dining room.

Kayla turns back to me, her face positively glowing, and smiles. "Sorry about that."

"Never apologize for being happy." I smile sincerely, even though I'm still a little jealous of how content her love life seems.

She glances around, probably looking for luggage. "So are you staying at the inn?"

"Yeah. Well, no. I mean, Jack and I stopped in late last night, on our way back from Louisiana."

"Oh that's right! You guys were on a road trip. How was it?" She wiggles her eyebrows and I have to bite back a sigh.

She thinks we just went on a romantic getaway, bless her heart.

Bless her heart? WHAT? I don't say shit like "bless her heart." Kayla's prettiness must be getting to me. It's either that, or the fact that a pair of gunmetal-gray eyes is currently sound asleep upstairs. Alone.

Cold fingers of guilt wring my gut and I nearly choke on my heart, which is somehow lodged in my throat, as I try to answer. "It was good. Fine. It was fine."

She scans my face, her big blue eyes softening. "I see."

I clear my throat and she continues, "So things with Daren are going pretty good now. He's definitely the most *interesting* thing that's ever happened to me." She winks and I throw her a small smile.

When I ran into Kayla a few days ago, I told her that I tolerated Jack because he was so interesting. And I encouraged her to go after Daren for the same reason.

"So tell me, Jenna," she says, quieting her voice like she knows this is a touchy subject. "Do you still find Jack interesting?"

Oh, God yes. More so than ever before.

But my voice doesn't seem to be working so I simply nod, the threat of tears burning behind my eyes at what I have in the palm of my hand, what I'm throwing away every minute I'm not confessing how I feel to Jack.

Kayla watches me for a moment, knowing my glossy eyes are

more than just the morning sun, and silently leans in to give me a hug.

I hug her back in a desperate way, holding on to this sweet girl who knows nothing about me but cares anyway. Bless her heart, indeed.

Pulling back, I clear my throat again with a laugh. "God, why are you so nice?"

She shrugs with a grin. "It's my curse, I guess." A clatter of dishes falling draws her attention back to the dining room. "Shoot. I have to get back to work. I'll see you around later?"

I nod with a smile and she spins on her heel and scurries back to work, waving to me before disappearing through the dining room door.

Looking around, I see a beautiful lavender field behind the inn and quietly I step outside and suck in a deep breath. The fresh air eases the guilty fingers around my gut. Not much, but enough for me to breathe easier. I inhale again. Much better.

"Good morning!" Ellen says, startling me.

She's standing to my right, fidgeting with a broken shutter and doesn't appear to have any clue that I'm going through a small personal crisis.

"Morning." I smile.

"How did you sleep?" she asks.

It's hard for me to keep my face under control as the answer to that question invades my mind. *I slept well, thanks. Lots of great, hot sex and orgasms with Jack. And oh yeah, I'm pretty sure I fell in love with him even more last night than I was already. Which terrifies me. But I slept fantastic.*

"Good," I say.

Her smile stays put. "Good."

I like Ellen. She's forty and single and runs her own business. She's pretty awesome and somewhat of an inspiration to me. She has the right idea. No man. Just her and her success. It worked for her, right?

My feelings for Jack only make me weak. I don't need a man. I'll never need a man, even a man as great as Jack. Right?

But then I think about all the people in my life that I love. My grandma, my mother, my sisters, Pixie, my cousins. My love for them is pure, and not a weakness at all. And Jack's love for Drew isn't a weakness either. In fact, his love for his family was the strength he needed to protect them.

"Hey, can I ask you something?" I say, stepping closer to Ellen.

"Of course." She dusts her hands off and gives me her full attention.

"Do you think love is something we can control?"

She snorts. "Not at all."

I frown. "So you don't think you can talk yourself out of loving someone?"

"Nope." She inhales deeply. "Love isn't an obedient whim. It's an unruly force. And it answers to no one."

I kick at the ground. "But then how can I ever be an independent woman if love has that kind of control over me?"

She wrinkles her brow in concern then glances upstairs where Jack is probably still sleeping. "Is this about the attractive guy in your room?"

I pucker my lips. "Maybe."

She nods knowingly. "Choosing to love a man, and letting that man love you back, is the most independent thing a girl can do for herself. No independent person is truly successful on their own."

"But you're successful and you're on your own."

She smiles sadly. "I'm on my own at the moment. But I wasn't alone when I made my dreams come true." She gestures to the inn. "I had a great man who loved me deeply and made me who I am."

That surprises me. I had no idea Ellen had some epic love story in her past. "So what happened?"

She shrugs and goes back to the shutter. "I was *too* independent. And yes, there's such a thing as being too independent." She swallows. "For years, I tried pushing him away before he could break my heart. And then one day, he let me go. I've been free and 'independent' ever since." She looks up at her beautiful inn with a hollow sigh. "But I've been lonely as hell." She looks back at me. "It's funny. I was so desperate to be on my own, and now that I am, I'm more codependent than ever before. This inn is my lover, if that makes any sense. But the inn can't encourage me or kiss me. The inn doesn't care if I hurt or when I cry." She shakes her head. "I traded one lover for another, and I lost."

Emotion clogs up my throat as I listen to the mournful tone of her voice. Is that what I'm destined for? Trading Jack in for some fabulous career that might be wildly successful but will never be able to hold me, to argue with me over radio stations?

"You okay, Jenna?" Ellen steps forward.

I blink at her. "I have to go." Then I turn and race back upstairs to room number four. Ellen was right. Love is an unruly thing and I've already been overcome by it.

I just need to be brave and finally say it out loud.

Bursting through the bedroom door, my heart slams into my chest when I realize Jack is gone. He's nowhere in sight. The bedsheets are rumpled and my bags are still in the corner, but Jack and his beautiful silver eyes have vanished.

Tears burn the back of my eyes as my worst nightmare begins

to unfold. Did he leave me? Did he get sick of waiting around for me to come to my senses and call a cab to take him home?

Oh God.

Have I already lost him?

On the verge of a hysterical breakdown, I'm about to hustle back downstairs when I hear the shower turn on in our room's small bathroom.

My chest heaves in relief as I realize Jack hasn't left me. And maybe that means he hasn't yet given up on me. Without thinking, I run into the bathroom and step into the shower with my clothes on.

"Holy shi—" Jack jumps as I climb under the spray in front of him.

"Don't let me go," I beg, as water tumbles down my face and clothes. "I know I'm difficult and I've put you through hell but I know what I want now. I don't *need* a man. I want one—and only one." Swallowing all my fears, I say, "I am hopelessly ridiculously in love with you, Jack. I AM IN LOVE WITH YOU.

"Please don't give up on me," I say, searching his eyes. "Don't let me push you away. I want to do this—this thing between us. I want to give it a shot. Even if that means I become some bumbling girl of mush who watches romantic comedies and cries every time she has sex with her man. I don't care." I shake my head, water flinging off of my eyelashes and nose. "I love you, Jack."

Standing naked in the shower, with his tattooed body glistening in the spray, Jack's silver eyes pierce me once again. But this time they see into me with love and hope and the promise of things to come.

A slow grin stretches across his beautiful face as he leans down and kisses me with the passion of heaven and hell colliding. I wrap my drenched body around his and let the water fall over us as I kiss him back with, yes, another tear running down my cheek.

Pulling back from the kiss, just barely enough to speak, Jack's eyes sparkle with his smile. "Told you so," he says.

I grin so big my face hurts.

He takes me in his arms, water falling on us like a beautiful storm, and brings his mouth to my ear to whisper, "Say it again."

Beaming, I look into his eyes. "Jack Oliver, I love you with all my heart."

His mouth is on mine again, kissing me and smiling against my lips like he's the luckiest guy on earth. And I'm the happiest girl in the world.

Grandma was right. I was brave enough to confess my feelings.

And it was totally worth it.

EPILOGUE

*A*ll I'm saying," Ethan says as he stuffs a pair of red leather pants into a cardboard box, "is that the three of us could have some really fun times together. As roommates."

"This is not up for discussion," Jack says. "You're moving out. Jenna is moving in. End of story."

I bite back a smile at the look of betrayal on Ethan's face. "Aw, come on, man. What does she have that I don't have?"

Jack doesn't hesitate to list things off. "Manners. Grace. Good hygiene—"

"Boobs," I add.

Jack nods at me. "That too."

I grin at Ethan. "Contrary to what your shoe collection might suggest, you don't have lady parts. So you're out. I'm in."

The beautiful October weather is rolling into Arizona and with the change of seasons comes a big change for Jack and me. He asked me to move in with him two weeks ago, and despite my history with commitment and vocalizing how I feel, I instantly said yes.

It's hard to believe our road trip was only a few months ago. It feels like years have passed since then. Good years. Happy years.

Ethan huffs as he carries the box out of the apartment. "This is the last box I'm loading today. I'll be back tomorrow to collect the rest of my belongings when I'm in a better mood and not thinking about Jenna's lady parts."

"Okay, ew," I say.

Ethan exits the apartment, and the moment it's just the two of us, alone, in our new home, Jack's face lights up with a big smile. "I love you."

He says that. All the time. It's like he thinks he needs to remind me or something.

I playfully tug at his shirt collar, pulling it down to trace the lines of his tattoos there. "I love you too."

He tugs the waist of my yoga pants down a bit and brushes his thumb over the tattoo there. The midnight bird we share, taking flight in hope of finding something more. Jack's flew him away from a life of crime. Mine flew me away from my fear of love. A lucky tattoo indeed.

"You know what I'm thinking about?" he says, his voice husky and low.

I arch an eyebrow. "My lady parts?"

"You know me so well."

I giggle—yes, I giggle now—and he lifts me into his arms and carries me down the hall to his room. Excuse me—*our* room.

God, I love saying that.

Our home. Our bed.

Our true love.

Maybe I believe in happily ever after, after all.

———

Later that night, I watch Marvin the goat try to eat my shoe again and curse under my breath. "I'm not kidding, Pixie. This goat has got to go."

Pixie smiles over at me. "But he likes you."

We're sitting in the stands at Levi's football game, along with Levi's parents and Ellen, and somehow I got stuck babysitting Levi's friend Zack's pet goat. Zack's a teammate of Levi's and currently on the football field, otherwise he'd be getting an earful from me about this goat that keeps trying to eat my footwear.

"Here, I'll take the damn goat," says Jack, arriving with the pretzel he got me from the concession stand. He scoots past everyone else to come sit down by me and trades the pretzel for the goat.

After he situates the goat far away from my feet, Jack leans over and kisses me. "Hey, baby."

"Hey." I smile and kiss him back more fully.

Jack is pretty much my whole life, and while that overwhelms me sometimes, it still rocks my world. Every day seems to be better than the one before, and I still feel independent.

Ellen was right—choosing to love Jack was the best thing I could have done.

"Okay, ew," Pixie teases. "There are children here." She looks around at where there are clearly no children anywhere. "Okay, well, there's a goat here. Get a room."

"Oh, we will," I say with a wink. "Later."

She mocks a gag but not before I catch the look of joy on her face.

"Sorry we're late!" Kayla says with a smile as she and Daren climb up the bleachers. "*Somebody* was perfecting a recipe and just couldn't leave the inn's kitchen until he had it perfect." She playfully rolls her eyes at Daren as they scoot in beside everyone else.

"Only because *somebody* insisted on adding potato soup to the lunch menu." He winks at Kayla.

"Hey." She points at him defensively. "Potato soup is a classic and everyone is going to love it."

"Yeah. Because I perfected the recipe in the kitchen just now," he says.

"Aw, lovebirds," Pixie sighs dramatically. "Aren't they adorable?"

I watch Daren kiss Kayla's nose and I make a face. "They're something all right."

Pixie scoffs. "Like you two are any better."

I hold a hand up. "Oh, please, Miss '*You hang up first...no* you *hang up first*'! You and Levi are disgusting on the phone."

Jack takes the hand I have held up and clucks his tongue as he examines it.

"What's this?" he says, holding up my ring finger.

Earlier today, I slipped Grandma's gris-gris ring off my ring finger and replaced it with the beautiful red stone ring Jack bought me. It's a reminder of that trip—and all the moments that brought me to this very happy point in my life—and it looks perfect on that finger.

"Why?" I say. "Does it freak you out to have a ring you bought me on my wedding ring finger?"

He watches me for a moment. "Not at all."

He's serious, which both terrifies me and makes me want to sing. God, I love him.

Biting back a smile, I shrug. "Good. Because I figured it was time to take off Grandma's ring since, you know, I feel all settled now."

He smiles. "Do you now?"

I nod. "I do."

He leans in and lowers his voice. "And would that have anything to do with me?"

"No," I say with a smile. Then I lean over and whisper in his ear, "It has *everything* to do with you."

Jack might have been all wrong for me and my plans, but he was just the kind of wrong I needed. The right kind of wrong.

Pixie Marshall hopes that working with her aunt at the Willow Inn will help her forget her past. Except there's a problem: the resident handyman is none other than Levi Andrews. Now he's right down the hall and stirring up feelings Pixie thought she'd long buried...

Please see the next page for an excerpt from the first book in the Finding Fate series,

Best Kind of Broken.

I

PIXIE

*I*f my bastard neighbor uses all the hot water again, I will suffocate him in his sleep.

I listen as the shower finally goes off and huff my way around my room, gathering my shower supplies. I don't politely wait for him to leave the bathroom, oh no. I stand outside the bathroom door—which has steam escaping from the crack at the bottom—with a carefully applied scowl and wait.

Still waiting.

The door swings open to a perfect male body emerging from a billow of hot fog. His dark hair is loose and wet and frames his face in a haphazard way that manages to look sexy despite the fact that he probably shook it out like a dog before opening the door, and of course he's wearing nothing but a towel.

Kill me now.

I peek into the bathroom, totally pissed, and block his exit with my body. "A thirty-minute shower, Levi? What the hell?"

A smile pulls at the corners of his mouth. "I was dirty."

Oh, I bet.

"I swear to God," I say, "if I have to take another cold shower—"

"You shouldn't swear to God, Pix." He brings his face close to mine and the steam from his skin dampens my nose and cheeks. "It's not nice."

This close up, I can see the tiny silver flecks in his otherwise bright blue eyes and almost feel the three-day scruff that shadows his jaw. Not that I want to feel his scruff. Ever.

I curl my lip. "I want a hot shower."

"Then shower at night."

"I'm not kidding, Levi."

"Neither am I." His eyes slide to my mouth for a moment—a split second—and there it is. The electricity. The humming vibration that never used to exist between us.

He snaps his eyes away and pulls back. The damp heat from his body pulls away as well, and some stupid, primal part of me whines in protest.

"Now, if you'll excuse me…" He waits for me to move out of his way. I don't.

I jab my finger at his chest. "I haven't had a hot shower for three days—"

Cupping my upper arms, he lifts me off the floor and moves me out of his way like I'm light as a feather. Then he walks the ten paces down the hall to his room and disappears inside without a look back.

Jackass.

With a muttered curse, I stomp into the small bathroom and try not to enjoy the smell of spearmint wafting into my nose and settling on my skin. Damn Levi and his hot-smelling soap.

My freshman year of college ended two weeks ago, and since Arizona State dorms don't allow students to stay during the summer, I had to find a new place to live and, consequently, a job. So I started working for my aunt Ellen at Willow Inn because one of the job perks—and I use that term loosely—is free room and board.

And my free room shares a hallway and a bathroom with the only person I was hoping to avoid for the rest of my life.

Levi Andrews.

Hot guy. Handyman. My long-lost…something.

Ellen conveniently forgot to tell me that Levi lived at the inn, so the day I moved in was chock-full of surprises.

Surprise! Levi lives here too.

Surprise! You'll be sleeping next door to him.

Surprise! You'll be sharing a sink, a shower, and a daily dose of weird sexual tension with him.

Ellen is lucky I love her.

Had I known that Levi lived and worked here, I never would have taken the job, let alone moved in. But Aunt Ellen is one conniving innkeeper and, honestly, my only other option was far less appealing. So here I am, living and working right alongside a walking piece of my past.

Since we're the only two resident employees, Levi and I are the only people who sleep in the east wing—a setup that might be ideal were it not for the giant elephant we keep sidestepping during these epic encounters of ours.

Memories start creeping up the back of my neck, and a hot prickle forms behind my eyes. I quickly blink it back and turn on the shower, scanning the bathroom for safer things to focus on.

Little blue dots on the wallpaper.

Purple flowers on my bottle of shampoo.

Dots. Flowers. Shampoo.

With the threat of tears now under control, I thrust my hand into the shower and relax a tinge when hot water hits my fingers.

Stripping off my pajamas, I step into the spray with high hopes, but water has just hit the right side of my neck when it goes from warm to ice-cold.

Sonofabitch.

There will be suffocation tonight. There will be misery and pain and a big fat pillow over Levi's big fat scruffy face.

Biting back a howl of frustration, I turn off the water and wrap a towel around my half-wet body. No way am I taking another cold shower. I'll just have to be unclean today. I hastily grab my stuff and yank the bathroom door open just as Levi leans into the hallway.

He's traded in his towel for a pair of low-slung jeans but hasn't gotten around to throwing on a shirt, so I have to watch his chest muscles flex as he grips his bedroom doorframe.

He looks me over with a smirk. "Done so soon?"

I flip him off and enter my room, slamming the door behind me like a fourth grader.

I throw on some clothes, pull my hair into a messy ponytail, and step into my paint-stained sneakers before looking myself over in the mirror. Ugh.

I tug at the V-neck collar of my shirt for a good twenty seconds before giving up and changing into a crew-neck shirt instead. Much better.

My phone chirps on the dresser, and I knock over a jar of paintbrushes as I reach for it. As I pick up my phone, paintbrushes go rolling off the dresser and onto the floor, where they join piles of discarded clothing and crumpled college applications. I glance at the text message and frown.

Miss you.

It's from Matt.

Miss you too, I text back. I do miss him. Sort of.

Call me. I have news.

I start to call Matt but pause when I hear Levi's footsteps in the hallway, making their way back to the bathroom. I hear him plug something in, and the sound of his electric razor meets my ears. I set my phone back on the dresser as a wicked smile spreads across my face.

Levi should know better by now. He really should.

Casually moving around my room, I plug in every electric item I own and wait until he's halfway through shaving. Then I turn everything on at once. The electricity immediately goes out and I hear the buzz of his razor die.

"Dammit, Pixie!"

Ah, the sweet sound of male irritation.

Plastering on an innocent look, I open my door and peer across the hall to the bathroom. Levi looks ridiculous standing in the doorway in just his jeans—still no shirt—glowering at me with half of his face shaved.

He stiffens his jaw. "Seriously?"

I mock a look of sympathy. "You really should charge your razor every once in a while." I exit my room and move down the hall, singing out, "Have fun rocking a half-beard all day."

As I head down the stairs, the wet side of my ponytail slaps against my neck with each step. Another smile pulls at my lips.

If Levi wants to play, it's on.

2

LEVI

*T*welve days.

Pixie's been living here for only twelve days and I already want to stab myself with a spoon. Not because she keeps blowing the fuse, though that reoccurring shenanigan of hers is certainly stab-worthy, but because I can't do normal around Pixie.

But fighting? That I can do.

After pulling a shirt on, I march downstairs and out the back door. The large lavender field behind the inn sways in the morning breeze, and thousands of purple flowers throw their scent into the wind, reminding me of things better left forgotten. Things I used to have locked down. So much for all that.

I blame Ellen. Maybe if she'd given me a heads-up about Pixie moving in, I could have prepared better.

Another breeze blows by and shoves more lavender up my nose.

Or maybe not.

The sky hangs above me, bright blue and free of clouds, and the early sun slants across the earth, casting a long shadow behind me as I walk the length of the building. I squint up at the white siding and notice one of the panels is cracked, which is nothing new.

Willow Inn is nearly one hundred years old, and parts of it are just as broken as they are picturesque. It's a quaint place, with white cladding and a wraparound porch beneath a blue-shingled roof, and it sits on ten acres of lavender fields and swaying willow trees. It has two wings of upstairs rooms and a main floor with the usual lobby, kitchen, and dining space.

The newly remodeled west wing has seven bedrooms, each with its own bathroom. That's where all the guests stay.

The east wing has yet to be remodeled, which is why Ellen allows Pixie and me to stay there and why I'm a live-in employee. Along with my other handyman duties, I'm also helping Ellen gut the old east wing so she can have the area remodeled to accommodate private bathrooms in every room.

I reach the fuse box at the edge of the inn and, flipping a breaker I'm far too familiar with, restore electricity to the east wing.

Fortunately, all the gutting and redesigning requires the east wing to run on its own electricity and water supply, so guests are never affected by my hot water usage or Pixie's electricity tantrums, but damn. We really need to find a less immature way to be around each other.

I turn and follow my shadow back to the door, holding my breath as I pass the purple field. The wooden floors of the lobby are extra shiny as I walk inside, which means Eva, the girl who cleans the main house, probably came in early and left before anyone saw her. She's tends to work stealthily like that, finishing her work before anyone wakes. Sometimes I envy Eva that. The solitude. The invisibility.

Back inside, I see a figure up ahead, and a string of curse words line themselves up on my tongue.

Daren Ackwood.

I hate this douche bag and he's headed right for me.

"What's happening, Andrews?" He gives me the chin nod like we go way back. We went to the same high school and I think we had a class together senior year, but we're not pals. He looks over my partially shaved face. "What the hell happened to you?"

"Pixie," I say.

He nods and looks around. "Is Sarah here?"

Sarah is Pixie's real name. The only people who've ever called her Pixie are me and Ellen and...

"Why?" I cross my arms and eye the case of water he's carrying. "Did she order water?"

Daren is the inn gofer, delivering groceries and linens and anything else the place needs, so unfortunately he's here twice a week with his preppy-boy jeans and nine coats of cologne. And he's always looking for Pixie.

"No, but you never know." He lifts a cocky brow. "She might be thirsty."

"She's not thirsty."

He looks over my facial hair again. "Oh, I think she's thirsty."

And I think Daren's throat needs to be stepped on.

"Morning, Levi." Ellen walks up with a smile and hands me my To Do list for the day. Her long dark hair slips over her shoulder as she turns and throws a courteous smile to the gofer. "Hey, Daren."

"Hey, Miss Marshall."

As Ellen starts talking to me about the fire alarm, I watch Daren's eyes cruise down her body and linger in places they have no business lingering in.

More than his throat needs to be stepped on.

Ellen Marshall is a very attractive forty-year-old who's used to guys checking her out. Not me, of course—Ellen's like family to me and I respect her—but pretty much any other guy who sees her instantly fantasizes about her, which pisses me off.

"...because the system is outdated," Ellen says.

"Routine check on the fire alarms," I say, my eyes fixed on Daren, who is still ogling her. "Got it."

"Can I help you with something?" Ellen smiles sharply at him. "Looks like your eyes are lost."

He readjusts his gaze. "Uh, no, ma'am. I was just wondering where Sarah was."

"Sarah is working. And so are you." Her hazel eyes drop to the case of water. "Why don't you take that to the dining room? I think Angelo is stocking the bar this morning."

He gives a single nod and walks off.

Ellen turns back to me and looks over my face. "Nice beard," she says. "Pixie?"

I rub a hand down the smooth side of my jaw. "Yeah."

She lets out an exasperated sigh. "Levi—"

"I'll check out the fire alarms after I finish shaving," I say, quickly cutting her off. Because I don't have the time, or the balls, to undergo the conversation she wants to have with me. "Later." I don't give her a chance to respond as I turn and head for the stairs.

Back in the bathroom, I stare at my reflection in the mirror and shake my head. Pixie timed it perfectly, I'll give her that. My facial hair is literally half-gone. I look like a before and after razor ad.

I think back to the irritated expression on her face and a small smile tugs at my lips. She was so frustrated, waiting outside the bathroom door with her flushed cheeks and full lips and indignant green eyes...

Why does she have to be so goddamn pretty?

I turn on the razor and run the blades down my jaw, thinking back to the first time I saw those indignant eyes cut into mine. My smile fades.

Pixie was six. I was seven. And my Transformers were missing.

I remember running around the house, completely panicked that I had lost my favorite toys, until I came upon Pixie sitting cross-legged in the front room with my very manly robots set up alongside her very dumb dolls.

I immediately called in the authorities—"Mom! Pixie took my Transformers!"—and wasted no time rescuing my toys from the clutches of the pink vomit that was Barbie.

"Hey!" She tried to pry them from my hands. "Those are the protectors. They kill all the bad guys. My dolls need them!"

"Your dolls are stupid. Stop taking my things. Mom! *Mom*!"

Haunted eyes stare back at me in the mirror as I slowly finish shaving.

I wish I would have known back then how significant Pixie was going to be.

I wish I would have known a lot of things.

Kayla Turner has lost everything. So when her late father leaves her an inheritance, she breathes a sigh of relief—until she learns the inheritance comes with strings... in the form of handsome playboy Daren Ackwood.

Sometimes when perfect falls apart, a little trouble fixes everything...

Please see the next page for an excerpt from the second book in the series,

Perfect Kind of Trouble.

I

KAYLA

*O*n the other side of the casket, a middle-aged woman wearing a navy blue dress glares at me.

The man in the wooden box has only been dead for three days and this woman already has me pegged as the slutty mistress he kept on the side. I'm probably an ex-stripper with a coke problem as well, based on the way she's sizing me up. But this isn't my first rodeo—or my first funeral—and deadly looks like the one Navy Nancy is angling at me are nothing new, unfortunately.

Now feeling a little self-conscious, I slowly slide my black sunglasses on and tip my head down, concentrating on the casket in front of me as the preacher/priest/certified-online minister drones on about peace and eternity.

It's a nice casket, made of polished cherrywood with decorative iron handles and rounded edges. I should care more than I do about the deceased man within, but all I can think about is how that casket probably cost more than any car I've ever been in, and how the man inside is probably tucked against velvet walls lined with Egyptian cotton.

And now I'm angry. Great.

I promised myself I wouldn't be angry today. Bitter? Sure. That was a given. But not angry.

Taking a deep breath, I raise my head and try to avert my attention. Behind my dark shades, I glance around the cemetery. More people showed up than I had expected, most of them looking like they're sweet and respectable. I wonder how well they knew James Turner. Were they friends of his? Coworkers? Lovers? Folks around here probably show up at funerals regardless of their relationship with the deceased. That's the thing about small towns; everyone cares about everyone else—or at least acts like they do.

"James was a good man," the minister says, "who lived a solid life and has now gone on to a better place…"

A roll of thunder sounds in the distance and I turn my eyes to the heavy gray clouds above. The weatherman said it's supposed to rain tonight. They'll bury James, cover his casket with dirt, and rain will fall and seal him into the earth. What an ideal passing.

Screw him.

A woman beside the minister begins to sing "Amazing Grace" as the pallbearers lower him into the grave. Across the way, a teenage boy openly gawks at me, his eyes gliding up and down my body like I'm standing here naked instead of fully clothed. I'm wearing a knee-length, long-sleeved, turtlenecked gray dress, in *July* no less. I'm ridiculously covered, not that Navy Nancy and Gawking Gary care.

When the boy catches me watching him, he quickly looks away and his face burns bright red. I turn away as well and play with the bracelet on my wrist as I focus my attention on the back of the crowd.

A huddle of women dab at their eyes with handkerchiefs. Beside them, a young family stands quietly with their hands clasped together. Nearby, an older couple mouths the words to "Amazing Grace" as the singer starts on the third verse. Looking around, I realize everyone else is singing along as well. *Of course* the people of Copper Springs would know the third verse of "Amazing Grace."

I really need to get out of here. I don't belong in this tiny town. I never have. One last obligation tomorrow then I'm gone.

In the far back of the congregation, a guy moves out from under a large oak tree and I tilt my head. He looks vaguely familiar but I can't quite place him.

He's average height, with dark brown hair, and a dark purple button-down shirt covers his broad shoulders. The long sleeves of his shirt are rolled up to his elbows and he's got on a pair of dark jeans to match the dark sunglasses that cover his eyes. Dark, dark, dark.

He's attractive. Dangerously attractive. The kind of attractive that can suck you into a sweet haze and undo you completely before you even know you've surrendered. I know I've seen him before but for the life of me I can't remember where, which is probably a good thing.

The singer wraps up the fourth verse of "Amazingly Depressing Grace," and a long silence follows before the minister clears his throat. He glances at me and I subtly nod. With a few last words about what a *wonderful* man James Turner was, he concludes the funeral and I let out a quiet breath of relief.

The end.

People disperse, most of them heading to their cars while the rest pass by the lowered casket and throw a handful of dirt or a flower onto the shiny cherrywood top. I step to the side, sunglasses strictly in place, and watch the mourners. Navy Nancy glares at me again and I look away. Wow. She really must think I'm some sort of James Turner hussy.

As offended as I am, I know she's probably just hurting. She was the first person to arrive at the funeral today and she teared up several times during the ceremony so I'm assuming she and James were pretty close. And if judging me makes her feel better on this sad day, then I'll let her hate me all she wants. I watch her leave the cemetery with a small group of other mourners. It's not like I'll ever see her again, anyway.

The guy in the purple shirt steps up to the grave and drops a handful of red dirt on the casket. The red stands out against the brown dirt beneath it and I wonder what its significance is. Then I wonder about the guy in purple. He doesn't seem to be here with anyone else, which is only strange because of how good-looking he is. Hot guys don't usually travel places without an equally hot girl on their arm. But this guy is definitely alone.

He strides to the parking lot and climbs into a black sports car, and all my wondering comes to an abrupt halt. I no longer care about who he is, or how he knew James, or why he looks familiar. Spoiled rich boys are the last thing I care about.

When everyone has left the area except the funeral home people, I carefully walk up to the casket. The heels of my black pumps slowly sink into the soft grass as I stare down at the last I'll ever see of James Turner. I try to muster up some sort of sadness, but all I come up with is more anger.

With a long inhale, I toss a soft white rose petal onto the brown and red dirt, and quietly say, "Rest in peace, Daddy."

2

DAREN

*S*ome people don't name their vehicles. Most people, probably. But there's something about a black Porsche that just makes you want to call it...Monique.

I climb inside my sports car, close the door, and look through the windshield at the dark clouds. Looks like Monique might need a bath tomorrow. My eyes fall back to the cemetery and my chest tightens. I still can't believe Old Man Turner is gone.

When I was thirteen, my life took a sharp turn to the shitty side of the street and Turner offered me a job mowing his lawn for fifteen dollars a week. A year went by before he asked me to start taking care of his garden as well, then gave me a raise. Shortly after, I was taking care of his entire yard and did so until last year when he requested that I focus my energy on my "real" jobs.

I didn't know he had cancer at the time. Hell, I didn't even know he was sick until he passed away. We lost touch for only a few months, but apparently, during that time Turner fought a short and intense battle with cancer and lost.

And I didn't even have a clue until last week.

My gut coils as I think about the day I found out—and all the days after—and I let out a heavy exhale. This past week has not been my finest. And now I'm at the funeral of the only man

I ever really considered a father. I didn't even get a chance to tell him good-bye.

I inhale, slow and steady, and I crack my knuckles. It's just been a shitty few years, all around.

Through the windshield, my eyes catch on a gray dress walking away from the casket with hips swinging and blonde hair swishing. I almost didn't recognize Kayla Turner behind those black sunglasses and that cold look she had on. But looking at her now, there's no mistaking.

She used to visit her dad in the summer, so every once in a while I'd catch glimpses of her inside the house while I was out mowing the lawn. And there are some faces you just don't forget.

Back then, she was all elbows and knees and freckles. But damn if Kayla Turner didn't grow up to be a total knockout. There wasn't a breathing soul in the cemetery today that didn't openly gape at her. I thought the kid in the front row was going to choke on his own drool, the way he was drinking her in.

I'm surprised she bothered to show up. She stopped coming around a few years ago and I saw how it tore Old Man Turner up. He missed her fiercely, but that didn't bring her back.

It's nice of her to finally visit again. Too bad she waited until her father's funeral to grace him with her presence.

With a clenched jaw, I start the engine, back out of my spot, and pull out of the parking lot. Monique purrs as I drive away from the cemetery and I want to purr right along with her. Cruising down the road eases the pressure in my chest and I feel like I can breathe again. I put the convertible top down and suck in a lungful of fresh air. Much better.

A distant roll of thunder echoes around. I pass a large gated community and a sour taste slips down my throat. Westlake Estates. The place I lived when life was good.

Well, not good exactly. But easier.

Turning onto the road that leads out of town, I head for work. I have two part-time jobs: one at the cell phone store in Copper Springs and one as a stock boy at the Willow Inn Bed & Breakfast outside of town. My job at Willow Inn is the only one I actually like, though.

Willow Inn is fifty miles south of town, in the middle of nowhere off the freeway, but I make the drive every week because of my awesome boss. Ellen owns and operates the quaint little inn and, in her spare time, she's a guardian angel.

Glancing at the time, I realize I have to be at Willow Inn in an hour and it takes at least that long to get there. Shit. And Monique is low on gas. Double shit.

With a muttered curse, I pull into the nearest gas station—a run-down fill-up place that looks closed except for the blinking neon sign that reads O_EN—and pull up next to a grime-coated gas pump before turning off the engine.

Getting out, I count the money in my pocket with a groan before shoving it back inside. As I start to fill Monique up, my phone beeps and I glance down to see another missed call from Eddie.

Eddie Perkins is the closest thing Copper Springs has to a professional lawyer, and lately he's been the bane of my existence. He's left me eight voice mails in the past week, none of which I've bothered listening to because I'm sure they're all about my dad. But ignoring him doesn't seem to be working.

Stepping away from the car, I listen to the most recent voice mail.

"Hello, Daren. It's Eddie again. I'm not sure if you've received my previous messages but I've been trying to reach you regarding James Turner. As I'm sure you know, he's passed away. A reading of his will is scheduled for tomorrow at 11:00 a.m. at my office, and Mr. Turner's last wishes specifically request that you be present. Hopefully, I'll see you there. If not, still give me a call so we can discuss... the other thing."

The message ends and I stare at my phone. Why in the world would Turner want me at the reading of his will?

Unless...

A thought hits me and it's almost too ridiculous to grasp.

Could this be about the baseball cards? Would Turner have remembered something from so long ago?

A small smile tugs at my lips.

Yes. He absolutely would have. That's just the kind of guy he was.

When I was thirteen, my dad gave me a set of collectable baseball cards for Christmas. I remember that Christmas clearly. It was the same Christmas that our housekeeper, Marcella, gave me a copy of the book *Holes*. It's about a boy who digs seemingly pointless holes as a punishment for something he didn't even do wrong. I was obsessed with the book; I must have read it ten times, and talked about it every day.

My mother and father barely paid attention to my interests. I doubt they ever even knew I'd read a single book, let alone one in particular over and over. But Marcella knew. She always made a point to care about the things I cared about. "You are my favorite boy, *mijo*," she would say.

She always called me *mijo*.

Son.

That Christmas, she'd wrapped the book in a green box with a red ribbon. I remember because that was the same box I decided to keep my collectable baseball cards in.

I brought the box to Turner's house one day to show off my new cards and proudly informed him that I had looked up the value of each one and knew I could sell the lot for at least a hundred dollars. Money was important to me back then. Money was all that mattered. My dad taught me that.

But later that day while I was mowing his lawn, Turner took my box of cards because, according to him, I was "too spoiled to appreciate them."

He was right, of course, but at the time I didn't care. I was furious, convinced he was going to sell the cards himself so he could have the money. But because I was just as spoiled as he'd claimed, I only stayed mad until my father bought me more baseball cards a few days later.

That's how things worked in my family: My parents bought me whatever I wanted, whenever I wanted, as long as I stayed out of their hair. I was an only child and I'm pretty sure I was a mistake. If my parents had *planned* to have me I'm sure they would have put a little more effort into... well, me. But I was an accident and, therefore, an inconvenience. An inconvenience easily soothed with a few new toys.

When I announced to Turner that I no longer cared about my stolen box of baseball cards, he laughed and said, "Someday you might." Then he promised that, someday, he'd return them to me.

I stare at my cell phone where the voice mail screen blinks back at me. Maybe this is Turner's way of coming through on that promise, after death.

The pressure starts to wind its way around my chest again,

thick and tight, and I feel the air seep from my lungs. I can't believe he's gone. Really gone.

A clanging noise startles my thoughts and I whip around to see a tow truck backed up to Monique and hauling her onto its bed. My eyes widen in horror.

"Hey!" I shout at the overweight truck driver, who's got a toothpick in his mouth and a handlebar mustache. "What are you doing?"

He barely glances at me. "Taking her in. Repo."

"Repo?" I start to panic. "No, no. There must be some mistake. A year's worth of payments were made on that car. I still have until next month."

He hands me a crumpled statement stained with greasy fingerprints and an unidentifiable smudge of brown. "Not according to the bank."

I quickly scan the paper. "Shit." I was sure those payments were good through August. I rub a hand over my mouth and try to clear my head. "Listen," I say, trying to stay calm as I appeal to the driver. "We can work this out. What do I need to do to get you to unhook my innocent car?"

He looks bored. "You got four months of payments on you?"

"Uh, no. But I have..." I pull out the contents of my pocket. "Forty-two dollars, a broken watch, and some red dirt."

A few grains of the dirt slip through my fingers and I think about all the weekends I spent taking care of Turner's yard. The lawn was healthy and the garden was abundant, but Turner's favorite part of the yard was the rose garden. I could tell that he was especially fond of his white roses, so I cared for those thorny flowers like they were helpless babies, and Turner wasn't shy about praising me for it. Every Saturday, I'd rake through the rare red topsoil Turner planted around his precious roses, making sure the bushes could breathe and grow. I pricked my fingers more times than I can count, but those roses never withered, and for that I was always proud. I think Old Man Turner was proud of my work too.

The tow truck guy shrugs. "No cash, no car. Sorry." He starts to lift Monique off the ground and I swear it's like watching someone kidnap a loved one.

"Wait—wait!" I hold up a hand. "I can get it. I can get you the money. I just—I just need a little time."

"Talk to the bank."

I quickly shake my head. "No, you see. I can't talk to the bank because the bank hates me—"

"Gee, I wonder why." He doesn't look at me.

"But I can get the money!" I gesture to Monique. "Just put my baby back down and you and I can go get a beer and talk this whole thing out." I flash a smile. "What do you say?"

He scoffs. "You pretty boys are all the same. Used to getting whatever you want with Daddy's money and pitching fits when someone takes your toys away." He shakes his head and climbs back into the tow truck. "See ya."

"But that's my ride!" I yell, throwing my arms up. "How am I supposed to get home?"

He starts the engine and flicks the toothpick to the other side of his mouth. "You should've thought of all that before you stopped making payments." Then he pulls out of the gas station with sweet Monique as his captive and I watch the last piece of my *other* life slowly disappear.

Motherfu—

"Sir?"

I spin around to see a scrawny gas attendant wiping his hands on a rag.

"What," I snap, frustrated at everything that's gone wrong in my existence.

"You gotta pay for that," he says.

I make a face. "For what?"

He nods at the pump. "For the gas."

"The ga—" I see the gas nozzle dangling from where poor Monique was ripped away and I want to scream. "Oh, come on, man! My car was basically just hijacked! I wasn't paying attention to how much *gas* I was using."

He shrugs. "Don't matter. Gas is gas. That'll be eighty-seven dollars."

"Eighty-se—" I clench my jaw. "I don't have eighty-seven dollars."

He scratches the back of his head. "Well I can't let you leave until you pay."

I scrub a hand down my face, trying to contain the many curse words that want to vault from my mouth. With a very calm and controlled voice I say, "Then do you have a manager I can speak to about settling this issue?"

He tips his head toward the small gas station store. "My sister."

Through the store's front window, I see a young woman with curly red hair at the register and a smile stretches across my face.

"Perfect," I say.

As I head for the entrance, a few drops of rain fall to the ground, plopping on the dirty concrete by my shoes. I look up at the dark clouds, fat with the oncoming storm and frown. I really don't want to walk home in the rain.

A string of gaudy bells slaps against the station door and chimes as I enter the store, and the sister looks up from a crossword puzzle. Her name tag reads WENDY. I file that information away.

Roving her eyes over me, her face immediately softens. "Why, hello there," she says in a voice I know is lower than her natural one. "Can I help you?"

I give her my very best helpless-boy grin and sigh dramatically. "I certainly hope so, Wendy."

Her eyes brighten at the sound of her name on my lips. Girls love it when you say their name. They melt over it. It's like a secret password that instantly grants you their trust.

She leans forward with a smitten grin and I know I've already charmed my way out of an eighty-seven-dollar gas bill. And maybe even found a ride home.

"Me too," she says eagerly.

I smile.

Sometimes it pays to be me.